These Dark Places

ALSO BY HILARY TAILOR

The Vanishing Tide

Where Water Lies

Between the Waves

These Dark Places

HILARY TAILOR

LAKE UNION
PUBLISHING

Published by Lake Union Publishing, Seattle

www.apub.com

EU Product Safety Contact:
Amazon Media EU S.à r.l.
38, avenue John F. Kennedy, L-1855 Luxembourg
amazonpublishing-gpsr@amazon.com

ISBN-13: 9781662526831
eISBN: 9781662526824

Cover design by Emma Rogers
Cover Image © nblx / Shutterstock

Printed in the United States of America

For Ruby, with all my love.

Chapter One

The phone rings out into the empty house, the sound of digital birdcall filling the dead air. Della hears it as she approaches the back door of the cottage, she separates it out from the noise of the woods, the urgent song of robins in spring, desperately trying to find a mate. Swearing under her breath, she pats down her pockets. How could she be so careless? It's the number one rule: *take your phone when you go into the woods.* Della quickens her pace, fighting down a feeling of unease that begins to swell in the base of her throat. A flock of magpies rise from the trees, screeching.

Three weeks from now, when things are at their worst, Della will look back at this moment, trying to remember how many magpies she saw, and whether they were an omen of what was to come.

There are two locks on the back door. It takes a few seconds to release them and, finally, when the door swings open, the ringtone dies. Her shoulders slump and she turns around to look for Marmite, who is emerging slowly from the trees, nose to the ground, his tail waving steadily side to side, as he treads carefully on arthritic legs.

'Come on, old man,' Della says with urgency as she holds the door open for him. He passes her with a brief glance of appreciation, and he slumps, gratefully, on to his large and smelly bed in the kitchen, near the fireplace.

Della shuts the back door, locks it and unwinds her scarf, walking over to the kitchen table to look at her phone. Three missed calls from Leo. He told her he had meetings today, that he was going to be busy. Why is he calling her in the early afternoon? Her mind lurches to Alex. Della barely spoke to her before she left for school this morning. She remembers making her eat a piece of toast, arguing absent-mindedly with her about needing a waterproof coat while Della tried to get Marmite to take his pills. Della's heart gives a painful squeeze. Leo never calls in the middle of the day.

The phone rings again and Leo's name lights the screen. Della snatches it up. 'Leo,' she demands before he can say anything. 'What's going on?'

She can hear the sound of a busy road, the chainsaw noise of a motorbike fading into the distance. There is a long hesitation on the other end of the phone and the feeling of dread inside her rises once more like a dark tide.

'Leo?' Della says, hearing the blood beat in her ears.

'It's not Leo,' says a voice, eventually. A woman's voice. 'Your husband isn't . . . he's not . . .'

The voice trails off as there is some sort of commotion in the background. Della can hear more voices, the sound of traffic, a car horn or a siren, she can't make it out. Another voice, a man, asks a question in the background, but Della can't decipher the meaning, just the inflection at the end of a sentence. The woman answers back, but her words become muted as her hand covers the phone.

'Hello?' shouts Della, frustration overtaking her fear. Alex can't be in danger, the woman would have said. Her daughter is safe, in school. Her husband is the most capable man she has ever met. She relaxes a little and allows herself to become impatient. 'Who is this?'

'You need to come. Now.' The tone of the woman's voice is pierced with anxiety, conjuring up Della's fear once more like a clairvoyant summoning a spirit.

'Where?' Della asks helplessly. 'What's going on?'

There is more discussion between people she cannot see or imagine. The phone is covered again, and the voices become muffled and indistinct.

Then suddenly, loudly, 'Go to the hospital.' The woman's voice is filled with urgency. 'Meet him at A&E. Go right now. *Right* now.' The line goes dead.

Della knows fear when she hears it, and this woman is frightened. Her fear connects with something in the very centre of Della. She understands immediately that she must obey. Glancing over to Marmite, who is already fast asleep, she grabs her keys, her phone, winds her scarf back around her neck and – even though she is panicking – draws the bolts across the back door. One at the top, one at the bottom, before double-checking the key is turned and removed from the lock.

The car is waiting on the dirt track. As Della pulls the front door closed and operates the deadbolt, she glances up at the house, as she always does, noting that the windows are all shut. When she opens the car door, her hands are trembling. She fumbles with the keys, stabbing at the ignition.

'Come on, idiot,' she scolds herself, wincing at the rock music that shrieks out of the radio when the car springs to life. For a brief moment, Della is transported back to an evening, two nights ago, when she picked up Alex from the library and they had sung together in the car to a tune they both knew, a rare moment of synchronicity. Then Della's mind snaps back to the present as she wonders what is happening now, why she has to go to the hospital, and why Leo didn't phone her himself.

Please don't let it be bad, she chants, over and over, as she swings the car around, driving away from the house down the dirt track, the car see-sawing and lurching over potholes and tree roots. The branches that arch over her head thin out and let in more light as she reaches the road, and when the tyres finally meet tarmac she floors the accelerator and heads for the hospital.

Chapter Two

By the time she reaches the hospital car park, Della's jaw aches from gritting her teeth. She runs to the entrance, ignoring the sign asking her to stop and sanitise her hands. Breathless, she confronts the receptionist at the Accident and Emergency department and gives her what little detail she has.

'Wait here,' says the receptionist, picking up the phone. A clinician of some sort – she doesn't know if he's a doctor or a nurse – comes to the reception desk and draws her to the side.

'Leo's your husband?' he says pleasantly.

'Yes. I got a call telling me to come here. I don't know what's going on.' She looks at this man, hoping he has all the answers.

'Leo collapsed and we want to give him a CT scan. He's in Radiology now. I'll take you up.'

Something cold slips down Della's spine, and she shivers. 'Collapsed? Where?'

'I don't know, I'm sorry. He was brought in by ambulance about twenty minutes ago.'

Della knows the National Health Service doesn't have the time or the resources to escort relatives around the building, but she remembers the fear in that woman's voice.

'Somebody called me from his phone. Do you know who it was?'

'No, I'm sorry. Shall we?' He motions for her to walk with him up the stairs, past a busy canteen, up another flight of stairs, until eventually they reach the radiology department. They make their way down a corridor which opens out to a large and busy waiting area with a curved reception desk. Della scans the room. Leo isn't there. A bleep goes off and the clinician who is with her looks down at his pager before silencing it.

'I'm going to leave you here as I'm needed . . . elsewhere.' He nods towards the crowded desk. 'The receptionist will tell you where he is.'

Della wants to beg him to stay, to grab hold of this man's hand like a tearful toddler to keep him by her side. She begins to think of questions she should ask him. She doesn't even know what a CT scan does, or how long it takes, or what they're looking for, but he is already walking away from her, and she is alone in a sea of people who are all navigating their own paths through the department.

Della turns to the reception but there is a nurse and a porter with a semi-recumbent patient on a trolley ahead of her. She fights the urge to barge past them and, with all the self-control she can muster, stops behind them and waits.

The nurse is arguing with the receptionist.

'It's urgent, didn't they say?' the nurse asks, exasperated.

'I don't have a record of it,' says the receptionist, shaking her head.

'There must be. He was admitted half an hour ago.'

'I've only just started my shift,' replies the receptionist, patiently, not looking at the nurse, but staring with a frown at the screen in front of her. 'Let me just . . .'

Della looks at the porter standing in front of her. His back is broad and muscular. He smells faintly of fresh sweat and detergent. But then the porter steps away, greeting another member of staff with a fist bump while the nurse continues to argue with the receptionist. Della looks down at the patient now revealed to her, lying on the trolley. His head and shoulders are elevated so she can't see his face, just the top of his head, which is covered in damp waves of hair, streaked with grey. There are small pieces of black grit clinging to his scalp. It is only when she sees his feet, poking out of a hospital blanket, his shoes still on, that she recognises the loafers she bought Leo for Christmas last year.

'Leo?' Della leaps around the trolley to see his face, ashamed she did not recognise her own husband. She pounces on him, looking him up and down. There is no blood, he has all four limbs. His eyes are screwed tightly shut and his shirt has been ripped open, the top two buttons missing. In the hollow of his collarbone, a place she has kissed more times than she can count, there is a round white pad with a silver press stud in the centre. She wonders why it isn't attached to anything and her eyes run down his body, noticing the pulse oximeter clipped to his index finger, the oxygen mask that has been pulled off and left around his neck. There is a drip attached to a cannula in the back of his hand and the liquid that runs into his body is as clear as water.

'What happened?' she asks him, stroking his head.

He winces, opens his eyes, and doesn't seem to recognise her.

The nurse spins around. 'Do you know him?' she asks in a completely different tone of voice to the one she just used on the receptionist.

'I'm his wife,' replies Della. 'Someone brought me up just now. Do you know why he's here?'

'He's having a CT scan,' the nurse replies kindly. 'That's all I've been told, I'm afraid.'

'Do you know—?'

But the nurse turns away from Della to answer a question from the receptionist. The porter is deep in conversation with his colleague.

'Leo?' His name is a question because Della can hardly believe this is her husband. His skin is grey with a faint sheen of sweat.

Suddenly, his eyes widen and he stares at her with incredulity, as if he is witnessing something beyond comprehension. Then his eyes snap shut once more as if he has seen too much.

'What's going on?' she asks the nurse, her voice rising, but the nurse is now taking matters into her own hands, leaning across the reception desk, looking at something on the computer screen.

Della turns back to Leo and realises that there is something very, very wrong with her husband. He is disorientated. There is vomit at the corner of his mouth.

Is he drunk? she thinks, picking a piece of grit out of his hair. She can't believe it. Leo has more self-control than anyone she knows. It's barely two o'clock on a Thursday afternoon. Della reaches once more to touch his head, so he opens his eyes, but she remembers how he flinched when she did that earlier, so she calls his name softly and reaches for his hand instead.

'Leo? Can you hear me? It's Della.'

He opens his eyes, slowly this time, and there is something different about him now. He looks more composed, and he recognises her.

'Della. You're here,' he breathes.

She feels inexplicably glad. 'I'm here, yes. Tell me what happened to you.'

'Headache.' He squeezes his eyes shut in pain.

'Did you hit your head? Did you fall?' Della looks for signs of damage. 'What do you remember?'

'I heard it. In my head. A pop. Something bad.'

Della can see it brings Leo distress to talk about it, so she shushes him and tells him it will be alright.

But Leo shakes his head, gravely, and opens his eyes, wide. 'It's bad,' he repeats. 'I can feel it.'

Della catches the fear in his voice, and it stirs something in her. Leo isn't frightened of anything.

'What can I do?' she asks, stroking his hand.

'Very important. Very important things to discuss.' His words are slurred, and she sees him sinking back into soft focus.

'Leo. What things?' She is suddenly overcome by an urge to keep him awake, keep him talking. Something nibbles at her consciousness, a premonition that tells her she shouldn't let him sleep. That if she lets him go to sleep he will never wake up. 'Tell me the important thing, Leo,' she says, squeezing his hand harder. 'I'm listening.'

He looks at her then, a pure and direct gaze. 'Don't sell the house.'

She almost laughs in relief. 'I'm not planning on selling the house. What do you mean?'

'Promise me, you'll never sell the house after I'm gone.'

'You're not going anywhere, Leo.' Della swallows the lump in her throat and tries to keep her voice steady. 'You're here, with me, and you'll be home before you know it.'

'Promise me. On Alex's life.'

'What— Why?' Again, that creeping feeling of fear moves through her bones, and she shivers. He is so filled with intensity she can barely blink in his gaze.

'Ethan,' he says in a low, frightened whisper.

Della spins, looks wildly around the room. Her brother's name enough to elicit a ripple of dread, even here in the safety of a hospital.

She lowers her voice to match his. 'What do you mean, Leo?'

'He's there.' Leo looks just beyond her shoulder. 'I saw him.'

Della can feel a thump in her chest like a hammer blow. She makes a fist and holds it to her sternum, trying to breathe. Her knuckles dig into the bone, a distraction from the pain coming from within her. 'You've seen him? When? Why didn't you tell me?'

Leo shakes his head. 'Sorry, sorry. So sorry. My fault. All my fault. I wrote it down. It didn't help.'

Della fights back tears of frustration. 'Leo, you're not making any sense.'

'I'm going to die, Della.'

An unfamiliar expression crosses Leo's face and Della realises with horror that he is scared. She has never seen her husband look like this. Della tries to muster words of support, but is so floored by this shift in him she is temporarily lost for words. 'Please don't. You're not going to die, you're just . . .'

'I am. I'm going to die.' His voice trembles, his eyes move around the room, although she can see it gives him pain to do it. 'Where's Alex?'

Alex. She had forgotten about Alex. 'She's at school. She'll be home soon, and I'll bring her straight over to see you.'

'Tell her I'm sorry. I'm so sorry, Della. For everything.'

Her vision mists with tears and she blinks them away. 'Leo, you have nothing to be sorry for. You are the best man, the most amazing, lovely man I ever met.'

'You wouldn't say that if you knew what I'd done,' he whispers.

Della whispers back, 'You haven't done *anything*, Leo, everything is going to be alright.'

His lips part and she cannot hear what he is saying. He strains with the effort.

She leans over him, willing him well with the strength of her love. 'Darling Leo, please don't worry—'

He brings his hand up to touch his head. 'The accident . . .'

'I know, sweetheart. You're in the best possible place now. They're going to find out what happened.'

'. . . I wanted to tell you.'

Della looks around helplessly for the nurse, willing her to come back and take charge. 'Just focus on getting better,' she says, feeling the weakness of her words.

'It's very important. Listen to me.'

Della stops, paralysed by the tone of his voice. She holds her breath and listens.

'He's there. In the woods.'

'Who's in the woods?' she asks, the back of her neck prickling with fear. She knows the answer before he gives it to her.

'Ethan.' Leo's eyes close with exhaustion.

She is silenced by the name, the creeping understanding of what it all might mean.

'Leo,' she whispers. 'Has Ethan come back?'

He looks in her direction, but his gaze is far away, fixed on something she cannot know. Then he stiffens and his breath comes deep and slow. When his limbs begin to tremble, the trolley shakes, and the noise of it is something she knows will live with her for the rest of her life.

Chapter Three

It is a strange thing, to be swept aside in the most critical moment of your husband's life. To know you are superfluous, unnecessary to his survival. That twenty years of knowledge, seventeen years of marriage, counts for nothing. You are a hindrance. Only strangers can help.

Della is led away to a stuffy room by the same nurse who called the crash team. The walls are a pale duck-egg blue and there are pictures of wheat fields blowing in soft breezes. There are armchairs and sofas in natural, nourishing colours. Della is brought a mug of tea, told that Leo is in good hands, that there is nothing further she can do but wait. After almost an hour, when the tea has formed a dark skin on the surface and the mug is cool to touch, the door opens, slowly. Before anybody speaks, Della knows that Leo is dead.

It is gently explained to her that it can happen like this. That a weakness in the wall of a blood vessel can rupture and bleed into the brain, causing a severe headache, nausea, disorientation. That a sub-arachnoid haemorrhage can re-bleed, and of those that do, it is common for this to occur in the first six hours. There will be an autopsy, and they are certain this is what they will find.

'Would you like to see him?' asks the nurse, eventually, when the conversation has run dry.

For a second, Della thinks she has misunderstood, that Leo is alive and waiting for her in a ward somewhere, sitting up in bed with his arms folded impatiently. Then a slow, sad resignation creeps over her like a shadow as she understands.

Stiff-limbed and mute, Della retraces her steps to the radiology department with the nurse, back down the corridor, her feet shuffling and heavy. There is a small room to the left, just before the reception desk. She hadn't noticed it before. She would have paid it more attention if she'd known.

'Take your time,' says the nurse. 'I'll be waiting for you at reception. There's no hurry. Take as much time as you need.'

The nurse opens the door to the small, dark room and, for a moment, Della is afraid to go in. But Leo is there, flat on the trolley, now, the blanket neatly folded over his chest, so she steps inside. The door closes gently behind her, and Della waits for a moment, knowing she is in a liminal place, that when she confirms what she has been told with her own eyes, there will be no going back to her old life. She takes a few steps forward, sees there is a chair for her, but she doesn't sit on it. Instead, she leans over, and she touches Leo's chest, putting her fingers in the hollow of his collarbone. She feels the curve of the sticky pad, the metal of the press stud under his shirt, which has now been closed with the buttons that remain. It is this detail that touches her the most, that someone has done this small thing for him. For her.

Leo's face is free of the pain that altered it earlier, but even so, there is something about him that doesn't quite look like her husband. She searches his features, trying to figure out what it is, and she can't make herself understand. He doesn't look dead, but he doesn't look as if he is asleep, either. Leo never slept on his back, he always curled up like a child in the womb, a stubborn frown creasing his brow. This man's face is smooth, and his body is straight. Della touches his forehead gently and it is warm. She reaches for his hand and it, too, holds a familiar heat. She feels his wedding ring rub against hers.

'Leo?' she whispers, hardly daring to hope. Her voice sounds strangled and raspy. His eyelashes are a fine, inky sweep against pale skin, and the fragile beauty of them breaks her heart. She traces the arch of his eyebrow with the pad of her thumb and leans closer. 'Leo?'

He doesn't reply. Yet still, she searches his face for answers, and when her back begins to ache from bending over, she sinks into the chair next to him, still holding on to his left hand. Gently, she bends his arm and brings his hand up to her face, resting her cheek in his palm, letting her tears run into it. She thinks about all the times he has caught her tears like this, cupping her face in his hands, telling her it will all be alright. Now, she looks at his profile, and drinks in every detail of him as she feels the minutes slip away, the time she must leave him narrowing down at a speed she cannot slow.

Della reaches out with her other hand and traces the small lump on the bridge of his nose, the faint scar on his temple, the mole on his neck. She makes herself remember him, the contours of him, searing them into her own memory with the touch of her fingers. An old habit from childhood tries to take her mind away, making it wander and float from the terrible reality in front of her. With great effort, she prevents this from happening, focusing solely on what lies before her, ignoring the questions that have already begun to clamour in her head.

Eventually, something crumbles within her, and she clings to him, a drowning woman to a life raft, moaning softly into his skin. She rests her head where his heart used to beat, a place that is as familiar to her as her own voice, smelling the laundry softener she used only yesterday morning on this shirt. Della closes her eyes tightly and still the tears cannot be stopped. Her eyelashes are wet and stuck together, her damp fingers still intertwined with his. Finally, when she cannot think of him gone any more, she listens to the sounds of the radiology department beyond the closed door. She can hear patients being summoned, a constant roll call of names she can't quite make out. She gives herself over to the hum of noise, a steady percussion that plays in the background as the heat quietly leaves the love of her life.

Chapter Four

Leaving the room is like leaving the quiet sanctuary of a church and emerging into a light-filled, noisy hell. The reception area in the radiology department is busy. People are going about their lives as if nothing extraordinary has happened, and Della wants to scream into the room, *Don't you know? Don't you realise what just happened?* She cannot believe the world looks and sounds the same. She stands, paralysed, searching for the nurse who said she would be there, and when she sees her at the desk, she is talking to another woman who turns to meet Della's gaze, then rushes towards her.

'Della! Oh my God, Della!'

'Tash?' says Della, weakly. 'How did you—'

'They won't tell me anything. They just said to come.' Tash looks her up and down, holding Della's shoulders at arm's length. 'You look awful. Are you OK?'

Della is confused. 'Who?'

The nurse approaches. 'Della, you asked us to call your friend, Tash. This is Natasha, right?'

Della can't think straight. 'What?'

The nurse explains, slowly. 'When we asked if we could call someone to come and drive you home, you said to call Natasha, and you gave me your phone.' As if to prove it, the nurse hands Della's phone back to her.

Della has no memory of doing this. It feels like a surreal magic trick. *Everything* feels surreal.

'When I phoned Natasha, I asked her to come and pick you up,' repeats the nurse. 'I haven't told her what's happened. I wasn't sure if you wanted me to.' She looks from Natasha to Della, an expectant expression on her face, as if it is Della's turn, now, to say something.

And then Della feels it, the grind of a gear belonging to a machine that has suddenly sprung into motion. A machine that will continue to hum in the background for the rest of her life. She will have to tell people. Forms will need to be filled in to make it official. There will have to be an autopsy, a funeral, anniversaries marking this horrible day. Leo's birth date will stop being a day to celebrate, it will become something else, something dark and sad. And she will change, her name will change.

She will have to call herself a widow.

'Della?' Tash looks scared. 'What's going on?'

'Leo died,' says Della, in a flat voice. It is the first time she has to say this, and she is conscious that however many times she says it in the future, the words will never lose their weight. The shape of them will never stop them feeling wrong as she expels them from her mouth.

'*What?*' Tash takes a step away from her as if scalded. Della feels the burden of an unwanted role reversal. She has to comfort Tash now, break it to her gently, just as the nurse did for her. How has she graduated from being the receiver of bad news, to delivering it, in such a short space of time? She feels the unfairness of it cut through the fog of grief as she repeats, almost word for word, what the nurse told her in that stuffy little room.

Tash doesn't react like Della did. She isn't quiet and stoical. She doesn't contain her grief for a place where it can be explored privately. Tash lets out a wail like a fox in the night and several people in the waiting room stop what they are doing to look at her. She clutches on to Della, allowing her to feel the full weight of her body, dragging her down. Then just as quickly, she pulls herself together, as if she realises she is there to support Della, not the other way round.

'I'm sorry, I'm sorry,' she moans. 'It's such a shock. You must be . . . you must feel . . . I don't know.' Tash gulps as a fresh wave of tears course down her face. 'What can I do?'

Della turns to the nurse. 'What happens next?' What she really wants to say is, *Where do I go? What do I do now, without him?*

'We need to do an autopsy,' says the nurse. 'To confirm the cause of death.'

'When will that happen?' asks Tash, who has now regained her composure.

'Usually within the next twenty-four hours. Then we can release his body to you.'

Della notes the words *his body*. The absence of his name.

'You'll need to come back in and register his death, but there's plenty of time for that.'

Della wants to ask her what is going to happen to Leo now, where he is going to go. She knows he can't stay in that room. 'Will he be alright?' she asks, instead. But the nurse seems to understand.

'We'll take care of him,' she says, touching Della's arm lightly. 'We'll look after him, I promise.'

At first, they are taken up with how to get Della's car safely out of the car park. Tash is used to driving something much newer with automatic everything. Not something as old as this car, which demands the driver use their own eyes to judge distance and hazards. Tash swears, loudly and liberally, as the car finally jerks out of the space and on to the road.

'I can't believe it. I can't believe it,' she keeps repeating, like a mantra. 'I just can't.'

Della is silent as she watches the road slip past. Again, she marvels that nothing has changed in the outside world. It all looks exactly the same.

'I remember meeting him in the student union at university. He was playing pool with Robin. He thrashed us both. He was so good at sport. Everything, really. He was good at *everything*. I can't believe I'm talking about him in the past tense. Oh my God.' The car swerves slightly. 'I'm going to have to tell Robin. This is going to kill him.' Tash grips the steering wheel tightly. 'I didn't mean that. I'm sorry. I don't know what I'm saying.'

'You knew him longer than I did,' Della says, feeling jealous of the extra months that Tash and Robin had with him when they were all students.

'He didn't really come into himself until he met you. I mean that. He lived for you.'

Della lets out a sob, fights to regain control. 'What am I going to do?'

Tash reaches over and squeezes her knee, fiercely. The strength of her touch, the violence of it, is a balm. 'You have me. You've always had me. I'm not going anywhere. We've known each other since we were kids. We will get through this together. Robin might be my husband, but I love you like my own sister. Robin and I will be right there for you and Alex.'

'Alex,' repeats Della, fresh panic coursing through her like adrenaline. 'She doesn't know yet.'

'Where will she be right now?'

Della looks at her watch. 'She'll be at home. School finished ages ago. She'll be wondering where I am.' She pulls out her phone from her coat pocket, but there are no missed calls from her daughter. Della imagines her, a carefree seventeen-year-old making peanut butter toast and watching something on her phone, blissfully unaware that her life is about to implode.

Tash turns the car into the woods, finding the dirt track and driving expertly down it, avoiding the worst of the roots. 'You can't stay here, you know,' she says. 'Not now Leo's gone. It's not safe.'

And then Della remembers the garbled conversation with Leo in the waiting area. She turns to Tash. 'Leo told me he saw Ethan, just before he died.'

'Where?' Tash loses her grip on the wheel for a moment as the car hits a hollow in the ground. She swears loudly as she shifts the car into a lower gear.

'Here, I think. In the woods. But he seemed really mixed up, the way he was talking. I couldn't understand if he meant what he was saying. I got the impression Leo had found him living there, though. Camping out.'

'But he would have mentioned that, surely. And he would have called the police, knowing Leo.'

Della shakes her head. 'Yeah. He would. Leo must have . . . I don't know. I don't know what he was thinking. He was so distressed. He was frightened, Tash. He knew he was going to die.' The tears come again, making her eyes smart.

'Either way,' says Tash in a grim voice, 'we need to plan for Ethan. When was the last time you saw him?'

'Not since last year. He's probably moved in with somebody. He sometimes gets a girlfriend in the winter, so he doesn't have to sleep out.'

Tash takes her eyes off the track when the house comes into view and looks at Della. 'Eventually they'll get sick of him. They'll kick him out and then he will come for you, Della. It's always the same. When he finds out that Leo is dead, it will give him free rein. He'll move himself in or set fire to the house. He'll never change.'

'Stop it.' Della puts the flat of her hands to her ears. 'I can't think about Ethan right now.'

'OK, but maybe Robin should come over and talk to you about finances. Let you know what your options are.'

'No. I don't want that. It's too soon.' She feels like she is drowning. The idea of Robin coming into the house without Leo being there is too much. 'I just want to be left alone.'

The car draws up outside the house and Tash switches the engine off. She turns to Della and takes her hand into hers. 'That's what I'm worried about. I don't think you should be left alone. This house is in the middle of nowhere. No neighbours for miles. You and Alex need to be looked after. You're vulnerable.'

Della pulls her hand away. 'No, we're not. Leo made sure of that. The house is like a fortress.'

'I'm just saying—'

'Leo is barely cold. Just let me deal with that. I don't want to think about Ethan right now.' She can't articulate how Ethan's name brings about a chain reaction of conflicting feelings. Dread. Compassion. Fear. Guilt.

'OK, sorry,' says Tash. 'I'm just trying to plan. You know how I am. But I do think Robin should come and see you as soon as possible. He'll want to make sure you're OK. We both want that. We love you.'

They both stare at the silhouette of Della's home. The shape of it has all the makings of a gingerbread house. The original structure was large until it was divided into two halves. The right-hand side is in darkness and has been since old Mrs Winters died almost five years ago. The left-hand side, Della's half, is lit up like a Christmas tree. Alex has illuminated her journey through the house. The hallway, the bathroom, her bedroom. Now, Della can see the silhouette of her daughter moving around the kitchen, slotting bread into the toaster, opening the fridge and staring at its contents as she nods her head in time to something she can hear through her headphones.

Della cannot take her eyes off her. Tash is silent. They are both thinking the same thing. They want to give Alex a few more minutes of normality before they snatch it away.

'I'm going to do this by myself,' says Della, eventually.

'Of course,' sniffs Tash, grabbing her hand and squeezing hard. 'I'll walk home. Robin can drive me to the hospital to pick up my car. I'll call you later when I get back, OK?'

Della nods, gets out of the car and watches Tash walk back up the dirt track. Then, when it is quiet, she stands in front of the house, raises her face to the sky and breathes in the woods. The air is damp and smells of spring. The birds are still calling to one another, darting back and forth across her vision, nest-building, defending their territory. The branches of the trees are already spritting green. Even the beech trees, always last, are beginning to turn to leaf. There is so much life here, waiting to burst forth. Della cannot reconcile the optimism with the misery she is bringing home.

Chapter Five

Alex is already waiting for her in the hallway when Della pushes open the front door. Her headphones are huge, like industrial ear mufflers. She pulls them off and they curl around her neck, tangled up in her hair, which is a bright, pure blonde at the tips, growing darker, more reddish at the roots. She is wearing Doc Martens boots, a pair of oversized men's dungarees with a T-shirt covered in logos underneath. A black hand-knitted cardigan she picked up from a second-hand shop is slung around her body, falling off her left shoulder, the sleeves covering her hands, and poking out from the cuffs are the tips of her nails, which are painted a bright, electric blue. Della takes in these details, absorbing the pain of knowing that Alex laced up those boots, buttoned that cardigan, when her father was still alive, and that when she takes these clothes off tonight – *if* she takes them off – they will be different, somehow. The fabric will be permeated with loss.

'Mum?' Alex's voice breaks into her thoughts. 'What are you doing? I saw you standing outside like a loon, and wasn't that Tash I just saw, walking off? What's going on?'

'Let's go in the kitchen,' says Della, wanting to snatch a few more seconds of normal before she ends everything. But Alex is alert now, like a fox scenting prey.

'What's happened? You look weird.'

'Alex, I . . .' Della stops, because she can't form the words. They are stones, cold and heavy in her mouth.

'Oh my God, what?' The fear in Alex's voice is so close to the surface it makes her voice tremble.

Della tries to stifle the sob that rises out of her, an animal sound, guttural and deep.

'Is it Dad?' Alex cries, a frantic look on her face. 'It's Dad, isn't it? Tell me.'

But the words don't come out. They can't. She can't tell her daughter the worst news of her life. She just nods her head, pulls Alex towards her, and in this moment, Alex's face crumples with understanding.

As Della does her best to explain to Alex that a part of her life is over, she becomes aware that grief is a shape. Leo, Della and Alex formed a structure under this roof, and now Leo is gone, that structure has been compromised, like a milking stool that has lost a leg. She sees it, feels it collapse before her eyes as Alex turns from her, pushes her hands away. Like a fire, needing to devour fuel, it does not take long for Alex's grief to turn on her. Della wonders if she knew this was going to happen, and that's why she sent Tash away.

'Why didn't you come and get me?' Alex wails. 'You had to practically drive past my school to get to the hospital. It would have taken five minutes. *Five minutes!*'

The heavy black eyeliner that Alex carefully applied this morning has streaked and run down her face. There is a piece of buttered toast on the kitchen counter. A single, perfect bite taken from the corner. Della can't tear her eyes away from it as she struggles to reason with Alex, with herself, why she didn't do that.

'I just didn't think,' she says eventually. 'I didn't know he was so ill. I thought I— we, had more time.'

'It doesn't matter how ill you thought he was! You know I would have wanted to see him as soon as possible. I could have said *goodbye*.'

Della shakes her head. It seems so simple now, with hindsight. To go and pick Alex up, take her too. But she didn't, and she can never change that. 'I just didn't think,' she repeats. 'It's such a critical time for you at school, Alex, you begin your exams in two months.' Della hears her own voice, spouting these ridiculous, meaningless words. The deluge of emotion that is pouring out of Alex drowns her own feelings. The rawness of it all, at the hospital, in the car with Tash, it is buried under the onslaught of Alex's grief, and she stops talking, feels herself turn to stone.

Alex puts her hands up to her tear-stained cheeks as if she is stopping herself from splitting apart. Her electric-blue nail polish is chipped, her hair is wild. 'Oh my God, seriously? You think I can do exams now? After this? My dad just *died*. He's *dead*.'

Della wants to throw her arms around her daughter, but everything about Alex's body language tells her to stay away. How can she possibly fill the hole that Leo has left? She couldn't even compete with him when he was alive.

'Of course, yes. You're right,' Della reasons, desperate to wrestle the conversation back to safer territory. 'I know this is awful, terrible. I don't know what I'm saying.' She glances out of the window. The sun is sinking through the trees, casting long shadows that reach for the house. A force of habit commands her to remember if she has bolted the doors, closed the windows. For a shameful second, she has an urge to run out of the house and lock herself in the studio. The idea of being surrounded by her work in that calm whitewashed space is so seductive she can almost smell the clay.

'I didn't mean it like that, I'm sorry,' she murmurs, forcing herself back into the room. Della watches as her daughter rages and cries, helpless to do anything about it.

'You were *always* jealous of Dad and me,' sobs Alex, throwing herself on to the floor next to Marmite, who is watching them warily from the safety of his bed. Alex buries her face in his neck.

Della's heart cracks open. 'No, that's not true, Alex. I love the relationship you have together.'

'*That's* why you didn't pick me up today. So you could have him all to yourself.'

'That's absolutely not—'

'Did he ask for me?' Alex looks up at her, pleading. Her face has gone white, now, she looks like a ghost. 'Did he say anything about me?'

Della hesitates, remembering Leo looking wildly around the room, asking for his daughter. Her face tells Alex all she needs to know.

Della sinks to her knees next to Alex and Marmite and, finally, Alex's anger is spent, and she allows herself to be comforted. As Alex wraps herself around the dog, Della tries to hold her, but she can't, so she rubs her back with her hands, trying to impart some kind of strength she knows she does not have. And Della begins to see beyond this day to the future. The gap that Leo has left for Alex will have to be filled by her. It is up to her to be the strong one now. The shape of their family must change and become something else.

As she feels the shudder of Alex tearing through her ribcage, she plays back Leo's words as his brain shut down.

I saw Ethan. He's in the woods.

Chapter Six

Tash calls that evening when Alex is in her room. A tray of uneaten food remains outside her door, and Della is desperate to have someone to talk to. The atmosphere in the house feels suffocating, as if the air is dense with something she cannot see. It bears down on her, bowing her head, opposing every movement. She can hardly pick up her phone she feels so tired. But she must talk to Tash, because she is Della's lifeline. The only person left who can hold her together.

'How is she?' asks Tash.

'Awful. She doesn't want to speak to me.'

Tash sighs. 'She was the apple of Leo's eye. Poor Alex.'

'The backbone of our family has gone. I can feel everything disintegrating already.' Della sits down heavily on to a kitchen chair and puts her elbows on the table, her head in her free hand.

'You're her mother, Della.'

'Yes, but what do I actually *do?* Leo was the breadwinner. I'm not qualified to do anything.'

'You've spent the last seventeen years rearing a child and looking after Leo. That's a job in itself. Don't knock motherhood, Della. I'd lose my job and give back my degree in a heartbeat if I could have a child with Robin. But there we are. We can't have everything,' she sniffs.

Della hears the rebuke, knows the pain Tash and Robin have gone through trying to conceive. 'Tash, I'm sorry, I didn't mean it like that.'

'If you moved . . . if you moved into the village. Close to me and Robin. We could look after you.'

Della feels the warmth in those words, the seductive pull of them. She could leave all of this behind, start again. She's done it before. But then she hears Leo's words.

Don't sell the house.

Tash continues, 'If Ethan has come back, you can't stay in the woods without Leo. Ethan was frightened of Leo.'

'I told you,' says Della in a quiet voice. 'I don't want to talk about Ethan.'

'You have to, Della. Alex is seventeen now. Almost eighteen. Old enough to know about him.'

'I don't want to talk to her about my childhood. Why would I want to burden her with that?'

'You wouldn't have to. You could just say he's dangerous. That he's a threat.'

'And how is that going to help Alex? She has enough to deal with right now. I'm not going to add to her worries by telling her about Ethan. I want her protected from all of that. Leo wanted it too.'

'Could you go to the police?'

Della snorts. 'And say what, exactly? That my brother is hanging around in the woods? What are they supposed to do about that? They never did much about it before.'

'It's a public space, I suppose,' Tash concedes.

'All Ethan wants is to put his family back together. He's lonely, really. We lost our father, and he was made head of a dysfunctional family.'

'Stop apologising for him.'

'He was only fourteen when Dad died.'

'And you were ten. If your mother hadn't been so feeble . . .' says Tash, who hasn't got a feeble bone in her body and doesn't understand why others cannot cope.

'It was a terrible shock for her when she lost Dad,' says Della, a vestige of compassion still circulating in her bloodstream for her mother. 'She expected Ethan to hold everything together. It wasn't fair on him.'

Ethan had stepped into their father's shoes, running the newsagent's before and after school until he was old enough to work there full-time. She remembers the door to her mother's bedroom, closed for what seemed like months; her inability to step up and take control of a terrible situation, her willingness to dump all of the responsibility on to her son's shoulders. 'We would have lost the business, and the flat, if it wasn't for Ethan,' Della says, thinking back. 'That's what made him the way he is. The pressure.' She remembers her mother, always passive, turning into a shadow overnight. With a start, Della realises she is the same age her mother was when she was widowed, that she is about to walk the path her mother did. She vows she will do better.

'That's no excuse for what he did to your hair. Or your home,' Tash mutters.

Della reflexively touches her hair, which is now feathered into a pixie cut. Back then she had long hair halfway down her back. Her father had loved her hair, he made no secret of it.

Someone's gonna steal you away with that hair, Rapunzel, he would say before swinging her over his shoulder and cantering out of the room. She kept the fairytale in a little bookcase by her bed. It was the most tattered book in her collection. She lost herself in its strange illustrations and thumbed through the pages long after her father stopped reading them to her. As a child, she didn't question the story, that the only means of escape was not available to the person who could provide it, that Rapunzel was reliant on her captor for survival. It was a thought that came to her later, though, and it lingered long into adulthood.

After their father died, it was Della's job to stack the newspapers and magazines on the shelves every morning before school. That morning, Della had settled down to read on the step stool she should have been using to reach the shelves. She knew she wasn't allowed to read *Just Seventeen* because she was too young, but she snuck a peek whenever she could.

From total crush to true love! Della understood none of it, but those forbidden pages brought a delicious sense of escape she badly needed. Her hair swung around her shoulders like a curtain, blocking out the shop, cocooning her for a moment as she lost herself in another world.

The smell of burning took longer than it should have done to filter through to her consciousness, and by the time it did, it was too late. Half of her hair had been singed away before she leapt to her feet, using the magazine to frantically beat it out. The stench was horrendous, but worse than that, as she brought up her fingers to feel the damage, the left side of her beautiful hair was shrivelled and crispy. She knew she would have to lose the right side to even it out. Amid her panic, she was acutely aware that this was the part of her that her father loved most, and now, like him, it was ashes.

She spun around to see what had caused the fire, but all she saw was Ethan, standing by the till, a lighter in his hand. She recognised the lighter. It had belonged to their father. An old-fashioned American Zippo that was never far from his reach. It was another memory of him, tainted.

'My hair!' Her voice came out as a sob.

His face looked impassive.

'Why did you do that, Ethan? Why did you do this to me?' she cried out, hardly able to believe it.

'I don't want someone to steal you away,' he explained, putting the lighter in his pocket. 'Now you'll be safe.'

Della walks through to the sitting room and sinks into an armchair, closing her eyes, preferring to wallow in the past than confront her future. She can't remember when she realised Ethan had changed. It was a creeping understanding, like bindweed strangling a garden. By the time she concluded her home environment was toxic, a normal life seemed unattainable. She has vague memories from before their father died, memories of Ethan's kindness. Sharing a bath with him when they were little, Ethan singing to her and soaping her hair with shampoo. She remembers holding his hand to cross the road on the way to school, telling her to look right and left and right again. His was the name she called when she couldn't sleep at night. These memories are little points of light in a darkened room.

'I wouldn't blame you if you had a drink, you know,' says Tash, sympathetically, breaking Della's recollection.

Della bites down, hard. She feels the muscles flex in her jaw. 'I don't do that any more. You know I don't do that.'

'It's not like you were an alcoholic or anything.'

'That's not the point. I don't drink any more because it took me to the edge of something . . .' Della thinks back briefly, painfully, to that time. A time of indistinct conversations, bruises that appeared on her skin from events she had no recollection of, the company of men whose names she never asked. The sound of her front door opening and closing early in the morning while she pretended to be asleep in a bed whose sheets she hadn't changed for weeks.

'Don't you think it would be helpful to lose yourself, to get blind drunk, for the night? I'd be more than happy to oblige. I can come round. Stay over?'

'No,' says Della, firmly. Although, when she says this the idea of getting drunk and falling into a dreamless sleep seems appealing. She shuts down the thought.

'I can't imagine going as long as you have without a drink,' muses Tash, and Della thinks she can hear her pouring herself a glass of wine.

Della doesn't remind her she had to stop when she became pregnant with Alex. She doesn't want to rub Tash's nose in it. And then she smiles briefly as she remembers the many evenings they had together as teenagers, dancing on tables and running barefoot home, their shoes in their hands. A different kind of intoxication to the one she put a stop to.

'At least you'll have company soon, which makes me feel better,' says Tash.

'Company?' Della sits up, looks around, as if somebody is about to enter the room.

'Robin told me the other half of your house finally got sold. Didn't you know?'

Della looks to the adjoining wall, as if to divine what might be happening on the other side of it. 'I thought it was still the subject of some probate row.'

'Not any more.'

'But we would have heard if someone had bought it, seen them looking around.' Della's mind turns to Ethan, even though she knows he has no money. It would be the kind of thing he would do. A nasty surprise.

'I think they might have had a buyer lined up, so they didn't advertise. The estate agent told Robin it was an easy sale. It's a dump next door, isn't it? He must've been delighted to find someone who wanted to take it on. You own all the land that surrounds the house, so not a very attractive prospect for most people.'

'But nobody has been here to look at it. I would have known,' persists Della.

'You're in your studio most of the time, throwing pots. That's well away from the house. Alex is in school. It's possible somebody could poke about without you knowing.'

At this idea, Della's stomach drops.

Tash continues, 'And Marmite's a useless guard dog now. He's deaf, isn't he?'

'He's not deaf,' says Della, defensively. 'Just a bit hard of hearing. Which reminds me, I need to feed him.' Suddenly, Della wants to get away. She feels anxious at the thought of someone coming here, looking at the house next door and, by extension, her own home.

'OK,' replies Tash. 'I'll see you tomorrow. I'll bring Robin over, you can talk about your options.'

'I don't want that, it's too soon.'

'It needs to be done, Della. The sooner the better. You'll thank me for it in time. Tash knows best.'

Della feels Tash is a torrent of water, a relentless breeze wearing her down. She hears herself reluctantly agreeing. 'You'll definitely come, too, though, yeah? Alex would like to see you.'

There is a pause, a pocket of silence, when Della knows they are both thinking about Leo. 'Are you going to be OK?' Tash speaks in a soft voice, and Della is reminded of the countless times Tash has asked her that, from a sad little girl in the playground to now. And then, she doesn't want to get away at all, she wants to stay on the phone talking to her best friend, all night if necessary.

'I'll be fine,' whispers Della, her eyes squeezed shut, not bothering to wipe the tears away. She stays like that, her cheeks wet, not wanting to put the phone down until Tash does it first.

Eventually, she gets up, looking for tissues, and walks through to the kitchen, where the fire is burning low. The log basket is almost empty and Della feels a moment of annoyance that Leo didn't fill it last night when she asked him to. She looks around the kitchen, at the dishwasher that needs emptying, the bins that need hauling up to the road so the rubbish can be collected. These jobs will fall to her, now.

There are signs of Leo all over this house. His spare reading glasses are on top of the microwave. The novel he was reading lies on the chair by the fire with a page turned down. She picks up his mug, left in the sink this morning, a puddle of coffee staining the porcelain. She tilts it to the light, trying to make out the shape of his lips on the rim. What is she supposed to do with these everyday things? These are the last things he touched. They are so filled with significance she can't bring herself to get rid of them. Yet at the same time she is suffocated by them, scattered around the house. Reminders of a life that once dominated this space, vanished in an afternoon. Feeling aimless and jittery, she feels the loss of him like an addict deprived of a fix.

Marmite raises his head, and she kneels down to him, cupping his face in her hands, breathing in his comforting smell. He looks at her with compassion and a profound understanding. He knows something is terribly, terribly wrong.

'Did you see anyone, Marmite, hmm?' She talks to him gently as she looks deep into his beautiful golden eyes, the irises edged with black. He moves his head gently to the side, his brown ears cocked, listening intently.

'You would have told me, wouldn't you, if you heard somebody looking at the house next door?'

Della trusts Marmite implicitly. He may be old, now, but he has been her guardian angel for the past fifteen years, because there was a time, when Alex was a toddler, that Della was afraid of the woods. Whenever she breathed in its own peculiar scent of moist earth and vegetation, she could sense something waiting, just under the surface of the soil. The trees seemed to reach for the house, their branches tapping at the windowpanes, clawing at the glass. When she looked out at night, she saw shadows, sinister shapes dropping silently from the canopy, slipping like liquid through the darkness, moving in a steady, stealthy path towards the house. She stopped venturing out of the back door. In saner moments, she knew it wasn't the woods she was afraid of, not really. It was who they might conceal.

She began to get into the car every morning with her daughter, after Leo had left for work. Alex was used to running around, unfettered, through the trees. Della drove her to the soft play on an industrial estate. Alex sat among the colourful plastic balls, nursery rhymes playing loudly over the sound system, a strip light flickering above her head. She looked so shocked, so bewildered, Della died a little inside.

Leo noticed. He always noticed when Della was on edge. He suggested, casually, that they get a dog. 'It will be good for Alex,' he said. The implication in his words was a kindness that Della loved him for. Alex was fine. It was Della who needed the dog.

Leo brought Marmite back to the cottage when he was only a puppy.

'What is he?' asked Della, taking in his large paws and long legs.

'Apparently, he's a Giant Schnauzer mix,' replied Leo. 'They're supposed to be very intelligent. Territorial. I think the guy said this one is mixed with German Shepherd.'

'So he's going to be big?' she said, looking into his golden eyes, stroking his black-and-tan fur.

'Yes,' said Leo, and then he took her hand. 'Big enough to give a man pause for thought.'

There was a silence, then. Neither of them said his name, but they knew they were both thinking about Ethan.

Chapter Seven

Della opens her eyes and, for a few blissful moments, she forgets. The day is bright. There is sunshine creeping around the closed curtain. She hears the rooks calling to one another mournfully like neglected babies, *wah, wah, wah.*

She turns her head to look for Leo, moves her leg to seek his out. When she sees the pillows next to her are untouched, the duvet flat and undisturbed, the weight of remembrance bears down on her so she can't breathe. The urge to close her eyes and crawl back into the safety of unconsciousness is strong, but she recalls her mother doing this, the resentment it caused, the damage it did to her and Ethan. She makes herself get up.

Della emails Alex's school, letting them know what has happened, that Alex won't be in for a while. She tiptoes up the stairs to Alex's room and sees the tray from last night has been taken into her room. Relieved, she walks back down the stairs to the kitchen and writes a note for Alex, propping it up on the kitchen table.

Out with Marmite, back soon x

Della feeds Marmite and unlocks the back door, taking her keys and phone with her. She waits for him to finish his breakfast, and he follows her, slowly, stiff from sleep, into the woods. She locks the door behind her, looks up at the house to make sure there aren't any open windows, before taking the path to the trees, all the time her eyes sweeping the fringes. A flock of starlings rises above her head, bubbling like water in a cloudburst of chatter. It makes her jump, and her mind turns to Ethan, how exposed she is now without Leo.

Della moves deliberately, her eyes scouring the ground. As she wanders through the trees, she becomes increasingly aware that this is not a dog walk, it is a patrol for signs of her brother. She walks some way into the thick of the trees, looking for signs. Of what, exactly, she's not sure – a tent, perhaps, the ashes of a fire. He never stays in the same place for long. Last year, he told her he was doing farm work, sleeping in barns, until he got fired or told to move on. He shows up periodically, usually around her wedding anniversary, to push a sarcastic card through the door. Once he posted an envelope stuffed with ashes. Sometimes he asks for money, but really, Della believes, he wants to usurp Leo, to feel the power of being the head of a family again.

As she moves methodically around the land at the back of her house, everything seems normal. Until she sees a flicker of colour in the lower branches of a beech tree. It's a bright, kingfisher blue, a small, shredded piece of fabric, like something from a tent or an anorak.

A spark of fear pulses through her, and she touches the back of her neck to halt the goosebumps. Ethan had a jacket this colour. She remembers him wearing it the last time. He'd set a small fire in a bowl on the doorstep. Leo had put it out without much trouble. When she took the bowl, sodden with water, she'd tipped the ashes into the sink. It was the remains of a page from the local newspaper profiling Leo and his business. Shards of Leo's face circled the plughole before they finally succumbed and disappeared down the drain.

Alert, her mouth dry, her eyes dart around the ground. It has been disturbed. The autumn leaves have been kicked about, scraped away. She bends down and sweeps the detritus lightly with her fingers. There are a couple of fairly fresh cigarette butts on the ground. She snaps her head up, scanning the surrounding trees, with a creeping sensation that someone is watching. Then she catches sight of her own house through the barest branches, and realises it is in a direct sightline. She imagines Ethan standing here, smoking, watching the house in the dark. Waiting for . . . what, exactly? She cannot imagine. She doesn't want to imagine. In her mind's eye, Della sees Leo coming upon him, alerted to the smell of cigarette smoke on his way back from work. But why didn't he tell her Ethan was here? Why didn't he warn her?

And then she wonders if Ethan came back more than she realised, that Leo saw him off more than she knew, that Leo has been battling with her brother and keeping it from her to protect her.

And now, that protection is gone.

Horrible scenarios run through her head. Petrol splashing against the wall of her house in the darkness, she and Alex asleep in bed. Or worse. Alex, alone, unable to get out. Della pinches her lips together with her fingers to stop the sound she wants to make. Ethan is much better at controlling fire now. What happened at their childhood home was a mistake. All he wants is obedience and respect. The fires he sets now are small. They are messages. He doesn't want to harm her. But what if Leo knew more than he let on? How many fires has he stopped without her knowledge? How many times has he sent Ethan away? There are cameras installed outside the house and studio. She would know the answers to these questions if she could access the software that Leo used to control them.

Panicking, she looks for Marmite, who is sniffing around the roots of a tree. She calls to him, and his reluctance to come makes her go over and see what he is looking at. But there is nothing there, only some unnamed animal smell that seems to have him hypnotised. She grabs his collar and moves him gently away.

'Come on, time to go back,' she says, her anxiety rising as she feels his stubborn resistance give way to her encouragement. He glances back, licks his lips and gives her a look that seems to say: *killjoy.*

Della's mind jumps to the studio. The studio is the most convenient place to break in to. If she were Ethan, it would be the studio she would try. There is running water. A kettle and a fridge. It is a stone building, the size of a large garage, a hundred-yard walk from the house. The windows are long horizontal strips of glass set high in the walls, too narrow for a man to climb through, wide enough to fill the space with light. Even so, she approaches the door with caution and tries the handle, puts the key in the lock. When she sees there is no damage, that her brother is not waiting for her inside, she lets out a breath she didn't realise she was holding. She is safe, for the time being.

The day Leo brought her here for the first time, he had already put an offer in on the house.

'The lady who lives here is finding it too much,' he explained to Della. 'She just wants to live out her days without any of the responsibility. Everything you see will be ours, apart from the other half of the house, of course.'

'You can't own a whole wood, surely?' Della had asked, her head spinning.

'There's a boundary. It's not all ours, it merges into the rest of the woods. But look, our land goes down to a lake, see? Imagine owning a whole lake.'

Leo was a different person here. He had a boyish glint in his eye. She felt, very keenly, she wanted to keep that look on his face. She didn't want to dampen his enthusiasm for this special place. He led her through the woods. She saw trees she couldn't name, towering over her like the forests in the fairytales her father used to read to her. She glimpsed tall mounds of holly that stretched metres high, thinning out to a large pond with a jetty. Water irises pushed their way out of the fringes and a family of ducks was swimming from one side to the other. A little boat, broken up and half sunk into the water, was still tethered to the jetty.

'This is unbelievable,' said Della. The whole place seemed to be filled with a soft, citrus light. 'How can you afford it?'

'My parents are going to help. Mrs Winters knows them, actually. She wants somebody decent living next door. She's used to having the whole place to herself, but she's had a health scare and knows eventually she'll need a willing neighbour to keep an eye on her. It's pretty hard to get out of here, especially in winter, and she won't be able to drive for ever. There'll be a tacit agreement we'll help her as much as we can, within reason. She's a nice woman, I promise.'

Della looked around, at the woods, the pond, the house in the distance, which was still covered in scaffolding. It had been split down the middle, each half a reflection of the other, two new front doors. The only difference was their half of the house owned the land, and the studio.

'She's a potter like you,' said Leo as they stopped at the studio. 'Look, it even has a kiln around the back.'

She felt swept along by his pleasure, giddy with the possibility he was opening up.

'She built the kiln herself,' he explained, gesturing to the odd-looking structure.

'It's wood-fired,' said Della, delighted. 'I've never seen one of these in the flesh. It looks like a large pizza oven.' She walked around the brick structure, noting the hatch at the back where logs would be loaded and fired up, the small chimney that protruded from the top. She swung open a large fire door through which the pottery was loaded. It was lined with a thick, heat-proof board. 'This is quite unusual. Nobody really uses wood-fired kilns any more.'

'But look!' said Leo, gesturing to the trees that surrounded them. 'Free fuel.'

'It's bigger than what I'm used to,' said Della, doubtfully, looking at the size of the kiln. She used smaller, top-loading kilns the size of a washing machine. Kilns that plugged in or were fired by gas.

'You always said you wanted to upscale. It'll be more cost effective.'

Della hesitated, not wanting to burst his bubble. 'Isn't it better to live in a community? To have neighbours?'

'Neighbours talk. Neighbours know your business, your routine. Especially in a close-knit village like this one. If Ethan went sniffing around the village, he'd hear about you in a second. But here?' He looked at her with certainty. 'Ethan won't find you here,' said Leo. The conviction of his words felt like a balm. 'You have no connection to this village. I can put my own name on the mortgage. He won't even be able to find you on the Land Registry, if he's clever enough to look. And anyway,' he said, a smile stealing over his face, 'you can change your name.'

'What?' asked Della. She didn't understand.

'Marry me, Della. This house, coming on the market like this, it's a sign we should be together.'

'But if Ethan finds us . . .'

'If Ethan finds us here, I can deal with him. You're worth the hassle. We can make this house a fortress.'

Della thought about the life that was already making its presence felt inside her. The man who stood in front of her, who didn't yet know he was going to be a father. The house that rose out of a tangled, secluded wood. It seemed beyond belief that finally, *finally*, she might be given her happily-ever-after.

Chapter Eight

For two whole years after Alex was born, they lived a life whose narrative seemed to come from the storybooks of her childhood. This was a time when they didn't check that the house was locked. The back door was left open to welcome the sunlight across the stone floor; windows were unlatched to let in the breeze. Leo found office space near to the village, less than half an hour's walk from the house. He set off every morning, a packed lunch in his backpack, cutting through the woods like a well-dressed rambler. He took the car when the weather was bad, or Della offered to drive him, but he loved the walk, the time it gave him to be among the trees and think his own thoughts. His affection for the landscape was scored into him, like woodgrain.

For Della, the love was learned. Like a goldfish that has lived its life in a bowl suddenly put into a lake, she explored the area closest to the house at first, cautiously circling wider and wider as she became acquainted with the paths that wound through the woods, first with Alex strapped to her chest in a sling, then with her toddling, hand in hand. It wasn't a lonely place, as she had first thought, it was a place filled with conversation, as the birds called to one another and the wind rattled the trees and stirred up the leaves. Everywhere she turned, everything she saw, seemed to be filled with the urge to live. From the bare branches of the blackthorn that budded and broke on the coldest of days to the nests that were built, destroyed and built again after a storm. The will to succeed, to survive adversity, shone like sunlight through the boughs.

It wasn't just the wildlife, though, it was the optimism of the villagers that touched her most. Every now and again, she would come across little memorials. Small bunches of flowers that were left in places of meaning. Notes that were tied to branches or folded carefully and pressed into the hollows of tree trunks. Not all of them memorialising the dead, though plenty were, but some of them filled with hope. Wishes for babies to be born healthy, for loved ones to get over an illness, for good fortune to smile upon families that were experiencing hard times. It became clear to Della that this was a place where people found nourishment, that the woods gave people strength. When she mentioned this to Leo, curled up on the sofa one night, her head in his lap, he already knew.

'There's a very old oak, somewhere in the middle of the wood,' he said, gently pulling the wisps of her hair through his fingertips. 'We used to call it the wishing tree. It supposedly had the power to grant wishes, but when we were kids we used it to get girlfriends.'

'Of course you did.' Della laughed. She reached up to his face, cupped his cheek in her palm.

He pulled her palm away and kissed it down to the wrist. 'If you fancied someone you'd put their name on a piece of paper and feed it to the tree.'

'Feed it?'

'Well. The idea was you stuffed your note into the soil around the trunk. The tree would absorb the information and consider your request.'

'And did it work?' Della asked, amused.

'Not very often. Not in my case, anyway. Some of the villagers, though, they used it as a kind of confessional. Some still do.'

'And how does that work?'

'You write your sins down and feed them to the tree. If you can't find your piece of paper when you come back it means your sins have been absorbed by the roots, drawn up through the trunk and expelled by the leaves. *Poof.* Gone. All is forgiven.'

'How convenient,' smirked Della. 'Did you ever do that?'

Leo smiled at the memory and shook his head. 'No, I did not. Half the kids in the village used to scratch around that poor tree, trying to dig up other people's secrets. Only the desperate left their notes there.'

Della walked the woods every day after Alex was born. The more time she spent with her baby, watching the turn of the seasons, the more Della understood. As the rain soaked into her skin, and the wind lifted her hair, as she drew the earth-scented air into the deepest part of her lungs, she understood why Leo had been so passionate about buying the house. This was a magical place. It would heal her. It would nourish her new family and everything from now on would be better.

Alex was between the ages of two and three when it all came crashing down. They had taken to walking part way with Leo to his office. Through the woods they all went, like a family from a fairytale. Della and Alex waved Leo off by the pond and turned to go back, playing hide and seek among the trees. Alex never got the hang of hiding. She thought that if she couldn't see Della, she couldn't be seen. Della usually made a big pretence of not being able to find her, which delighted Alex as she watched her mother calling in vain through the trees. But on this occasion, Alex did disappear. They were in the deepest part of the wood, away from the house, beyond their own boundary. Della called, amused at first that her daughter had outfoxed her, but then more urgently. Her voice became edged with panic as Alex's name echoed through the wood without an answer.

'Alex?' she shouted, at the top of her voice. 'I really mean it. You have to come out now. You're giving Mummy a scare.'

From behind her, she heard footsteps on fallen leaves, but it wasn't the light and rapid noise her daughter's feet made, it was the slow, heavy tread of a man who wasn't in a hurry. A man with Alex sitting on his shoulders.

Ethan.

His hair had grown. It fell unwashed around his face and shoulders, a dark, burnished brown. He had stopped cutting it, and now he looked feral. She noticed a tattoo on his dirty neck. Two words in black ink. *Love Burns.*

Della fought the scream, pressed it down, down, into her stomach. Tried to compose herself. Reminded herself that this was her brother, the boy who had once soaped her hair and held her hand to cross the road. Della looked up at Alex, who was laughing at the joke she thought she was playing on her mother. Her little hands gripped Ethan's forehead and his large hands held her shins. Della imagined trying to prise Alex away from him. Ethan had grown taller, if that were possible. There was no way she could manage it. Persuasion, then. Humour. Deference. All the things she used to employ to get him to cooperate. The words fell into place like an old language she had forgotten she'd mastered.

'You are a hard woman to find, Della,' he said, ignoring her platitudes. He looked pleased with himself. 'I almost gave up on you, until I saw your picture on Facebook last week.'

'Facebook?' repeated Della, feeling weak. She forced her shoulders back, smiled what she hoped was a casual smile.

'You were in a pub. Celebrating your third wedding anniversary. Looks like they put quite the party on for you. Tash reposted it. She should be more careful about her privacy settings. I feel like I know this village like the back of my hand.'

Della cursed Tash and the pub landlord silently.

'I can't believe you got married on the twentieth of March,' continued Ethan in a low voice. 'And that you didn't even invite me.'

Della swallowed and kept her face neutral. 'We didn't invite anyone apart from Tash and Robin, to be witnesses.'

'But that date. Did you have to do it then? The date you left me?'

The date you burned our lives down, she wanted to say.

For a second, she saw the hurt in his eyes. She connected with it, and a trickle of compassion escaped the place she thought she'd locked it up. A thought came to her, one that had resurfaced many times as the years passed and these encounters were repeated. *How is it possible to feel frightened of the person you love?*

'I didn't have a choice, Ethan,' she said softly. 'I was pregnant and there was a cancellation at the registry office. Leo booked it. He wasn't to know.' Della glanced quickly at Alex, high on his shoulders. Her little girl shifted her legs uncomfortably. Ethan's grip tightened.

Twisting his head to look up at her daughter, Ethan said, 'She's beautiful. Just like you. She has your hair. Do you remember how long your hair used to be?'

'Yes, I remember,' said Della, involuntarily touching the wisps that curled around the nape of her neck.

'Do you remember that wonderful smell? There's no smell like it.'

For a frightening second, she smelled her own hair burning and her hands clawed at her scalp to be sure.

Ethan laughed, lazy and slow. 'It's the same, you know. Redhead, blonde, brunette. It all smells the same in the end.'

Glancing desperately around, she wondered if there was anyone else in the wood nearby. She occasionally bumped into the odd dog-walker. Her eyes darted from tree to tree. She prayed that someone would come.

'This one isn't quite as good at hiding as you are.' He looked up once more at Alex, who was beginning to realise it wasn't a game. 'I didn't know I had a niece. You should have told me. She's my family too. I have rights. She needs to know who I am.'

Della tried to look unconcerned. 'She must be heavy, Ethan. Why don't you put her down, so we can talk properly.'

Alex had begun to kick her legs, and Ethan's hands stilled them. She started to sob. 'Be careful, Alex, or I might drop you,' he said, his smile shifting to something Della didn't want to contemplate.

'Maybe she wants to go to the toilet,' said Della with a flash of inspiration. 'She's not very reliable.' She saw Ethan consider the consequences and he roughly slid Alex from his shoulders and put her down. She tried to run towards Della, but Ethan was quicker and grabbed her hand, jerking her little body back to him. 'Their bones are still soft at this age, aren't they?' he said, examining her daughter's fingers, encased in his. 'Hard to break.'

Alex looked at Della, and the expression on her face, the bloom of understanding that this was beyond her mother's help, was something Della never forgot.

'What do you want, Ethan? I'm happy to talk. Let me know what you want.' Della swallowed. 'Let me help you.'

He tilted his head, like a predator sniffing the air, and for a moment, Della wondered if he could smell the fear rolling off her. 'You shouldn't have to ask me that. You know what I want,' he said softly.

She felt sick. 'Tell me.' She couldn't get the air into her lungs.

He spoke to her in a sing-song voice as if she were a child, and it transported her back to her bedroom at night, a frightened girl balancing a glass on the handle of her door, trying to eke out a few seconds of warning if Ethan tried the handle. 'I want you back, Della. The insurance money for the fire has come through.

You're my family. My blood. We should be together again, working side by side.'

'I'm married, Ethan,' Della pleaded. 'My life is here. You can keep the money. It's all yours. Please, Ethan . . .' She hated the whine in her voice.

'I wasn't offering it, Della. But thanks anyway.' His voice dripped with mean sarcasm.

Unable to escape, Alex began to call out to her mother in a high, thin voice. Della's heart twisted. Even if he lost his grip, they couldn't outrun him. Alex was too heavy and Della wasn't fast enough.

'Please, Ethan,' said Della, unable to keep the note of desperation at bay. 'I'm sure we can work this out. Just let her come to me.'

'I don't think so,' said Ethan, enjoying himself. 'You can't just run away from me. I'm your brother. I'm supposed to look after you, and you're not letting me. It's time you came home.' His voice had dropped, a sign he was getting angry. Like a switch, his face changed.

She counted the time to when Leo would return to find they were gone. Eight long hours.

And then, mercifully, a dog shot out of the thicket and raced around them, sniffing. Ethan held his hand out. The dog ran over and jumped up. When Ethan let go of Alex's hand to fend it off, Alex ran to her mother and as Della scooped her up the owner of the dog appeared. To Della's intense relief, she knew him. He was a man called Harvey, a friend of Leo's parents. Dressed in expensive waterproofs and carrying a long stick, he greeted Della loudly and immediately sized up Ethan, a suspicious look on his face.

'Everything alright, Della?' he asked, standing his ground.

'This gentleman is lost,' said Della, trying to keep her voice steady. 'I was pointing him to the road.'

Harvey used his stick and jabbed it, hard, beyond Ethan's shoulder. 'That way,' he said, brightly but firmly, and Della could have kissed him.

There was a silence when Ethan looked from Harvey to Della before he decided to go. 'I'm sure we'll bump into each other again,' he eventually said as he gave them all a cheery wave. 'I may even settle here myself. It's a beautiful spot.'

In the space of a morning, the life she had built crumbled before her. She saw, now, how naïve they had been. Della's happiness had blinded her to this forgotten fact: that fairytales are not pleasant stories. They are all edged with violence and darkness.

Chapter Nine

Now she knows that Ethan is not here, it is all Della can do to stop herself from locking the studio door behind her and hiding there for the rest of the day, submerged in clay. But first, she walks back to the house, checks the doors are still locked. She sees the bathroom window on the top floor misting up with the shower that Alex is taking. Loud music blasts out through the fan vent in the wall and, for once, Della is glad to hear it infusing the forest air.

Feeling guilty for wanting some time away from the house, Della opens the door to the studio and a familiar smell of clay and dust mingles with the damp smell of moss and earth. The smell calms her. It is as if she is entering a sacred space, a place of meditation. It soothes away some of her misery; she can feel it lifting off her like a heavy garment dropped at the door. The walls are plastered and whitewashed inside the stone building and when she switches on the lights, the spotlights in the ceiling illuminate the space in a neutral, gallery white. Two of the walls are covered in shelving, some of it built on castors so it can be moved easily. The wall furthest away from the door displays pieces she will never sell. On the wall without shelving there is a long table where she sketches and prepares pots for glazing. There is a double sink at one end of the building, and at the other an electric kiln for firing smaller items. It is a tranquil space, a country mile away from the noisy classroom where she first discovered the alchemy of clay.

Della remembers vividly the first time she threw her own pot. She was ten or eleven, freshly bereaved. Her teacher, Miss Abramovich, took a perfect ball of grey clay and threw it with surprising aggression on to the centre of the wheel. It seemed to Della that she worked some kind of magic with it, wetting it so it was pliant and smooth, cupping it with her hands and building it up to a cone, when all the while the wheel spun fast, throwing out cloudy drips of water into the basin underneath.

'I centre the clay for you.' Miss Abramovich nodded, dipping her hands into a bowl of water and drying them on a tea towel. 'Now, is your turn.' Her voice was deep, her accent rich and mysterious. She stood and gestured for Della to take her place.

Della lowered herself on to the stool, opened her knees wide, rearranged her apron so it covered her legs and leaned over the wheel. The clay was now the shape of a thick disc. It looked like an oversized hockey puck, or a mountain that had been sliced horizontally through the middle.

'Wet it,' said Miss Abramovich. 'The clay is always thirsty.'

Della leaned over and wetted her fingertips, dripping water sparingly over the clay.

'More, more like this.' Miss Abramovich threw a handful of water, wetting the wheel, making sure Della's hands were covered. 'Don't be shy about it. Now start the wheel. Fast.'

Della pressed on the foot pedal, gently, and the disc began to revolve slowly in front of her like a weird record player.

'Faster,' said Miss Abramovich. 'Is easier to work when it goes fast. Be bold. Show the clay who's boss.'

Della did as she was told. She was a little frightened of Miss Abramovich, who rarely smiled and didn't suffer fools. She pressed the pedal to the floor and the clay spun faster.

'Now. Take your index finger and your middle finger, put them together, like this, and touch the middle of the clay with your fingertips, firmly, so you make a dent.'

Della lowered her two fingers on to the surface of the spinning clay. It felt cold, smooth and slippery. When she pushed harder, the clay gave way willingly and bloomed like a strange flower.

'Now open it out,' Miss Abramovich said. 'Push those fingers to the bottom, not all the way or you'll make a hole in the base, but just enough. Then pull your fingers out to the sides so you widen the base.'

Miraculously, everything Miss Abramovich said, happened. When Della moved her fingers, the clay obeyed. She began to understand the pressure it needed to respond and, as she did so, something overtook her. This was the one thing in her life that she could control. She couldn't alter the fact her father had died so suddenly. She couldn't stop her mother from shrinking into grief. She hadn't the strength to combat Ethan's growing anger. But she could do this. She burrowed her fingers into the solid mass and stretched it out. It began to drag under her fingertips, and she knew it was time to wet it again to make the surface slippery once more.

'That's good,' nodded Miss Abramovich in approval. 'Very good. Now you pull up the sides of your vessel.'

Della noted the word *vessel.* It seemed a grown-up word somehow, more important than *pot.* She followed Miss Abramovich's instructions, using both hands now, her left hand inside, her right outside, bringing up the sides, making the vessel taller. The ridges her fingertips made on the surface of the clay were beautiful to her, the spinning shape that bent and flexed under the lightest touch.

'Play with it now, Della, see what it can do.'

Della put her fingertip gently to the rim of the vessel and it flared gracefully out. She wet her hands once more and took her finger to the middle of the vessel wall. She poked it in, softly at first, and then a little harder. The vessel gained a waist before the whole thing began to wobble and lose its balance. She cried out as her creation spun and collapsed in front of her eyes into a sodden, crumpled heap. She looked up at her teacher, feeling cheated. But Miss Abramovich gave a throaty laugh before she scraped the mess off the wheel, dried the surface and gave her a fresh ball of clay.

'Don't expect perfection first time, Della. Throwing is like learning language. You have to understand the clay, and that takes time. Be patient, be persistent. I see you have these qualities. Now is time to put them to good use.'

Della has made many mistakes since that day, and she has discarded many ugly lumps of clay, but she has never lost the feeling of power that the clay gave to her, that unforgettable memory of it yielding with the same grace under her youthful and inexperienced fingers as it did with Miss Abramovich.

Now, Della looks to the pieces that are drying on the racks. Pieces she shaped when Leo was alive. She touches them one by one, feeling the surface of the clay, judging how ready they are to be trimmed. The clay must be leather hard before it can be whittled and perfected. If she leaves them too long they will become too brittle to work with.

Most of the vessels are functional tableware – cups, plates, bowls. She is good enough, now, to make sets, producing every piece the same size and shape as the last, as if they have come out of a factory. At the end of the rack, away from the sets, there is a large, shrouded shape. She lifts the muslin cloth that covers it. It is the biggest piece she has ever attempted, a Korean-style moon jar in porcelain. A huge, circular vessel resting on a narrow, round base, so, if lit correctly, it will look as if it is hovering, like the rising moon above a rice field. When it is glazed and fired, the surface will become milk-white, but the colour won't be flat and even, it will sing with texture. The nature of the glaze will give the surface its own unique character, resembling the surface of the moon.

Moon jars are hard to make because the shape is top heavy, inherently unstable at this scale. The vessel must be thrown in two parts and joined in the middle to make the sphere. It is impossible to make a perfect sphere; the imperfection is part of the charm. And it meant something to her, to do this, for Leo. She hadn't told him she was doing it. She was going to present it to him on March the twentieth, on the vernal equinox, the first day of spring and, more crucially, their wedding anniversary.

Della touches the pot, which has already been bisque-fired to drive out the moisture. The surface is a matte bone white. It feels dry and grainy to touch, like chalk. The clay was expensive because it was the purest Ming porcelain she could find. Della thinks about the hope she poured into this vessel when she formed it. She can acknowledge to herself, in this private space, that this was not just a gift, it was a question, an intention.

What is going wrong between us? We need to put this right.

Della has spoken to nobody about the way Leo changed in the past twelve months. She knows the reason. The illness and death of his father so soon after his mother. It has been a tough year for him. But there was something else, something she couldn't put her finger on, like a discordant note in a melody. Underneath his grief, Leo had changed. There was a disconnection, as if he were distracted with something beyond her help. She had never seen him like that. She began to wonder if it wasn't just the death of his father, that it was something to do with her. She tried to talk to him, but she sensed a resistance too subtle to comment on. Usually, Leo loved to talk. He was always ready to share the details of his day. But during the past year, and particularly the last week of his life, when she asked him, he became silent, and Della wondered if he was annoyed with her, or worse, bored.

In the early hours, when she couldn't sleep, she would often glance over to the sleeping form of her husband and worry how her whole adult life had been constructed around him, how exposed she would be if he left her.

Leo would never leave, would he? He was a rock in the ground. Unchanging, reliable, steadfast. But still, the thought that he might want to, was perhaps thinking about it, hummed away in the background of her life, like a low purr of static. The uncertainty this gave her ate into her days like a canker and she slowly became a version of herself she disliked. She trod on eggshells around him, she spent more time in the studio, hoping if she disappeared he might miss her and come looking. But he didn't come. He remained at the kitchen table after she had cleared away the meal she had cooked for him, holding a cup of coffee that had long since cooled. Sometimes, when she came back from the studio or from Marmite's evening walk, she could see Leo through the lit window, and she stood in the darkness observing her husband staring into space, immersing himself in thoughts he wouldn't share.

In September, only six months away, Alex will leave to go to university. It would have been just the two of them. A fresh start. They have never lived together, alone. Alex was born only weeks after they moved in here. Della saw this year as a turning point. And now . . .

Della covers the pot with the cloth.

'Mum?' Alex's voice is quiet and cracked with grief. Her hair is wet from the shower, there are delicate strands plastered to her forehead.

Della watches her cross the studio floor and fights the urge to tell her to wear something warmer. She has wrapped herself in a coat of Leo's. It hangs, mid-thigh, exposing bare flesh, a thick pair of woollen socks rumpled at her shins.

'Hey, how are you? Did you sleep? Are you hungry?' Della asks. She takes in the dark circles under her daughter's eyes. 'Let me make you some breakfast.'

Della makes sure Marmite is out of the studio before she locks up. They walk back to the house together and, immediately, all three of them hear it. A beeping sound coming from the dirt track, quiet at first, then louder. Della's heart leaps, thinking of Ethan, but she soon understands it is a lorry reversing, she hears the roof of it crash into the branches of the lowest-hanging trees. They both quicken their pace, and Della sees colour moving beyond the trees, which resolves itself into a logo on the back of the van: *Reggie's Removals*.

Alex turns to Della, a perplexed look on her face. 'Looks like someone's taken a wrong turn.'

Then Della remembers as the past twenty-four hours reassemble in a murky jumble of information. 'Tash told me yesterday that the other half of the house has been sold.'

'Our house?'

'Well, Mrs Winters' house.'

'When did that happen?'

'I don't know.'

Mindful Alex is still half dressed, she asks her to take Marmite inside while she finds out what's going on. The lorry draws up outside the front of the house and three men leap out.

'Number two, Beech Wood Cottage?' he asks.

'Yes,' says Della. 'It's been sold, then?'

'I hope so, otherwise I'm trespassing,' he says, signalling for the truck to be opened.

'Where's the new owner?' asks Della, craning her neck into the truck to see if anyone else is there.

'Following on. They were supposed to meet us here, but we were told they won't be moving in just yet.'

'Do you know anything about them?'

'I don't,' the man says, turning his attention to the truck.

'Male or female?' she presses, her mind never far from Ethan.

'No idea,' he replies.

Della turns back to her own side of the house, not wanting to watch. They have been here, alone, for almost six years. They never put fences up between the two houses, there was never any need. Della can't imagine sharing her space with anyone else, hearing noises coming through the walls once more. She wonders what kind of person would want to live here, whether they are going to get along, and how she will do it all without Leo.

Chapter Ten

The morning passes in contrast. Inside their own half of the house, the atmosphere is shrouded in quiet. Next door, there is a constant percussion of activity until, finally, at lunchtime, the truck drives off, empty, and the house is left in silence once more. When Della hears another vehicle coming down the track, a car this time, she wonders if it might be the new owners, so she stands behind the curtain in the kitchen and watches until she recognises the car, a huge four-wheel-drive Jaguar. Robin. Her heart sinks. She had forgotten.

'Alex?' she murmurs, still looking out of the window. 'I have to speak to Robin about finances, and we'll need the kitchen table.'

'Now?' asks Alex, looking disoriented, as if she has just woken up. She is sitting at the table, staring at her phone, a plate of half-eaten toast, the only thing she seems able to stomach, in front of her.

'Yeah. They've just arrived. Do you want to say hello?'

'Not right now. I'll go to my room.'

'Tash will want to see you.'

'Maybe later.' Alex gets up from her chair. She is bare-legged, dressed in the same baggy T-shirt as yesterday, covered by a knee-length chunky cardigan. Leo's cardigan, Della notices. Della swallows a lump in her throat when she catches Alex sniff the collar as she wraps it around her body.

The doorbell rings through the house and Della takes her time to answer it, struggling to compose herself, taking a long, deep breath before she opens the door.

Tash rushes in and gives her a hard hug, but Robin hangs back a little. It is the first time she has seen Robin looking uncertain. His face is drawn, a bad night's sleep perhaps, like the rest of them. He hesitates before he comes into the house, eventually giving her a too-long bear hug, not saying anything, which is also unusual. When he pulls back and looks at her, it is obvious he is trying to keep his composure and she is reminded that he knew Leo first, their relationship stretching back to freshers' week. Again, she gets the feeling that Leo's absence is a physical thing, destabilising them all until they can find a new shape to occupy.

'How's Alex?' asks Tash, already in the kitchen, looking for her.

'Upstairs. She's not dressed yet. Not quite ready for visitors,' Della says pointedly.

'I'll put the kettle on, shall I?' says Tash. 'While you talk to Robin.'

Robin puts his briefcase on the kitchen table, but he doesn't open it. He rests his hands on it and gestures for her to sit, clearing his throat in that pompous way Della associates with him. She sees he is dressed for the occasion. A full suit, even though they are friends. He even has a tie with tiny polka dots knotted at his thick neck.

Robin loves a suit, Leo said once. Della understood why. There was a reason Robin was such a success on the rugby field. He was built for it, and a suit made him look even more imposing. He's never been tall, like Leo, but he learned to command authority under expensive waistcoats and tailored jackets.

Robin clears his throat again, coughs, and Della realises he is struggling to talk. After a moment he mumbles, 'I never imagined . . . I never thought I would have to do this.' He shakes his head and says, almost to himself, 'I always assumed it would be me before Leo.' Again, that strangled noise in his throat as he masters his emotions. Della sees him take a deep breath, his jacket swelling to a bigger size, his shirt straining at the buttons across his chest. He lets the breath out, nods imperceptibly, and suddenly he is the old Robin again, commanding a room.

'Being Leo's financial adviser,' he begins, 'I can help you organise Leo's estate. He had a will, so from that perspective it will be very straightforward. Everything passes to you, and because you are married there will be no inheritance tax to pay. We won't have to apply for probate, but you'll need several copies of his death certificate to be able to prove to the authorities you have control of the family finances now. But that's easy to do.'

'Well, OK,' says Della. Her legs feel shaky. She sits down. 'That sounds good.' She wants to hang on to something positive, even though there is nothing positive about this meeting.

Robin sighs, his voice full of regret. 'Yes, it is. Leo was a very organised person. He hasn't left much to chance . . .' He pauses, his fingertips brushing the surface of the table, and it is then that Della remembers the last time Robin came here with a couple of his friends, to play poker. There is a beat of silence when, Della is sure, Robin is remembering the same thing.

Tash delivers three mugs of tea to the table, crashing through the silence.

Robin frowns. 'There is an outstanding mortgage on the house that will need to be paid. I can arrange for you to have a mortgage holiday. Mortgage lenders understand it's a difficult time, so they often give clients a bit of leeway if you want to stay in the property and take over payments. You might want to sell up, of course. We can talk about that. That might be the easiest thing to do.'

'But we've paid the mortgage off. Leo said he was going to do that when his father died.'

Robin hesitates. 'That didn't happen.'

'Why didn't it happen? Frank died a year ago.'

Robin pulls the waistband of his trousers up as if to check it is there. 'I believe Leo decided to invest it instead.'

'Well, he didn't say anything to me about it.' She looks at Robin and he breaks eye contact, frowning.

It is Della's turn to frown. 'Well, where's the money? Frank sold his house before he went into care, he had savings. Leo inherited the lot. It was a substantial amount. I could pay off the mortgage with it right now if I had access to it.'

Robin shakes his head. 'Did Leo mention anything to you about what he did with the proceeds of his father's house sale?'

Della feels a prick of annoyance. 'You're the financial adviser, Robin. Shouldn't you know?'

'I didn't advise Leo's father, just you and Leo. He had to pay care home fees for several months. It wasn't cheap. Some of it will have gone on that.'

'But not all of it! Not by a long stretch.' Della has the sensation she is in a room filling with water. That it will soon reach over her head. She pictures Robin and Tash, bringing in a dual salary in a house they can comfortably afford. She tries to see how she will be able to afford the mortgage for her and Alex. She has a hobby, not a job.

'So you don't know how the fees were paid? From which bank account?' Robin asks.

'Leo dealt with it.' Della feels helpless and stupid. She never took any interest in money because Leo always took care of that sort of thing.

'Della, if you sold this house and the land, it would solve everything,' says Robin. 'The land doesn't have any restrictions on it, so it could be sold for development, separately from the house. You could be comfortably off, if you did that, so don't worry too much about the savings.'

But I am worried, thinks Della. 'I might not want to sell,' she ventures, remembering Leo's words.

Don't sell the house.

'This is my home,' she continues. 'Alex's home. It's my workplace, too, and the idea of giving the woods over to developers . . .' It is typical of Robin not to care about an acre of wood being bulldozed to make way for houses.

'You may have to if you don't have savings to cover the mortgage. I'm not sure if your earnings—'

Again, that feeling of being overwhelmed by water, unable to breathe. How did she end up here? She cannot get over how her life has been upended in the space of twenty-four hours. She is standing on quicksand. Nothing is safe, nothing is stable. How could Leo leave her like this?

'What about his laptop?' Della says, suddenly animated. 'Won't that give us some idea?' She gets up and races up the stairs to the bedroom, where Leo's computer is hidden in a fire-proof floor safe. She pulls back the rug, opens the safe and brings the laptop back to the kitchen table.

'Here. He used this one for home stuff. His other laptop will be in the office, but he never kept anything personal on it. Maybe his banking stuff will be here?'

Robin gives a little laugh. 'He would have used the internet for banking, which you can access from any laptop.'

Della opens up the laptop, a brand-new Apple Mac. It blinks into life when she raises the lid and demands a fingerprint to proceed further.

'Can we bypass this?' Della asks, looking at Robin, then Tash.

'Don't you have the password?' asks Robin. 'You can use a password if you can't do the fingerprint.'

'I don't use this laptop. I use my phone for most things,' *or I ask Leo to do it.* This last thought is voiced privately. Her life is analogue: in the woods among the trees, in the studio with her hands in clay, in the house, cooking or cleaning, dropping Alex off or picking her up from somewhere. She doesn't have time to sit at a laptop, gazing into a screen. That was Leo's domain. IT was his job.

I'll take care of it. He used that phrase so often it became a catchphrase, an in-joke in their family. In her head, she lists the things that Leo took care of, the hidden things that greased their journey through life, and her stomach contracts. She knows she is an important member of this family, but she is nothing if she can't afford to pay the mortgage or get into their savings. The feeling of stupidity creeps over her again. How could she be so ignorant of the family finances?

'Look, let me think about this. I'm sure Leo must've left the password for me or something.' She doesn't feel confident when she says this, but she must try and take the reins of the situation. 'I can't think about this right now. Can I get back to you in a few days?'

'Are you going to be OK for money in the meantime?' Tash asks. 'We can give you whatever you need.'

'I have a bank card for the joint account,' Della replies, feeling nettled. She isn't a charity case. 'There's enough in there to tide us over.' *But not for long,* she thinks, trying to quell the panic. A clock has begun to tick, somewhere far away, and she knows the ticking will get louder and louder if she doesn't find out what happened to Leo's inheritance.

Tash breaks into her thoughts. 'Della, can I go and find Alex before we leave? I want to see her.'

'Sure.' Della waves absent-mindedly upstairs.

'Coming?' Tash asks Robin.

'In a minute, I'll catch you up,' says Robin.

They both wait until Tash has run upstairs.

'You knew, didn't you?' says Della quietly. 'You knew he hadn't paid off the mortgage and hadn't told me about it.'

'In all fairness, I thought he was going to invest the money and that he would discuss it with you first. He might have done that, actually. Invest it, I mean.'

'And not tell you about it? I doubt it. He did nothing financial without your say-so. Leo was planning on paying the mortgage off, we all discussed it over dinner that night.'

She recalls that dinner. Candlelight, Leo drunk because Frank's death was still so fresh, but optimistic something good could come of his legacy. Robin, who was always drunk at these dinners, suggested a list of frivolous things Leo should do, from ice driving in the Arctic Circle to flying lessons. But Leo was adamant he wanted to pay the mortgage off.

'Look,' says Robin, spreading his fingers wide on the briefcase, 'I admit, I should have been a bit more curious. I should have chased it up. But he's not my only client, Della. I have a whole list of people to look after, and they are entitled to change their minds about what to do with their money. As soon as you get access to his affairs, I'm sure you'll find out.'

'How? I can't get into his computer.'

'What about his phone?'

Della hasn't thought about that. 'I don't know.' She thinks about the last call that phone made. The woman's voice. She wonders what happened to it after the call ended. 'It's probably at the hospital with his things,' she says.

Robin looks at her, a different expression on his face. 'We would never see you starve, Della. It was an unspoken agreement between Leo and me that I would always look out for you and Alex.'

Della's stomach turns inside out. 'I don't need your help. I'll be fine.' As the words leave her mouth, she knows it isn't true.

'You know,' Robin says, his fingertips circling the leather of his briefcase, 'there was a time . . .'

'Don't,' says Della in a low voice.

There is a small silence, and then Robin says quietly, 'I miss him too, you know. He was my friend, too.'

Alex's door opens and Della can hear feet on the stairs.

'The offer's there,' he says before he walks over to Alex, arms outstretched. 'Come and give your uncle Robin a hug. Make an old man happy, will you?'

Chapter Eleven

It's been forty-eight hours since Leo died, and already a lifetime has passed. She knows she must return to the hospital to register his death and discuss the results of the autopsy, but the conversation she had with Robin yesterday is still ringing in her head. She must try and get into Leo's computer.

Della thinks about knocking on Alex's door, waking her up, but she wants to let her sleep, so she leaves a note on the kitchen table.

Just popped out to the high street. Back soon. Marmite has been fed. Text me if you want anything X

The village has grown since they moved here. It has become an attractive prospect for people who can't afford to live in London but have to travel to work there. The high street used to be a supermarket, a takeaway, a bank, an estate agent's and a post office, but now it has expanded and there are several gift shops that stock Della's pottery, some nice restaurants and bars, and everything else a person might need. Della parks outside the estate agent's and gazes into the window. She wonders who has taken the other half of the house. Then she gets out of the car, hyper-aware that this is the street Leo collapsed in. She looks up and down, for evidence of where this event happened, but there is nothing to see. There are no markers to commemorate the place her husband fell.

She walks, with Leo's laptop in her bag, and goes into the smallest shop on the high street, occupying a corner space that used to be a barber's. It's a phone repair shop that Della has often used to buy SIM cards and fix cracked screens that Alex has damaged over the years. Consequently, she is on friendly terms with Mo, the guy who runs it.

'Mrs Harkin!' Mo opens his arms wide. 'It's been a long time. Which is good, I think?' he asks, laughing.

'I haven't brought you a phone repair this time,' Della replies, wondering how much to tell Mo about Leo. 'It's a laptop. I need to get into it, but it's locked.'

She hands the laptop over to Mo, who inspects it admiringly. 'My son wants one of these,' he murmurs. 'Nice. Very nice. Too expensive for him, though. Let me know if you ever want to sell it.'

Della tries to smile at him, but it is hard. She is out of practice. 'I'm locked out of it. That's the problem. Can you get in?'

Mo opens the lid and, once more, the Apple Mac springs into life. 'It's fingerprint recognition. You just put your finger here, see?' He shows her, obligingly, how to do it.

'It's my husband's computer, that's the problem, and he . . . he isn't here to do it. I need to look something up and he didn't give me the password.'

'Oh.' Mo frowns, looking uncertain. 'You need his fingerprint to get into this. Apple take their security very seriously. It's probably why your husband uses it. He's an IT specialist, yes?'

'Yes. Look, Mo, is there any way you can bypass the fingerprint and just . . . get into the computer? I really need to look inside.'

Mo looks a little uncomfortable. 'Is he away for long? Your husband? I don't think it's going to be possible to circumvent this. Maybe you wait until he returns? Or you ask him for the password?

I don't want to get into any trouble. Phones are more my thing. Not so much the computers.'

Della nods and takes a breath. 'Mo, my husband died on Thursday.' She waits for the bomb to drop, and Mo's expression crumples with confusion and, then, compassion. The look on his face brings her to tears and she hunts for a tissue in her pockets. She cannot bear his kindness, this gentle, softly spoken man. It is too overwhelming, like a bright light she cannot look at.

'Mrs Harkin, I thought you looked sad when you came in. I am so sorry. Here . . .' He proffers a handkerchief of his own. It is ironed and folded into a neat square, and this simple act brings her fresh tears as she imagines Mo's wife ironing his handkerchiefs for him, making sure he has a fresh one before he leaves the house.

'Sit, please. Sit down. I'm so sorry. Let me see what I can do. Will you be alright here if I go for a few minutes to the back?'

Della nods, glad to be left alone for a moment so she can compose herself. Mo gently takes the laptop from her and disappears into the back while Della dabs her eyes and cleans up her face in a small mirror on the wall of the shop. She is going to have to do this many, many times, she thinks to herself as she waits for Mo. She will have to break the news to countless people, and every time she will have to absorb a little of their shock and their pain and their compassion and their kindness. The kindness particularly – it bruises her in a way she cannot understand.

Mo returns to the front of the shop after a few minutes. 'It is as I thought,' he declares gravely. 'If you don't have a fingerprint, you need a password. I can get you into the computer as a separate user, but you won't be able to see any of the documents already on there.'

'I don't understand,' says Della. 'You'll have to explain it to me like I'm an idiot.'

'So this laptop, it is like a book, see?' Mo puts his hands together and then opens them, hinged. 'I can get you into the book, but the pages your husband has written – that is, all of his files – these pages are glued together. Without his fingerprint, or his password, you cannot unstick them. I can only get you on to a different page of the book, a clean page, where you can use the computer and make your own files. Do you see?'

Della sees. And then she sees other things. The fact Leo never shared his password with her. The fact he never involved her in the household finances, or his father's legacy. If it was a kindness, it is coming back to hurt her now. She thinks about the countless times she asked him a question about money or technology or how something worked in the house. He always told her not to worry about it, that he'd take care of it. And then the mortgage. She was sure he'd paid it off. He seemed so certain he wanted to do it. Why did he change his mind? Why didn't he discuss it with her?

As she leaves the shop, an uncomfortable thought enters her head. There is an area of Leo's life she has been excluded from, and she is not sure how deliberate, how unkind, that exclusion was. As she gets into her car a small seed of resentment swells and grows. She will not be defeated by a laptop. She will tear the house apart, looking for his password. She will comb through his belongings, and if she can't find it, she will look for his phone. If she can find his phone, she might have more luck.

Chapter Twelve

When Della returns home, Alex is up, picking at a piece of toast. Her eyelids are swollen, and the whites of her eyes are pink. Her eyelashes are stuck together with tears.

'Shall I make you something?' Della asks gently. Alex screws up her face as if she might be sick. 'OK, OK,' Della reassures her. 'Just eat what you feel like.'

'Why did you go to the high street?' Alex asks.

'I needed to talk to Mo about getting into Dad's laptop.'

Alex snorts. 'Good luck with that. You know what he was like. Mr Security.'

Della looks at her hopefully. 'You don't know the password for it, do you?'

'No chance.' Alex grimaces, and her tone softens slightly. 'You can use my laptop if you need one.'

'It's OK, I was just . . . I don't know. Curiosity, I guess.' Della sits down opposite Alex. 'I'm going to call the hospital this morning and see if I can pick up the medical certificate tomorrow so I can . . .' She pauses, unwilling to say the words, wanting to protect her daughter from the bureaucracy of it all. 'So I can register Dad's death.'

Alex considers this for a moment, a grim look on her face. 'What does that involve?'

'It means going back there, and some form-filling, I think.'

'Is Dad still at the hospital? I thought, maybe—' Alex shakes her head. 'I don't know what I thought, actually.'

Della looks at her, saddened that she should even have to consider these things at her age. 'Yes, he is. They should have finished the autopsy by now. I think the funeral director will pick him up on Monday morning.'

'Can I come with you to the hospital? Can I see him?'

Della hesitates. 'Are you sure you want to do that?'

Alex nods, emphatically. 'Yes. I want to see him.'

'Of course. If it would make you feel better. Of course you can see him. I'm sure the nurse said it would be OK to visit. I'll call and arrange it.'

'Has Marmite been out today?' asks Alex.

'Just for a wee but not for a walk.'

'I'll take him out.'

'Actually don't,' says Della, thinking that there might be some truth in Leo's words, that Ethan might be near. Her mind turns to the blue scrap of fabric she found in the woods, still caught in the branches, still flapping like an injured bird.

'Why can't I walk him?' Alex presses.

'Um, someone said there was a guy in the woods, exposing himself to young women.'

Alex wrinkles her nose. 'Ew, Mum, yuck.'

'I know. You could do without that. I don't want you going out there for a while. Not until they've caught him.'

Alex rolls her eyes. 'What are the chances of that? Virtually zero.'

'I know. Just . . . humour me. Don't go in there for a while. Give it a few days, yeah?'

'OK. I might go to the library then.'

'The library?'

'Yeah,' says Alex quietly. 'I think we should find some readings for Dad.'

A dark wash bleeds through the fabric of Della's understanding. She sits at the kitchen table, her body thumping down on the chair as her legs give way. 'I haven't even thought about that.'

'That's OK. I'd quite like to do it.'

Della looks at her daughter. 'Would you? Really?'

'Well, the readings at least. I don't want to organise a whole funeral.'

A thought passes through Della's mind, and she shakes her head to dislodge it.

'What?' asks Alex.

'Nothing. I suppose . . . I was wondering why you don't look for readings on the internet, like every other teenager. But . . . It's none of my business why you'd prefer to use the library.'

'Dad would have liked it,' says Alex simply.

And Della understands what Alex means. That Leo would have liked the image of his daughter leafing through a book, illuminated by a shaft of sunlight, in the same library he used as a boy, to find readings to honour him, rather than surfing the web in between updating her TikTok account. The fact Alex has understood this affirms the closeness she had with Leo, and Della wonders if she would have the same level of understanding when the time comes for Della's funeral. She knows the answer and realises now is not the time to dwell on it.

'Shall I run you down there?' Della asks.

'I'd rather walk,' Alex replies. 'I need to get out.'

'As long as you walk up the track to the road and get the bus, OK?' Della insists. 'There and back. And take your phone.'

Alex nods, gathers her things and leaves.

The house feels quiet without anyone else there, but it isn't relaxing and calm. It's kinetic and wrong. Della feels agitated and unable to focus. She drifts aimlessly into the bedroom. The cottage is old, there are beams in the walls and ceiling, but the interior has been modernised. There are remote-controlled curtains and lights that can be activated by Leo's phone app, or discreet recessed buttons sunk into the plasterwork. Their bedroom and bathroom are painted in masculine, cool shades. It looks like something out of a boutique hotel.

Because of the odd, uneven shape of the house, they have fitted wardrobes that Leo organised through a local builder. Between drawers and shelves, there are little hidey-holes and storage spaces for smaller items. Some are covered with panels that click open if you press them in the right spot. There was always a worry Ethan could break in; he was often short of money. Leo wanted to make it as difficult as possible for him.

Della opens Leo's side of the wardrobe. His shirts hang together, neatly, laundered and pressed. His suit jackets, trousers and ties are all grouped in outfits, ready to be worn. Della inhales them, seeking his scent, but all she gets is the smell of fabric softener. She wishes she had thought to wear his cardigan, as Alex has done, so she could smell his body. By now it will reek of her daughter's perfume.

Without really thinking about what she is doing, Della starts looking in his pockets, at first tentatively, then with more urgency. When she finds nothing, she goes into the drawers and slides her fingers around every neatly folded T-shirt, every pair of socks. She picks out his favourite pair and holds it to her cheek for a moment, before using it to wipe her eyes. Then she decides to go through the cubbyholes. One houses spare change, spare keys for the windows and doors. There is a collection of stones Alex gave him when she was little, picked off the shoreline on a beach holiday. It touches Della he has made a place for them here, among his most intimate things. There is a slim space filled with old tickets for the theatre, an entrance ticket for the first time they took Alex to the zoo. A receipt for something she does not recognise. Handwritten, quaint-looking, issued only a few days ago. She scrutinises it. One hundred and ninety-five pounds spent on *Betula pendula,* whatever that is. Shocked at the price, she makes a mental note to look it up, folds it and puts it into her pocket. Then, moving on to a slim panel that looks insignificant, Della presses and shoves until it springs open.

There, in the narrow space, is a bank book. Della's heart gives a little leap. It is an old-fashioned building society book, and the name on the front is *Franklyn Harkin,* Leo's father, which makes sense, because Leo would never have an account like this with a physical book that could be stolen.

Della takes the book and sits on the bed, going through it from front to back. The account was opened when both Leo's parents were alive. Deposits are few and far between. But then, around the time that Leo's father, widowed and ill, sold the house to go into care, a huge amount is deposited, almost two hundred thousand pounds. Then, regular withdrawals are made, presumably to cover the cost of Frank's care. But there are other withdrawals, after Frank passed away. Della looks at the last date. The last withdrawal was made a few days before Leo died, and it has wiped the account clean.

Della stares into the pages of the bank book, willing them to make sense. She knows that Leo had power of attorney over his father, so although the name on this book is not Leo's, Leo would have had the right to use the money for his father's care. Della frowns at the dates once more, not understanding. She raises her head and stares out of the window. A woodpecker laughs and is answered by a mate. The trees whisper to one another, as if they might know the answer.

Della is overcome by the feeling she has lost something she never had, and a memory emerges from the darkness of her past, of waking up on the morning of her sixteenth birthday, going down the stairs to breakfast, where she knew birthday cards would be waiting for her. She still had a couple of aunts and uncles, a grandparent who sent her money on special occasions such as this. The anticipation of having her own money to spend on something nice was better than any gift. She wasn't allowed a job of her own. She had to work in the newsagent's, and she didn't get paid for that.

Usually, the cards lay, unopened, next to her cereal bowl. But today, they had all been opened for her and were arranged nicely around the table. Her mother was waiting, looking nervous, and Della felt observed as she read through every card. A couple of them referred to the money that had been sent. But there were no notes on the table. No cheques.

'Where's the birthday money?' she had asked her mother.

Her mother looked embarrassed. 'Ethan thought it best to keep it somewhere safe.'

As if her words had summoned him, Ethan strode into the room, a man now, at almost twenty years old. 'You're only sixteen,' he explained. 'You can't be trusted to look after that amount of cash.'

'But I might want to spend it,' countered Della.

Ethan rolled his eyes. 'Only when you tell me what you want first. I don't want you wasting it.'

Della thought quickly. 'I want a dress for the school dance. It's next month, and the whole year is going.'

'You don't need a dress, and you don't need to go to a stupid dance,' Ethan barked, taking a slice of toast that was meant for her.

'Ethan . . .' said her mother, faintly.

Ethan shot her a look. 'It's a waste of time. She's leaving school anyway, what's the point?'

'Leaving school?' echoed Della. 'Who said I was leaving school?' She thought about Miss Abramovich, their precious time together in lessons and the lunch hour, the only time Della felt she was truly understood.

And then something happened. A lifting, a clearing, a dawn of realisation. Ethan had no intention of giving her that money. She would never be able to stay on at school. She would be stuck here, working a full-time job with no pay, for the rest of her life.

Later, when Ethan had gone to the cash-and-carry, her mother took her to one side. 'I have some nice fabric,' she said. 'I'll make you something for the dance, I promise.'

Three weeks later, after many late nights of sewing when Ethan was asleep, Della tried the dress on. Her mother had worked magic with a length of emerald-green satin. It flowed to the floor like a river. She looked like a film star, like the models in the magazines she still tried to read when Ethan wasn't looking.

They hid the dress away until the night of the dance, and when Della couldn't find it, and she smelled an acrid burning in the back garden, she knew they had been found out. She couldn't help it. She looked out of the window. There, among the flames, was a sea of emerald being eaten by fire.

Della stares out of the window of her bedroom and on to the canopy of trees, remembering. And then she looks down at the bank book in her hands. Two hundred thousand pounds, gone in the space of eighteen months.

What has happened here? she thinks. *What has Leo been doing?*

Leo had everything in his name, because Ethan would have tracked her down if he hadn't, he said. But Ethan *did* track her down, less than three years after they moved into this house. That was almost fifteen years ago, and over that time, Ethan has appeared occasionally, demanding money, threatening Della. Leo has always sent him away. Leo has always taken care of everything.

It stopped being important, hiding her name. They had already decided this was their forever home and they didn't want to move. They would just make the house impenetrable. But Leo didn't put her name on the mortgage, or the deeds to the house.

An uncomfortable parallel begins to draw itself in her mind between the money that was taken on her birthday and the money that has been taken here. This was for their future, surely? That's what Leo said. The slow, thick feeling of stupidity runs through her once more, like oil.

She pulls out her phone and googles Ethan's name. He would be delighted at the lack of information she can find. The only trace of him is in an old newspaper article, which she can recite by heart:

The family-run newsagent's is no stranger to tragedy. The owner, William Locke, died suddenly of a heart attack nine years ago, leaving Imogen Locke and her two children struggling to run the business. Ethan, the eldest child, took over the newsagent's when he was sixteen and was making a success of it until everything was tragically wiped out by a fire last Friday night.

Twenty-three-year-old Ethan and his nineteen-year-old sister, Adele, managed to escape with minor injuries, but their mother, Imogen, died at the scene. She was forty-nine years old.

Chapter Thirteen

Della sits on the edge of the bed for some time, staring out of the window, wrestling with her thoughts. She thinks back over the past eighteen months. They had been tough for both of them, but particularly Leo. Frank became ill, unable to cope. Leo had to sell the house he grew up in and find a care home. Frank only lasted six months in there before he died. Della remembers coming into their bedroom with an armful of washing, expecting it to be empty, but instead she found Leo, sitting on the bed as she is now, crying.

'Leo, what can I do?' she had asked, putting the washing down and sitting next to him. There was nothing she could do, she knew that.

He shook his head. 'I don't know,' he said quietly. 'It just keeps hitting me.'

She took his hand. 'I know. First your mum, now your dad. Me and Alex and Marmite – we're right here for you.'

Leo had been depressed after his father died, there was no doubt. She'd encouraged him to do something for himself, and he started volunteering at a drop-in centre in the town, ten miles away.

'It's mainly pensioners who can't work their computers, but they find it helpful, and I like doing it, it's easy,' he said. She was proud of him for doing something with his grief, turning it into something positive.

They had weathered the last twelve months together, as a family. It had been hard. Leo was more withdrawn than usual, he went to bed early, and he dropped into sleep like a stone through water. But gradually, he began to improve. Every day, he seemed a little easier, a little lighter. He began to get over the death of his parents.

Della had assumed his recovery had been partly down to her support, but as she opens the bank book once more and looks at the dwindling figures, she wonders if he found succour elsewhere.

Could he have gambled it all away? she thinks. But Leo was always so contemptuous about gambling. He knew how the odds worked and knew it was always in the bookies' favour. It wasn't his style.

Ethan, then. That would be the most obvious explanation. That he has somehow been paying him off. But Ethan prided himself on living off-grid. Della knows that while Leo has, in the past, given Ethan money to go away, it was never amounts like this, not tens of thousands of pounds in one go. He must have been transferring it into some kind of investment account, just like Robin suggested.

Della becomes aware that this speculation is not good for her. She must put this uncertainty away. Whatever Leo has done with the money, he'd always acted in their best interests, and now it is her turn to be that person for Alex. The relationship Alex had with her father was so close, Della often found it hard to carve out a place between them. Della will not sully Leo's memory with her own dark thoughts about his secrecy. And Alex must be protected from any worry until Della can figure out what has been going on.

Once more, memories of her own mother prick her conscience. She must have lived with the same agony of being left behind, of not knowing what to do next. Being widowed at the same age must be the only parallel Della can allow. She will deal with her own family differently. She must step up.

The back door opens and closes. Della goes down to meet Alex.

'How was the library?' she asks, putting the kettle on.

'OK,' replies Alex, shuffling into the kitchen, her shoulders rounded, her head down. 'I took out a few books.'

'I thought you were going to stay there today?' Della tries to establish eye contact.

Alex looks away and dumps her book-filled bag on the kitchen table. 'I changed my mind. It's full of people from school, revising for A levels. I don't want to talk to them.'

Della feels a stab of concern. 'Is there nobody you want to talk to right now? I'm happy to give you a lift wherever—'

'No,' says Alex with finality. 'What's that?' she asks, pointing to the bank book which Della has left near the kettle.

Della looks at it, not wanting to upset Alex further. But she has no choice. 'It's your grandad's bank book. I was trying to sort out finances.'

Alex picks it up and flicks through it. 'This is so old-school,' she declares. 'Wow. He had a lot of cash.' She flicks to the final page, where the account total is zero and looks up at Della. 'What happened?'

'I don't know. Actually, that's what I'm trying to find out.'

'Dad told me how much Grandad's house went for, and he was only in that care home for six months. There should be loads left over.'

Della is caught out. She had no idea Leo had discussed money with Alex. He certainly never discussed it with her. Now she is not sure what to say next.

'Did he tell you what he planned to spend that money on?' she asks Alex, trying to sound casual.

'No. Don't you know?'

'Well . . . no.'

'How can you *not know* where all this money went?' Alex turns the pages of the bank book in disbelief.

'Your dad never told me.'

'And you never thought to ask him? This isn't the nineteen-fifties, you know. You are allowed to be involved in life-changing amounts of money like this.'

'I always left that kind of thing to your father,' Della says quietly.

'Like a good feminist,' says Alex in a mocking voice. Suddenly, her body language changes, the vulnerability she has shown Della over the past couple of days vanishes and is replaced by anger. She points to the window. 'I swear you spend more time in that studio churning out mugs than you do in this house with your own family. You always let Dad take responsibility for everything.'

Something twists, painfully, deep inside Della. She doesn't have Alex's respect. Perhaps she never did. And again, the parallel with her own mother is presented to her, raw and unbidden.

'I am truly sorry, Alex. I'll make it up to you.'

Alex makes a noise of exasperation. 'How can you make it up? You don't even have a proper job.'

Della feels afraid. 'There are things we can do. Alex, I—'

Alex's face is heating up now, and she looks at Della with horror. 'Oh my *God,* you aren't going to sell this house, are you? Don't you *dare* sell this house!' Alex cries. 'Dad built this world for us, and you're going to tear it all apart.'

Della is unprepared for the strength of Alex's feelings. 'I'm not, I'm not. It might not come to that.'

'It better not,' Alex says, her voice low and dangerous. 'This is where we belong. I'm not going to let you throw it all away.' As she sweeps her bag off the kitchen table, heavy with books, it takes a plate of half-eaten toast with it and the whole lot drops on to the floor. The plate smashes into two neat halves, scattering crumbs. Della flinches at the noise and sinks to her knees to pick up the pieces. As she hears Alex's footsteps pounding up the stairs, the slam of her bedroom door, Della cowers on the floor, a familiar feeling in her gut. She should have been more involved in the finances. Alex is right. But the feeling doesn't stem from the argument they had, it was the way Alex looked at her when she became angry. The way her voice lowered. The words she used. She sounded just like Ethan.

Chapter Fourteen

It is Sunday morning, three days after Leo's death, and Della does the hardest thing she has to do each day. She gets out of bed, and she dresses herself, recalling the argument she had with Alex yesterday. She approached her daughter, later, as a stalker approaches a startled deer, suggesting Alex might share her anger with a friend, that she might feel better if she had someone else to talk to, but Alex gave her a derisory look.

'I told you,' she said in a flat voice. 'There's nobody at school I want to talk to.'

Della's heart sank as she understood that, yet again, Alex has fallen out with a friendship group that was once the centre of her life. Alex has never found it hard to make friends, she just can't seem to figure out how to keep them. She is a leader, not a follower. But instead of seeking out girls who are happy with this arrangement, she is drawn to others just like her, alpha girls who also want things exactly their own way. There is always a honeymoon period when Alex finds a new group of friends. They are invited over for sleepovers, or Alex stays out after school. Then the obsession begins to sour as Alex jostles for position in the group. There is usually a difference of opinion, or Alex becomes dismissive and careless of someone else's emotions. This is followed by a dramatic falling-out, involving furious texting and late-night phone calls. Then, there is silence. It is a cycle that Della has become familiar with since Alex was at primary school.

'Surely if your friends knew what was going on at home . . .'

'I'm not talking to any of those girls. They're all losers. I can't believe I wanted to hang around with them in the first place.'

So much anger. Her daughter has so much anger. It spills out of her like a torrent that can only be dammed temporarily.

They both went to bed in stony silence.

As Della walks down the stairs, she looks out of the window that gives a view over the front of the house and sees there is still no sign of the new neighbours; the only vehicle is hers. She imagines having to meet them, putting on a brave face, trying to pretend everything is OK, knowing that whoever moves in next door, delighted with their new home, Della and Alex will be a disappointment to them. Leo always had a knack with strangers. Any awkwardness was smoothed away by his easy cordiality. She feels like half a person now, unable to meet new people without him. Foregoing breakfast because she has no appetite, Della puts her boots and coat on, and summons Marmite for a walk.

Her eyes scan the ground as she moves through the forest, looking for any disturbed ground, any evidence of a fire, any discarded rubbish. The low level of the spring sunshine gives the woods the quality of a film set, illuminated by hidden stage lights slanting horizontally through the trees. As she moves, she feels as if she is being watched by hidden eyes. She walks through the blackthorn blossom falling around her shoulders like confetti, as her eyes sweep the ground. There is a pile of fresh, bloodied feathers from something that's been taken in the night. There are holes in the ground, scraped by claws. It feels ridiculous, looking for her brother in her own back garden, and the more she searches, the more reassured she feels that Leo must have been raving.

In the early hours of the morning, when she is left with nothing else but her own grief, Della googled the process of dying on Alex's computer. Patients often say things they do not mean. There is a compulsion to voice your deepest fears when you are on the edge of death, and she knows Leo's main concern was to keep her and Alex safe from Ethan. Of course he wouldn't want her to sell this house. Leo feels the same as Alex does. He had turned it into the safest place for all of them. Toughened glass. Reinforced doors and window frames. Heat sensors. Unbreakable locks. Cameras, front and back. He wouldn't want them to leave it after he died. He had spent so long putting everything in place.

Della stops scouring the ground. All is as it should be. The forest floor is still covered with last year's leaves. Her boots tread through layers of oak, beech and hornbeam that fell to the ground in the autumn, brown and crisp, and are now blackened with damp and mud, rapidly turning to mulch beneath her feet. A wet morning mist clouds the air, giving it a milky, eerie quality, and she can hear woodpeckers drumming the dead oaks above her head, an ancient, prehistoric noise that gives her a shivering thrill every time she hears it echoing through the air.

Della reaches the pond. The temperatures plummeted at the turn of the year, and in February she started watching the progress of ice creep across the water. There is always a time lag between the frost on the ground and frost on the pond. The freeze has to be steady and relentless before it takes hold here. But when it does, it happens like this: little patches of milky ice begin to form around the shallows. Then, floating islands of clear ice appear on the surface where it is deeper. Eventually, if the frost holds, these islands seek one another out, as if by instinct. They grow larger, knocking against one another, slowly fusing together to make a glassy sheet. And then the most extraordinary, the most wonderful thing happens.

The ice sings.

The sound is like the snapping of a taut wire ricocheting through the cold air, or a ghostly finger running round the rim of a glass. It is a sound that is so hard to describe, so otherworldly, that Della came here every morning to listen to it until the temperatures rose enough for the ice to disappear. Now, in the first days of March, with weak sunlight struggling through the boughs, the hard ground has turned to mush, and the pond won't sing for another year. Still, Della stands there listening, absorbing the sounds of the pond, looking at the surface of the water, the weak sunlight turning it to pewter before the sun disappears behind cloud cover.

The mist thickens into rainfall. She hears it before she feels it, the new leaves on the oak trees above her catching the raindrops until they become weighed down with water and drop their burden on to the branches below, until, inevitably, the rain falls through the leaves and on to the ground in a pitter-patter of sound, like a thousand tiny footsteps passing through the wood. Della breathes in the soft air, filling her body. Marmite gives her a pleading look and, taking pity on him, she turns around and walks with him, slowly, back to the house.

When she unlocks the kitchen door, she hears voices. Alex is talking to Tash, a pot of tea between them on the kitchen table. Alex is nibbling a piece of toast and Tash pushes a plate of cut apple slices before her.

'Hi,' says Della, looking around for Robin. 'I wasn't expecting you.'

'I thought I would drive you and Alex up to the hospital. You were going to sort out the death certificate today, right?'

A rush of gratitude courses through Della at the idea of her constant chatter in the car, breaking up the crust of silence that has formed between Della and Alex.

'Great,' says Della, taking some apple. 'Shall we go now?'

'No time like the present,' says Tash, draining her tea and grabbing her car keys from the table. 'Ready, Alex?'

Alex nods, not looking at Della. Della wonders if she has said anything to Tash about their argument last night and decides she probably hasn't.

As they approach the hospital, Della is simultaneously repelled and drawn to the building. It is the place of his death, yet it is where Leo lies, right now. She feels the push and pull of it like a black tide.

It doesn't take long to pick up the medical certificate of the cause of death; the autopsy didn't provide any surprises. Alex is taken away to see Leo, and Della and Tash go and collect his belongings. Della is handed a plastic bag, rather like a crime-scene evidence bag. It is sealed and annotated on the back. She opens it, inhaling the scent of his jacket, his shoes, his shirt, and she fancies she can smell a vestige of Leo clinging to the fabric.

'There's no phone in here.' She frowns, looking at Tash. 'His phone should be here, too.'

'I'll go back and ask,' says Tash. 'Maybe it's in a separate bag.'

But Tash comes back empty-handed. 'They said that's all they have but they'll ask the person in charge and phone you if they find it. That's the best I could do.' Tash puts her arm around Della's shoulders. 'Come on, let's go to the canteen and wait for Alex.'

They find a small, square table in the far corner of the canteen. 'Are you hungry? Can I get you anything?' Tash asks.

'I can't eat anything,' says Della. 'I feel like I have a stone in my stomach.' She hugs the bag containing Leo's belongings and draws a small comfort from it. 'I wonder if the person who called me still has his phone,' she says, remembering the confusion she could hear on the street. 'Maybe in the drama, they kept hold of it.'

'They would have called you again, surely? They wouldn't have kept it.'

'I suppose,' says Della.

'Only one way to find out. Call it,' urges Tash.

Della pulls out her own phone, and it feels sad and strange to call Leo's number, seeing his name flash up on the screen as it has done thousands of times. But the phone is dead, it goes straight to voicemail, a man's voice that isn't Leo's tells her he can't come to the phone right now, and Della feels regret that Leo never recorded his own message for this purpose, that she will never be able to sit and dial this number, listen to his voice.

'What's wrong?' asks Tash, ever alert to her mood.

'I don't know . . . I just get the feeling that whoever called me that morning knew him. That they weren't strangers.'

'What makes you think that?' asks Tash.

Della can't articulate this feeling she has had since last Thursday. Her shoulders slump and she hugs Leo's belongings tighter. 'I don't know.'

Tash thinks. 'It was on the high street, yeah? It was busy, plenty of people walking by. Anybody would have stopped for him. If she'd known him, or if she was with him, she would have gone into the ambulance, wouldn't she? You're allowed to do that, aren't you, if you know the person? And she would have told you who she was.'

But Della isn't sure this woman wanted her to know who she was. She doesn't know why. 'I just . . . I just can't shake the feeling something was going on.'

'What do you mean?' asks Tash, cocking her head to one side like a watchful hound.

Della sits back in her chair and rakes her hands through her hair. 'The mortgage. He told me he was going to pay it off and he didn't. I found a bank book that belonged to his father and all of the money from the sale of his house has been transferred out. I don't know where it's gone.' As Della speaks, she can't explain the acute sense of shame she feels at being excluded from an important area of Leo's life. An area he saw fit to share with Alex.

'Does it say which account the money went to?' asks Tash.

'It was all drawn out as cash, I think. It's really weird. I thought about gambling . . .'

Tash snorts. 'I can't see Leo as a gambler. Robin would have mentioned it if he was. God knows, Robin loves a flutter every now and then. I think Leo used to take the piss out of him for it. That money has probably gone into some kind of savings account.'

'Robin would know about that, surely?'

Tash shrugs. 'Not necessarily. Leo doesn't need Robin's permission or advice to set up a simple savings account, or an ISA. Robin just did the more complicated stuff. Pensions, mortgages, stocks, that sort of thing.' Tash leans forward over the small table. 'Listen, Della, you might be over-thinking this whole thing. There's probably an innocent explanation and, in time, you'll find out what it is.'

'It would help if I could get into his phone or his laptop,' says Della, unable to shake off the uneasy feeling that has settled inside her.

'There are ways of finding bank accounts of dead people. Robin will take care of it. I'll ask him if you like. There's some sort of search you can do.'

Della feels a rush of gratitude for Tash. 'Thanks,' she says. 'I honestly don't know what I'd do without you.'

Tash takes her hand. 'I would do anything for you, you know that,' she says, looking serious. 'I'm here for you. I always have been, and I always will be,' she declares. Then her eyes fill with tears. 'If it were Robin, up there in a hospital morgue, you'd be with me every step of the way, I know it.'

Della feels herself well up too. Tash hands her a tissue, and as they both dry their eyes, she feels the truth in Tash's words. Tash is an open book, all her emotions, her inner life, her hopes and fears are right there for Della to see. Della loves Tash. She is the sister she never had. But alongside the force of her, the absolute loyalty of her friendship, there is a nagging feeling that a part of Tash is enjoying the drama. It was the same at school. They forged a friendship when Della's father died, and it deepened when Ethan became difficult and dangerous. Every morning in the playground, Tash would run up to her, asking if Della was OK, wanting to know what was going on in her house. And although it helped Della to talk about her crumbling childhood, there was something else she didn't acknowledge until years later; that Tash was sucked into Della's misery like a bystander at a car crash. Over time, as Della tried to slough off the skin of her past, Tash has been in the background, reminding her of it as a way to draw her close. Della understands now that Tash uses misery to create intimacy, and she doesn't blame her for it because, without Tash, she would still be living with Ethan. But there is a part of herself that she hides away from Tash. She feels the imbalance like a physical pull, the tip of a seesaw off kilter with the weight of it.

Sometimes, when they talk like this, when Della feels they are at their absolute closest, she almost blurts it out. But that would risk everything. A lifetime of friendship. And that is something Della is not prepared to do.

Chapter Fifteen

Tash drives Della and Alex home from the hospital and the silence in the car is deafening. As they approach the village, Della feels like screaming. Alex has avoided talking to her the whole morning and she is desperate to know how it went when she spent time with Leo in the hospital morgue.

'Alex,' she tries, 'are you glad you saw Dad? Did it make you feel better?' The words seem flimsy and hollow. Like she is talking to a child, not her almost-adult daughter. Leo would have known how to coax her out of a bad mood. He would have made a joke, said something insightful to make Alex feel seen, but Della cannot find the words to salve Alex's mood. It is the same feeling of helplessness she gets whenever she has to assemble a piece of flat-pack furniture. She has all the pieces, she has the instructions, but she can't seem to connect the two together. She only has a small amount of time before this pattern between them becomes set. She needs to earn Alex's respect somehow, and quickly.

'Actually, Tash,' says Alex, 'do you mind dropping me off in the village? There's a few things I want to do.'

Tash pulls over in the high street and. when Alex has slammed the door, loudly, and stalked off down the road, she turns to Della. 'What's going on between you two?'

Della drops her head down to the bag containing Leo's clothes and groans. 'She thinks I'm a bad feminist for not knowing where the money went. She knew we had inherited from Frank because Leo told her, but he never mentioned it to me beyond saying he'd take care of it. She thinks I'm an idiot. And she's right.'

'She's really angry with you, and you don't deserve it,' observes Tash. 'Don't talk about yourself like that. You aren't an idiot.'

Della turns to her. 'Her father just died. She'd be really angry anyway. She may as well have a focus.'

Tash purses her lips. 'You used to talk like this when you lived with Ethan, you know? I hated it then, and I hate it now. You're nobody's punching bag, Della. Not even Alex's.'

Della looks at her pleadingly. 'Does she remind you of Ethan? She's so angry. And not just now, but before Leo died. She's so . . . ready to have a fight. I worry about her.'

'She is not Ethan,' says Tash with conviction. 'She never will be. She's a teenager letting off steam. But if you fall back into the same routine that you did with Ethan – appeasement, mollification – I'm going to have a tantrum of my own. You are so ready to absorb the blame for everything, Della. It needs to stop. You can't make this situation any better for Alex by making yourself out to be a failure. You need to be strong for her.'

'Leo was the strong one,' says Della quietly, watching the back of her daughter disappearing down the street.

'You can be strong. Look at how much strength it took to escape Ethan.'

'I never really did, though, did I?' Della replies, bitterly. 'He always found me, no matter where I went.'

'All Ethan wanted was to have you with him, doing his bidding. You never went back to him, even when he came here threatening all sorts. You stood up to him.'

'Leo stood up to him,' Della corrects her. 'He listened to Leo, not me. What am I going to do, Tash, if Ethan comes back and finds out Leo is dead? What then?'

'How dangerous do you think he is, Della?'

'I'm not sure,' she replies, reluctant to elaborate. It sounds silly to give voice to what she is afraid of, that he will come and take Leo's place as the man of the house. She doesn't think Ethan intends to hurt her or Alex, but he might by trying to get what he wants. She imagines him as the big bad wolf, prowling around the edges of her life. What she does not articulate to Tash is the creeping worry that she might find Ethan hard to resist, now Leo has gone. Like a vampire emerging from the woods and knocking at her window, Della fears that in a moment of weakness, she will open the door and let him in.

It is hard to explain, the magnetic pull of Ethan. Hard to explain how, when he is in a room, he fills it up with the confidence of knowing what to do. It's the same kind of confidence that Leo had. It feels like standing in the brightest light. The warmth of it fills her up, and she misses that warmth with a deep, dark ache. To be next to someone who knows what to do, she craves that comfort with the urgency of a child. The shame that follows the desire is something she would never share with anyone.

Tash sighs. 'This is why I think you and Alex should move into the village. Where you will have a street full of neighbours and Robin and I can keep an eye on you. Promise me you'll think about it?'

Tash makes it all sound so easy. At this point there is nothing she would like to do more, but Della shakes her head, remembering the row she and Alex had. 'Alex won't tolerate that.' She looks into the distance, a multitude of worries clawing at her mind.

'Why do I get the feeling there's something else?' asks Tash, sternly. 'I can read you like a book.'

Della turns, reluctant to verbalise it, but she needs another opinion, and Tash is the only person she can ask. 'Do you remember last weekend, when Leo had that car accident?'

Tash looks out of the windscreen and shrugs. 'Robin described it as more of a bump. He hit the old oak on the top road, didn't he?'

Della nods. 'He could have died if he'd been driving any faster.'

'Thank God he didn't drive like Robin,' Tash remarks.

Della bites her tongue. Leo died anyway just walking down a street.

'Sorry,' mumbles Tash, realising at the same time. 'That was a stupid thing to say.'

Della ignores the apology, thinking instead of last weekend. 'I'd been away with Alex, in Edinburgh. It was too far to go there and back in one day, so we decided to make a weekend of it. When I called Leo on Sunday night to let him know what time our train was getting in, I knew there was something wrong as soon as he answered the phone.'

'What did he say?' asks Tash.

'He said it looks worse than it feels. That it was his own fault. He was more worried about the tree than his head. I wanted him to get it checked out in the hospital. But he wouldn't.'

Della remembers the swelling on his temple blooming into an impressive bruise. He had tried to bluff it out, but later that evening, after a few glasses of whisky, he confessed he was struggling with the anniversary of his father's death. He was finding it hard to focus. He missed his parents more than he thought possible. He wept at the kitchen table after Alex had gone to bed and Della had felt helpless in the face of his despair.

Della continues, 'I told him to take some time off work, or to stop the volunteering, but he wouldn't. He said he liked the drop-in centre. That it made him feel useful.' Della turns to Tash. 'I wanted to take him to the hospital, but he'd already dropped the car into the garage to get it patched up. It wasn't a big deal, he said.'

'Well, it wasn't, was it?' counters Tash. 'He told Robin it wasn't a big deal. He was just shaken up.'

'I should have made him go to the hospital. I should have called a taxi and made him come with me.' Della still recalls the feeling of relief as she got home. It had been a long journey back from Edinburgh and it was late in the evening, she was tired. She'd been too easily reassured by Leo, who always got his way in an argument.

'I don't have blurred vision; I can walk and talk,' he told her, sounding irked. 'I just gave myself a fright this afternoon, that's all. It could have been so much worse. It's shaken me up. This—' He pointed to his head. 'This is nothing compared to how much I'm beating myself up over it right now. I can't believe I took that bend too fast.'

Della allowed him to reassure her; she had been too ready to let it go. 'I think it might have contributed to his death,' she says quietly to Tash, hardly able to get the words out. 'I think when he had that car crash, something happened in his head. It weakened something.'

Tash looks at her. 'I thought sub-arachnoid haemorrhages just . . . happened. I didn't think they were caused by a bang to the head. And that accident was over a week ago.'

'I googled it.'

Tash sighs. 'Nothing good comes from googling anything to do with health. It always gives you the worst-case scenario. Half that stuff online is scaremongering.'

'This was from the NHS website, I'm not an idiot.'

'Sorry, no.' Tash swallows. 'Of course. But you're torturing yourself over something that you'll never get to the bottom of. How can you possibly ever know?'

'It could be my fault, all of this. If I'd taken him to the hospital, he could have had a scan. They would have seen whatever it was that caused him to die. Maybe all this could have been averted.'

Tash puts her hand on top of Della's. 'Whoa, slow down. This is too much. You can't blame yourself for Leo's death any more than you can blame yourself for him hitting that tree. He did that all by himself and he insisted he was fine.'

Della thinks back to the past week. He wasn't as right as rain. There were changes in Leo's behaviour. The tears that came, often, without warning. The distance between them opening up even more. Could it have been more than the anniversary of his father's death? Could he have damaged his head so badly, that afternoon, that something permanent changed, a precursor to a death that Della could have stopped?

Chapter Sixteen

Tash turns the car on to the dirt track and navigates the familiar bumps and turns before Della's house reveals itself, slowly, through the trees.

'Have you met your new neighbour yet?'

'No sign of them,' answers Della, noting that Robin's car is there, parked next to hers. He is peering into the windows of the other half of the house and Della feels a proprietorial irritation at his nosiness. He stands up, caught out, when he hears the car, but visibly relaxes when he realises it is his wife, and he bends down once more to resume his surveillance.

'I think you've got a hippie moving in next door,' he declares, brushing the palms of his hands together to wipe off the dust from the windows. 'There are several dodgy-looking musical instruments in there and lots of artisan cushions.' He makes his fingers into quotation marks around the word *artisan*. Della rolls her eyes. Only Robin would proclaim a musical instrument to look dodgy.

'I'll be sure to let them know when I meet them,' replies Della in a flat voice. She is not in the mood for Robin. She's too tired. 'That is, if they ever show up.'

'I wonder what's keeping them?' says Tash, joining Robin at the window. 'All their stuff is piled up in there for all to see. It seems weird they haven't come yet.'

'Maybe she's a woman of mystery,' says Robin.

'What makes you think it's a woman?' jokes Tash.

'Have you *seen* those fabrics in there? Headscarves and Turkish rugs. I'll bet you fifty quid it's a woman.'

Della lets Robin and Tash in, grateful her rift with Alex won't be witnessed first-hand by Robin, who loves to get in the middle of a disagreement. She hopes Alex comes back after he has gone.

'I'll just be a second, OK?' Della says. 'Can you put the kettle on, one of you?' Della races up the stairs. She puts Leo's things on the bed, not wanting Robin to paw through them, not wanting to talk about them. She will look at them later, properly, when she has had time to think. When she comes back down the stairs it is clear Tash has already told Robin about the bank book and the disappearing money. Della bites her tongue.

'Robin says he'll take a look in the business account for you and any other accounts he knows Leo had,' Tash says, sweetly, delivering three mugs of tea to the table. She sits down and looks up at Robin and Della.

'The money won't be in there, though,' declares Robin. He remains standing as if he is conducting a meeting. 'The business account doesn't earn interest, and he knew it would complicate his tax affairs if he put savings in there.'

'Oh,' says Della.

Robin carries on talking. 'You should have access to his business account soon, and anything else that doesn't have your name on it. I'll make a list of all the accounts I know about, and we'll take it from there. The death certificate will allow you to do that now. Get a few extra copies made, you'll need—'

'Yes, I know,' interrupts Della, trying not to feel patronised, unwilling to sit so Robin can talk down to her.

'At some point, you'll need to decide what to do with Leo's business, though,' continues Robin, undeterred. 'I've already started contacting all his clients I know about. It will take me a little longer to find the ones I don't if we can't get into his laptop, unless you have a list somewhere?'

'No,' says Della feeling defeated.

'In any case, you have to wind the business down. You won't be taking it over,' he insists. 'Maybe Alex . . . ?'

'I don't think so,' says Della. 'I'm hoping she'll be off to uni in September. She's not really interested in IT. Drama and politics are her main subjects.'

'She's doing maths too, though, right?' says Tash, unhelpfully. 'She has a good head for business.'

Robin jams his thumbs into his waistband and tucks his shirt more firmly into his trousers. 'There could be money in it. You need money right now.'

'It's not her responsibility to run this house,' Della reminds him. 'It's mine.'

'Suit yourself.' Robin shrugs. 'Tash says you don't want to sell up just yet, but you could parcel off some of the land and sell it for development. Have you thought about that?'

Suddenly Della feels very tired. She gives in and sits down. 'Do you mind if we don't do this now?' she says weakly.

'You look shattered,' says Tash, springing up and squeezing her arm. 'Go and have a lie down. Come on Robin, let's go.' Tash takes her car keys from the kitchen table and looks at Robin pointedly.

'I'll meet you back at home,' says Robin, not moving. 'Just want to run a few more things past Della.'

'Don't be long,' says Tash. 'She needs to rest.'

The front door closes and the sound of Tash's car making a three-point turn competes with the wind that races through the trees. Della listens, and the noise sounds like a river, coursing through the landscape. She looks through the window. There is a low mist blurring the tree trunks as the spring sunshine warms the earth, releasing the moisture that clings to the ground. Robin, still standing, smooths the table with his fingertips.

'In all seriousness, Della,' he says, 'I want to help.'

'I know,' says Della, bringing herself back into the room. 'I'm just tired, Robin. It's been a busy morning.'

'How's Alex?' he asks.

'Upset. Angry,' says Della in a flat voice.

Robin nods to himself and sits down opposite her. The mugs of tea that Tash made for them are cooling between them. 'Do you remember when we first met?'

'Vaguely,' replies Della, wondering where this is leading.

'I hadn't made up my mind about Tash. We were very much back and forth. And then she brought you into the flat. She rescued you, really, didn't she?'

'Robin, I—'

'I don't mind telling you, I fancied you straight away. I'm a sucker for a sob story. But Leo got there first, as usual. I didn't stand a chance. It was always that way with Leo. He was better-looking than me. Thinner. Girls always looked at him first. And he liked to win.'

Della says nothing; this conversation has happened before.

'I only really got together with Tash properly because she was so close to you. It made it easier to be with you.'

'Don't, Robin,' says Della, wearily.

'And I knew you were Leo's, and that you didn't find me half as fascinating as him. Until you discovered alcohol and turned into a bit of a party girl.' Robin leans back in his chair, smiling. 'Wow. What a change. Like night and day. A totally different Della.'

Della feels her skin begin to shiver. She feels weak; she hasn't eaten all day, she now realises. 'I don't know what this has got to do with—'

Robin continues as if she isn't there. 'Where did that party girl go, is what I could never figure out. I saw a completely different side to you. I rather liked it, I don't mind telling you.' He looks at her with open desire, and it repulses her. 'There was a time when I thought I had a chance with you. A little window that opened a crack, just a crack, for me.'

Della stands up, quickly, and the shriek of the chair scraping against the stone floor is everything she wants to say, at the volume she wants to say it. But Robin wouldn't understand that. He is the kind of man who needs things to be spelled out. 'Leo is the person I fell in love with. Nothing changes that. Nothing will ever change that. I've told you this before.'

'He's not here, though, is he?' says Robin, lightly, looking around the room as if Leo might be standing there, with them. 'He's gone. He's lost all your money, and he's landed you in the shit. And here you are, all alone, in need of help. My help.'

'Robin, don't. This is not welcome, or helpful.' Then she says, reproachfully, 'He was your *best friend*.'

Robin sighs, lightly, and examines his fingernails, which are expertly manicured. Then he looks up at her. 'All I'm saying is that you only have to say the word and I'll help you more than you thought possible.'

'What's that supposed to mean?' Della whispers, not wanting to hear the answer.

'You and I both know I would give Tash up in a heartbeat if you wanted me to. That's all it would take. If I got a glimpse of the old Della . . . I have a nice lifestyle, you know this. Alex and you would both be well provided for. Think about it, is all I'm saying. You know how I feel about you, how I have always felt about you.'

When she begins to speak to Robin, she realises she is using the same voice she uses with Ethan, and it kills her that she doesn't have the energy to lash out and yell at him. Now, without Leo, she can wreck this sham of a friendship. But she feels so tired she doesn't have it in her. And Robin is looking into Leo's finances in a way she never could. She needs him. 'Robin, I want you to leave,' she says quietly. 'Tash is my best friend and Leo is my husband. I know we have history, but just because I've known you since I was nineteen, it doesn't give you the right to talk to me like this. I'm not interested, and I never was. I don't know how else to tell you.'

Robin stands up, acknowledging that the game is over. 'Shame,' he says, an amused look on his face. 'No hard feelings, though.'

'He's been dead for three days,' Della says in a low voice. 'And this is how you honour him. The only reason I am still on talking terms with you is because of Tash. If it wasn't for her . . .'

'Well, it's a good job neither of us is going to upset the apple cart then, isn't it?' Robin replies in a friendly voice, safe in the knowledge she would never, ever tell Tash about the feelings Robin has always had for her.

'Don't come back here,' she says, trying to stop her voice from wobbling. 'I don't want you anywhere near me or Alex.'

Della doesn't see Robin out. She stays sitting at the table, her legs too weak to bear her weight. Conversations like these used to be few and far between. Drunken dinner parties when Robin would engineer a meeting on the staircase, or during a walk through the woods when Leo and Tash were up ahead. It was always hard, with Leo and Tash around, but now she is on her own, she wonders how many more times this will happen, and how she can put a stop to it. The only reason she ever put up with Robin was because he was Leo's best friend and Tash fell in love with him. Now Leo is gone, it's one less reason. But to cut Robin loose is to lose Tash, and she owes Tash more than the ugly truth.

Chapter Seventeen

Della wakes to the sound of Alex going down the stairs. For the first time since Leo died, she leaps out of bed and puts some clothes on without thinking about it. Alex came home late last night, too late, but Della refrained from telling her off. She will be eighteen soon, and an adult.

'Alex?' Della calls as she enters the kitchen, zipping up a hoodie. 'What are you doing up so early?'

Alex is dressed and fully made-up. Her eyeliner is done perfectly with a little flick at each corner of her eye. Her lips are deepest plum. She is wearing a carefully curated outfit, a pair of torn black tights, a black denim mini skirt and a T-shirt plastered with slogans, with Leo's cardigan buttoned around her thin frame. Alex doesn't reply, she butters a piece of toast, and Della is grateful to see she has already drunk a glass of milk. Then she sees Alex's schoolbag on one of the kitchen chairs.

'You're going to school already?' asks Della. 'Are you sure?'

'I'd rather be at school than here with you,' Alex says in a practised voice, picking up her bag and pushing past Della to the front door. 'Besides, I thought you hated me missing school.'

'Do you need a lift?' Della asks, helplessly. She looks at her watch. Alex is early. There is plenty of time for her to walk to school.

The front door slams and Della is left in a quiet house. Even Marmite remains asleep in his bed. She wonders what to do with herself. There are a million things she should be doing to sort out Leo's affairs, but she is overcome by worry for her daughter and the suspicion she is powerless to help her.

Sometimes, when Alex is unaware of it, Della studies her, searching for something familiar. She looks for a connection, a trace of herself in her daughter's face. A reflection in the way she moves. For a short while their hair was the same, white blonde, but over the years, Alex lost it somehow, shedding it like an unwanted gift. Now it is pale brown with a faint, coppery tinge. Strawberry, Leo called it. The blonde at the tips of Alex's hair comes straight out of a bottle, applied with a toothbrush over the bathroom sink.

But it's not that, not really. It's not the way she looks. It's the way Alex *is.* Her confidence staggers Della, sometimes. She is so sure of herself, so certain of her own ability, Della knows it comes from her father. Even when Alex was a toddler, Della felt at a disadvantage. When Alex mastered how to talk, she practised by barking instructions at Della, like a short-tempered factory foreman.

Not DIS way, Mummy, like DAT. You have to do it like DAT.

Della doesn't know if she lost confidence in herself, over the years, or if it was never there in the first place. She wonders, sometimes, if confidence is like a fire, a smouldering ember that just needs a little oxygen, or perhaps a seed, waiting for rainfall. She tries to imagine her own internal landscape and sees only a desert. She imagines Alex has a rainforest. Della shoves her hands into her pockets and pulls out a square of paper. It is the handwritten receipt she pulled out of Leo's wardrobe at the weekend. She reads it again – *Betula pendula* – and decides to ring the number running along the bottom.

'Hello, Longacre.' The voice, a man's, rises at the end in a question.

'Um, hi,' responds Della. 'I have a receipt from you and I'm not sure what it's for. *Betula pendula* is written on it.'

'That's a silver birch.'

'A tree. The receipt is for the purchase of a tree?'

'Yes. We're a plant nursery.'

'But the price is almost two hundred pounds. That seems . . . a little excessive.'

'Sounds like a twenty-eight-litre tree. That's five metres high.'

'Oh,' responds Della, none the wiser.

'Is there a problem with your order?' queries the voice, sounding a little impatient.

'I don't know. My husband bought it a few days ago, but I'm not sure what happened to it.'

'Give me the order number on the top of the receipt and I'll go and find out.'

Della does as she's told and waits for a few minutes, wondering what Leo has been up to. There is no reason to buy a tree. They are surrounded by trees. Then a thought creeps up on her. Was this a gift for someone else? This isn't the kind of gift you buy for a friend unless they are a very good friend, and the price indicates it was for someone special. An unpleasant thought enters her head. She can hardly believe she is considering this, but could it be possible he was having an affair? The woman's voice on Leo's phone telling her to go to hospital comes back to her. Who was he with that morning? Why was he so distant this last year? And now this tree. A very expensive tree.

There is a rattle as the phone is picked up once more.

The voice says, 'The tree is still here with instructions to deliver it. It hasn't left the nursery yet.'

'Can you confirm the address for delivery?' asks Della, her heart pounding. Her armpits prickle with sweat.

'Number one, Beech Wood Cottage.'

Della blows out a breath of relief. Her own address. She massages her temple with her free hand.

'It says here it's not supposed to be delivered for a couple of weeks. With a message attached.'

'What's the message?' asks Della.

The voice sounds a little awkward. 'It says *Happy anniversary, all my love, Leo.'*

The relief turns to a swell of joy. Their anniversary. Of course.

'Is that OK?' asks the voice. 'Maybe I shouldn't have told you that, if you're his wife.'

'Yes, yes, it's OK,' says Della, distracted. 'It's just a strange choice for an anniversary gift, that's all.'

'Not really,' says the voice. 'Silver birch trees symbolise new beginnings. It's not the first one we've sold for an anniversary. Are you renewing your wedding vows?'

'No, but I think I get it now,' says Della, thinking of Leo's interest in local folklore. He sometimes referred affectionately to silver birch trees as *the ladies of the wood.* The few they have in their own part of the wood are too far from the house to be able to see from the window. Once, a long time ago, she recalls Leo mentioning this was a shame.

Della thanks the voice on the phone.

'OK. I hope I didn't spoil the surprise.'

'You didn't,' replies Della, firmly. 'It's exactly what I needed to hear this morning.'

Della ends the call feeling guilty for suspecting Leo of being unfaithful, but this is quickly overridden by optimism. The tree was an affirmation Leo loved her and had been thinking about her only a couple of days before he died. She makes a decision. Today she will be less helpless. She will become the parent Alex needs. A leader, not a follower. She has orders she needs to fulfil. If Alex is going back to school, she should begin work, too. But now, pottery won't be a side hustle. She needs to step it up, make it earn. 'Marmite?' she calls.

His head raises, slowly, his ears cocked.

'Shall we go to the studio?'

He gets up, with effort, unable to resist a walk, and she unlocks the back door. They saunter together and Della breathes in the scent of sunlight on wet leaves as she follows the path that leads to the studio. A dog barks in the distance. Marmite raises his head and drops it again to sniff at the ground.

'Too tired to bark today, Marmite?' asks Della, gently stroking his ears. She feels absurdly happy, thinking about that birch tree. As a child, Leo absorbed forest folklore as if it were fact. Like rain falling down to earth, the stories nourished him, they became embedded in his soul. He used to tease her for not knowing what the trees were called when she first came here. Now, she remembers these stories, Leo's stories, as she passes through the wood. Blackthorn wards off evil spirits. Hawthorn brings bad luck if you take their flowers into the house. Rowan trees protect against the dead. Willows can uproot themselves and follow you if they are minded to. Every tree she touches, she recalls the stories that Leo told her, nurtured by the comfort they bring.

As she unlocks the door to the studio, she feels her troubles slipping off her like an old skin. There is an atmosphere of calm in here, the pots waiting to be trimmed, the clay waiting to be shaped. In Della's mind, they are promises, waiting to be fulfilled. She made these promises as a wife and mother, and now she must fulfil them as a widow. They are a link to the past. She can see her fingerprint on one of them, a marker of who she once was. The poured concrete floor has, over the years, taken on spills of milky water, drops of unfired glaze and lumps of raw clay. She looks at it now, her history here played out in muted tones of earth and stone.

Before Alex was born, before she fell into making functional ceramics for cafés and restaurants, Della spent her spare time making one-off, singular pieces as she sought to find her style. It would have been easier to go to college to do this with a teacher to guide her, but by the time she felt ready, when Tash and Leo graduated, they took Della with them on their journey through life. When they left college she abandoned thoughts of being a student and focused on teaching herself what she needed to know. She glazed pots differently back then, using bold and vibrant colours, art pieces really, but she felt a fraud presenting them that way, so she didn't. She gave most of them away. Of those she sold, she did with a confession.

I'm self-taught, she would say, an apologetic note in her voice. *I'm still learning.*

Now, Della works with natural colour because it sells well. The glazes she uses come from the earth in shades of deep, rich umber, warm stone and chalk. Sometimes, she makes a glaze of palest blue speckled with dark chocolate, exactly the same shade as a magpie's egg. There is one pot, in the centre of the shelf, that is different from the others. Its sides are a little too thick and it has a lopsided look that gives it an air of exhaustion, but this is because it has been patched up. You can clearly see the individual pieces it broke into and were then glued back together. This is the first pot she ever threw without the help of Miss Abramovich. When Della takes it in her hands, as she does now, she still remembers how the wet clay felt under her young fingertips. She remembers how thirsty it was, how much water she needed to throw on it for the clay to become compliant. By this time, she knew how much muscle she needed to raise the clay up in a cone shape, to push it down again, flexing it until it obeyed. Miss Abramovich had made her practise this coning process several times, before she was allowed to throw her own pot, unaided.

Della made a deep connection to the clay, she began to anticipate how it would behave and to manipulate it instinctively, without fear of it collapsing. It was the only thing in her life that bent to her will. It was also the first piece of work that Miss Abramovich had allowed into the kiln. A vessel had to be deemed good enough to save from going back into the clay bucket, and only Miss Abramovich could decide.

She helped Miss Abramovich load the pots into the kiln, stacking them close together, but making sure nothing touched. Miss Abramovich closed the kiln door and set the temperature.

'Now we pray to the kiln gods,' she said seriously, crossing her fingers.

It took several days for the kiln to reach the right temperature, fire the contents and cool down again. When the door was finally opened, Della's pot was still there, intact. But she hardly recognised it. It was a different colour, paler, and much smaller than she remembered. She questioned Miss Abramovich.

'In the kiln, during the first firing – the *bisque firing* – the water leaves the clay, and this makes it shrink,' she explained. 'Everything comes out smaller, Della. Even my work.'

Della looked at her pot. Her *vessel,* knowing it was entirely hers and hers alone. Miss Abramovich nodded, a look of contentment crossing her face. 'The kiln gods are pleased. This is a good vessel, Della. Now you must glaze.'

The range of glazes at the school was limited, but Della didn't care. Miss Abramovich stood over her as she dipped the pot into the glaze. 'If you don't work with care, it will explode in the kiln. *Poof.'* Her long fingers mimicked an explosion. 'There is nothing more disappointing than putting your heart into a vessel, only to see it gone when you open the kiln door. Be careful, and the kiln gods will be happy and look kindly on your work.'

Della wasn't sure if Miss Abramovich was joking, but she followed her instruction to the letter. After another firing in the kiln, the grey liquid she had dipped her pot in turned into a rich, glossy black. It made her vessel look sophisticated and grown-up. It was big enough to pass as a small vase, the shape of it like a tulip, and Della imagined it in the centre of their kitchen table, holding a small bouquet of flowers picked from their little garden. Miss Abramovich wrapped it in newspaper and put it into its own plastic bag. Della carried it carefully home, terrified of dropping it. She showed it to her mother, who seemed genuinely impressed.

'It's beautiful, Della, like something out of a shop. I wouldn't have known you'd made it by hand. It looks so professional.'

Della glowed under the warmth of her mother's praise. Just as she imagined, the vessel was placed in the centre of the only table in the flat above the newsagent's, and Della and her mother picked out a few flowers from their little garden. The black, glossy glaze set the colours on fire. Della sat at the table and ate her dinner, not taking her eyes off her creation.

The pot lasted less than three days. She heard her mother cry out before she saw what had happened, and as she raced to the kitchen, she knew what she would find before she saw it. She should have known better than to leave something so precious, so much admired, unguarded in the flat.

Ethan shrugged. 'It slipped,' he said. 'You should have kept it in your room.'

Nowadays, Della could probably take this pot apart and re-glue it back together so the joins can't be seen, but she doesn't. She keeps it as a reminder that she and it are kindred. That broken things can be put back together but the fractures will remain.

Chapter Eighteen

Her phone rings in the studio and Della stops, wipes the clay off her hands, hoping it is Alex calling. She looks at her watch. It is barely lunchtime, and when she picks up she can see it is Tash.

'Hey,' she says, trapping the phone in between her shoulder and her ear, scrubbing the clay from her fingers with an old tea towel.

'Robin just told me you don't want him coming over anymore.' She sounds hurt.

Della stops what she is doing and tries to guess what angle Robin is working. He won't have told her the truth of their last conversation. Della doesn't want that either.

'I'm sorry, Tash,' says Della, opting for contrition, moving the phone to her clean hand. 'I just need some time. I don't want to talk about finances and business stuff. I just want to get past the funeral. Then I'll feel more ready to talk about the future.' The ticking clock on her mortgage payments is never far from her mind. She glances at the orders she has spent the morning trimming. The payment she is due won't even touch the sides.

'He's only trying to help, you know. I know he can be a bit cack-handed, but he wants to do the right thing by you, for Leo's sake.'

'Look, let me just get through the funeral and then I can think about finances.'

Tash's voice becomes softer. 'Have you got a date yet? For the funeral? I want to help.'

Della recognises there are two sides to Tash. Her side and Robin's. Della is in a constant battle to reclaim the loyalty of her old friend as it cleaves towards her husband.

'Friday,' sighs Della, not sure if she wants it to come quickly or not at all.

'So soon?'

'I guess it's not a busy time of year. And he died in hospital, which makes things more straightforward, I think. Someone shoved a leaflet in my hand and told me what would happen soon after he died.' The staff at the hospital had meant to make things easier, but even so, Della was shocked by the speed of it all.

'Where will it be?'

'The crematorium. I can't face a burial, and I don't think Leo cared.'

'Can I do anything?'

'Yes,' decides Della. 'All the people you emailed to let them know about Leo last week. Can you email them again and tell them about the funeral? It's going to be held at midday. Tell them no flowers. If they want to make a gesture, they can make a donation to the hospital or the Woodland Trust.'

'Are you sure?' asks Tash.

Della thinks about the carpet of wood anemones that are beginning to cover the forest floor, the cherry trees that are blooming in the woods, a delicate pink and white, and the hawthorn that is just coming into leaf. The idea of shop-bought cut flowers, hothoused and shipped over in tightly packed crates, already dying in their cellophane, is too much to bear.

'I'm sure,' she says.

Tash is quiet for a moment. 'The last funeral I went to was your mum's.'

'I don't remember much about that,' replies Della. She had been taken by Miss Abramovich and taken away again before Ethan could get close.

'You were lucky to get out of that place alive,' murmurs Tash. 'If it hadn't been for that passer-by who called the fire brigade . . . why they didn't lock Ethan up for it, I'll never understand.'

'He didn't mean it to go that far,' says Della. 'He just didn't want me to leave. Do you remember, he found out I was applying to art school?'

'Bollocks. He's a bully, Della, plain and simple. People like Ethan, all they want is to destroy everyone else's happiness. It's like sport to them.'

Della sighs inwardly at having to go down this path again and again. It changes nothing, criticising Ethan. He went through so much at such a young age. 'He's mentally ill, really,' she finally says in a lame voice.

'See? Even now, you're making excuses for him. Sometimes I think you forget what he was like.'

But Della has not forgotten what her brother was like. She can still remember the first time she began to fear him. There didn't seem to be much of an age difference between them for a while after their dad died, but all of a sudden, Ethan grew taller, his muscles began to show under his T-shirt. And with his size, his temper grew into something sly and cold. She remembers, vividly, being pinned down, unable to breathe, the feeling of absolute helplessness under someone much bigger, much stronger than her. She learned to avoid him. She never went nearer than a few feet of him so she could always get a head start. She learned a whole new language to placate his moods. A language she aped from her mother. But there were other times when things were different. Little acts of kindness like the shafts of sunlight that warm the forest air. A bar of chocolate, dropped into her lap when she helped him do the accounts.

The fireworks he lit on Guy Fawkes night. The Catherine wheel he always saved for her. The look on his face when they exploded into the night. If only she could have known how to keep that version of him. She would have given anything.

Tash talks about Ethan until Della feels the air is tainted by him. It is unbelievable to her that even though it is Leo they should be talking about, four days dead, Ethan always finds a way to take centre stage. It is a conversation they have been having together since they were teenagers, and it feels familiar to retrace these steps with her old friend, but lately Della feels sick of it. She tries to end the call, several times, but Tash hasn't finished dispensing advice. And then Della's phone dies. She looks at the blank screen, annoyed she forgot to charge it last night. Grief has scattered the pattern of her day. Small inconveniences like this are depressingly frequent. She is not sorry to be cut off from Tash, though, and the strength of her opinions.

It is well past lunchtime. She cleans up, washes the wheel down and locks the studio door. But Marmite doesn't seem to want to go home; he turns to the woods, nose down, following the scent of something she cannot know.

'Come on then,' Della says, looking at her watch. 'Just a quick one, yeah?'

The woods are old, very old. There is plenty of magic, lying dormant. Leo told her once there are bodies buried deep in plague pits, that the trees have been here for centuries. Della wonders at the things they have seen, the things they have witnessed below their spreading canopy. They groan, like old men taking a seat, their branches like swollen knuckles, their fat trunks with thick bark rumpled and wrinkled like slipped, loose skin. The forest talks to itself. When the wind blows through the trees, their leaves rasp in reply. Their crowns nod to one another in understanding. Branches wave and gesticulate. As she walks further into the wood she looks to the forest floor, trying to imagine the vast network of roots and hyphae under her feet. Leo told her once about it, how it links the trees in some secretive way.

It communicates with everything it's connected to. Every living thing for miles and miles. It's a bit like an underground internet for trees. Some people call it the Wood Wide Web.

Della imagines a constant murmur of conversation rumbling under the ground. Above, all around her, she can hear whispering in the wind, the nodding scratch and squeak of branches, but thanks to Leo, she knows there are deeper, more important conversations going on directly underneath the soil.

She follows Marmite, sweeping the area as she goes, looking for signs of Ethan. The feeling he might appear through the trees is never far from her mind, gnawing away at her like a hungry animal. But all is quiet. Marmite, in a burst of energy, lopes into the undergrowth, following a creature that is faster and younger than he is. Instead of following him, Della is drawn to the pond, wanting to stop for a while to look over the water, to enjoy the ripples as the wind kisses its skin. But today it is motionless, grey and flat. There is a brooding atmosphere around the water, a sense of breath being held, and the thought crosses her mind: that somehow, this landscape, that has nurtured Leo for most of his life, knows that he will be returned to the earth soon. She shivers, turns, wanting lunch, pleased she is hungry for once.

'Marmite? Let's go,' she calls, making her way back to the house. But Marmite doesn't appear. There is no sign of him. He doesn't come when she whistles, loud and shrill, calling his name. Feeling uneasy, she calls a little louder, until finally, deep in the wood, a shadow at the foot of a tree resolves itself, and she sees him, lying down, unwilling or unable to get up. Before she realises where she is, her heart begins to quicken. She looks around, trying to quell the jitters. It is the same clearing she found herself in on

Friday. The bright blue fabric flaps in the breeze, still caught in the arms of the beech tree, still struggling to get away.

'Marmite?' She calls his name urgently, kneeling next to him, worried what she might find. 'Are you hurt?'

She tries to get him on to his feet, but he is too heavy. She checks his body, runs her fingers through his fur, in earnest now, squeezing him gently, then more firmly up and down his legs, looking for an injury she doesn't want to find. He doesn't react, doesn't seem in pain, but is unable or unwilling to walk. His head falls back, and he closes his eyes.

There is a moment when she considers leaving him to run back to the house, but they got rid of the landline years ago. They all use their mobile phones, now, and hers is dead. Alex would never forgive her if she left Marmite by himself, and she can't bring herself to leave him here, alone. The gnawing feeling that Ethan is not far from here becomes stronger and she begins to feel sick. What if he had something to do with this?

It takes a few seconds to pluck up the courage to use her voice, to admit to herself this isn't a situation she can resolve alone. And she feels it now, how utterly alone she is. She calls for help, sounding hysterical, knowing it is unlikely anybody will hear her. Her shouts rise in desperation. Her voice sounds thin and reedy and pathetically small. Then she remembers the dog that barked when she first came out and prays there are lunchtime dog-walkers elsewhere in the woods. Her voice gathers strength. It seems like an age that she sits on the cold, wet ground, cradling Marmite's head, calling and calling for help.

And then another voice. Far away at first, but nearer when Della yells for her to come over. Slowly, through the trees, the shape of a woman.

'Can I help?' she asks, looking uncertain. And then, 'Oh no! What's happened to your dog?'

Della slumps in relief and begins to cry, burying her face in Marmite's fur. 'I don't know,' she sobs, raising her head. 'He can't seem to move and he's too heavy for me to lift alone. I need to get him to a vet.' She looks up at the woman, who is a blurred shape through her tears. 'I just need to get him to a vet,' she begs. 'Can you help me?' She snivels, wiping her face with her coat sleeve. 'Please. I can't do it by myself. He means everything to me.' Fresh tears course down her face. She can't lose another family member. The universe wouldn't be that cruel, would it?

A part of her, the same part that nibbles and gnaws at the edge of her consciousness, whispers, *yes, it would.*

The woman looks out of her depth. She is about the same age as Della, with long, pale-red hair piled messily on the top of her head. Strands reach out to the sky and Della is reminded of a sea anemone, waving in the water. She is wearing jeans and boots and a donkey jacket that looks too big, like it should belong to a man.

'OK, stay here,' the woman says eventually. 'I'll be back.' And she runs in the direction she came from, returning sooner than Della expected with a chequered picnic rug. This time she seems more sure of herself. 'If we can get the dog on here, we can pull him to my car.'

The two women work together, not speaking. Della reassures Marmite, who seems half asleep. Finally they position him far enough on to the blanket that they can both grab the edges and, gently, they convey him to the path, which is spongy with leaf mulch.

'Your blanket will be ruined,' pants Della, though she doesn't care. All she can think about is Marmite.

'Don't worry. It'll wash,' says the woman, panting back.

They both pull Marmite, stopping briefly for the woman to change hands or get a better grip on the corner of the blanket. Della forgets that she is much stronger than most because pottery is so physical. Her arms are a tangle of muscle. She bites her tongue each time they have to stop. Then Della sees the path to her house. 'Here,' she says, 'we need to go there, to the house. My car is parked on the dirt track.'

The woman drops her corners of the blanket. She stands upright to stretch her back, putting her hands on her hips.

'I just need to go into the house to get my car keys,' continues Della, searching in her pocket for her house keys.

'*Oh*. I see.' The woman doesn't move and looks at her strangely.

'What's wrong?' says Della, catching something in her voice.

'I bought the other half of the house. You must be my neighbour.'

Even then, through her anxiety about Marmite, the burning pain of the muscles in her arms, Della is aware that first impressions last. She wipes her face with her forearm, knowing she is caked in snot and tears and she can't pull out a pleasantry to make this all seem better than it is. 'I have to go. Sorry . . .' she mumbles, unable to meet her gaze. 'I have to—' She turns to the house, runs towards it, wanting to get away from this woman, needing to get the car keys.

'I'm Carrie, by the way,' she hears the woman call after her. 'Pleased to meet you.'

Chapter Nineteen

Carrie offers to come with Della to the vet, but Della can't look at her, she just needs to focus on Marmite. She and Carrie lift him into the back of the car. Della leans in and whispers some words of comfort into his ear. Then she kisses him, inhales him, before she dashes to the driver's side and starts the engine. She drives slowly over the bumps in the dirt track; Carrie, arms folded, disappears in the rear-view mirror. Della listens out for any noise that Marmite might make, but he is silent, and she prays to a god she doesn't believe in that everything will be OK.

She parks outside the vet's and sprints in, shouting for a member of staff to help her. After she tries to explain what happened, her words garbled and incoherent, she is asked to wait while they examine him. In the long minutes that tick by, she takes some deep breaths and tries not to think about what could be happening in there, pushing away the similarity between this waiting room and the one she was ushered into at the hospital when they were trying to resuscitate Leo. Eventually, she is called in to another, smaller room, where she is asked to take a seat. Della looks around. 'Where is he?' she asks.

'We're just taking some blood. He's fine,' the vet reassures her. 'Has he shown any signs of being in pain? Whimpering, yelping, panting fast?'

Della feels herself relax a little. She shrugs and shakes her head. 'No, nothing. It's just like he gave up and didn't want to walk anymore.'

The vet nods. 'We've had a good look at him, he isn't in pain, so that rules out an injury he might have picked up in the woods, but he's quite sleepy. I'm wondering if he had a stroke, although it's rare in dogs. How old is he now?'

'Fifteen. Nearly sixteen.'

'That's very old for a dog like this. We could scan him to confirm there's no injury and see if we can detect any kind of tumour or bleed, but it would involve an anaesthetic, and I wouldn't recommend that at his age unless you insist.'

'No,' says Della, her heart sinking. 'I don't want him to be put through that.' Then the unthinkable thought resurfaces. She has to ask. 'You don't think . . . you don't think he's been poisoned, do you?'

'Poisoned?' The vet looks surprised. 'I don't think so. Has he been vomiting?'

'No. Not that I'm aware.' She wishes she had taken more notice of the area around him in the woods, but she is sure she would have noticed.

'In that case, let's keep an eye on him overnight. We'll do a blood-clotting test to rule out rat poison. But really, sometimes these things have a way of working themselves out. I'll give you a call tomorrow after we've had a bit of time to observe him. We'll see if we can get him walking and make sure he's hydrated and eating properly. Then we'll take it from there.'

'Can I see him?' sniffs Della, a lump in her throat. A feeling of shame spreads over her. She can't even keep her dog safe now Leo has gone. Leo would have been able to lift him and get him here sooner. Aren't strokes easier to treat if they're seen to quickly?

At least Leo would never have to see this. At least he has been spared that.

'Of course you can,' replies the vet with a kind smile. 'Follow me.'

She is led to the back of the building to a room with large cages arranged around the perimeter of the floor. A nurse has Marmite's cage door open, and she is depositing a bowl of water next to him. Marmite is asleep.

The nurse retreats to give her some space and Della kneels on the floor, leaning into the cage. She buries her face in his neck and savours the yeasty smell of him, stroking his ears and murmuring his name. She runs her hand down the length of his warm body, and he gives a contented sigh in his sleep. It is enough to reassure her. She withdraws from the cage and the nurse comes back to close it securely.

'We'll look after him, I promise,' she says. 'He's in good hands.'

Della turns away in despair, remembering the nurse in the hospital saying the exact same thing about Leo.

She drives home, the road a blur through her tears, and when she gets to the front door, the house keys have gone from her pocket. She pats herself down, once, twice, hardly able to believe it, and realises she must have left them in the house when she picked up her car keys. It is a joke between her and Leo that she refuses to keep her car and house keys together. Della maintains it is better to lose one set than both. As she peers through the letterbox and sees them sitting on the hallway table, far out of her reach, she hears Leo's voice – *I told you so, Del* – and realises he has won the argument one last time. She pulls out her phone to call Alex to find out what time she will be at home, but the screen on her phone reminds her it died long ago.

Without warning, an animal howl rages through her, forcing its way out of her mouth and clawing into the damp air. She sinks down on to the doorstep, weeping loudly at the injustice of it all, knowing she has failed Alex again by not being able to communicate with her to tell her the news, knowing that Leo would have done everything better.

She looks at her watch, thinking she might have time to catch her at school, but school kicked out half an hour ago. If Alex was coming straight home she would be here by now. If she was continuing her campaign of silence and punishment, then she's probably in the village.

Her face feels salty. She wipes it once more with her sleeve and realises her sleeve is filthy. Eventually, Della gets up, wondering what to do, until the door next to hers opens.

'Are you OK?' Carrie asks, peering around the doorway. 'How's the dog?'

Della tells her what has happened and Carrie nods to herself. 'Come in. You can charge your phone up and call your daughter. I'll make us something. You look like you could do with it.' She doesn't wait for Della to answer, she simply steps back inside, leaving the door open.

Della has not been into the adjoining house since Mrs Winters died. It has not been touched for many years and there is a neglected air about it. The walls need painting, the flooring is old, the windows are dirty and there is a big black smoke stain around the mouth of the fireplace. Carrie's possessions are scattered about, haphazardly, in boxes, in piles. But some of her possessions are unpacked and on display. Her stuff is brightly coloured. A lot look like vintage finds, and nothing matches. There is a set of orange melamine nesting bowls and a trendy Italian cast-iron stove-top coffee maker. The cushions on the sofa are sixties prints. There is a retro armchair, in the corner, that Della recognises as a design classic. She looks at the framed prints that are propped up against the wall, the bold-patterned curtains folded next to the windows, ready to be hung, and she realises this woman has the kind of taste that is respected and copied in magazines. She looks at Carrie, who is wearing a beautiful hand-knitted jumper in a deep rust colour that has unusual, old-fashioned ruched sleeves that tighten elegantly at the cuffs, showing her pale wrists. It is the kind of jumper you cannot easily buy in the shops. The more Della looks around, the more she realises nothing that Carrie owns can be easily bought. It has all been discovered, repurposed, restored.

Della thinks about her own house on the other side of the wall, where Leo ripped out all of the old-fashioned details and modernised. Tash and Robin have always said how they adore the sleek modernity of their house, the high-tech everything that Leo installed to make life easier, safer, more predictable. But now Della sees how Carrie has chosen to furnish her space, she feels wrong-footed somehow, ashamed of the way they obliterated the original features in favour of something shiny and new.

'Sorry it's such a mess. I only got into the house today.'

Again, Della senses an uncertainty in Carrie, a feeling she is watching her for reassurance. 'It's fine. I'd still be sitting on the doorstep if it wasn't for you. I can't believe I forgot to charge my phone and now I've locked myself out of my own house.'

'Well, I'm the clumsiest person alive, so no judgement here,' Carrie says, holding up her hands. 'How did it go at the vet's? Did you say Marmite was your dog's name?'

'Yes,' replies Della, trying to keep her voice even. 'They're keeping him in overnight. They don't know what's wrong with him, but it might be a stroke.'

'Poor dog. I hope he's OK.'

'Yeah.' Della takes a breath and decides to get it over with as soon as possible. 'It's particularly awful,' she says deliberately, 'because my husband died last week. I don't think I could take another death in the family. My daughter and I . . . Well, you can imagine.'

Carrie stops what she is doing, her hand flies up to her lips as her eyes fill with tears. 'Oh my God,' she says in a strangled voice. 'That's . . . that's . . .' And then she looks around, finds a tissue and blows her nose. 'Sorry. An overdeveloped sense of empathy. I sometimes feel things a bit too keenly. You've had a really terrible day. A terrible week.' She clears a space on the sofa and motions for Della to sit. 'Let me make you something.' She doesn't ask Della what she would like, just goes through to the kitchen, leaving Della in the sitting room, and Della can hear her at the stove, switching on the gas, moving a pan around, opening drawers. Eventually, Carrie comes back, and she has composed herself. She hands Della an elegant tea glass filled with something milky, and it smells warm and sweet and fragrant and spicy.

'What is it?' Della asks.

'It's my take on an Indian chai. I grind the spices myself. I live off this in the winter months. It's such a comforting drink.'

Della sips and tastes honey, ginger and mint. It soothes her throat, which has been tense all day from being on the brink of tears. She feels herself relax among Carrie's things.

'Don't forget to charge your phone,' Carrie reminds her gently, handing over a charging cable. 'What was your daughter's name?'

'Alex,' replies Della, plugging the phone in to the wall socket.

Carrie smiles. 'That's funny. You have a girl with a boy's name, and I have a boy with a girl's name.'

'You have a son?' asks Della, looking around for evidence of a child.

'Yes,' replies Carrie. 'He's at school today, though I guess he'll be exploring the village by now. He's seventeen, almost eighteen. His name is Jude.'

'That's the same age as Alex. Is he at Woodside Grange? Just up the road?'

'Yes. It's his first day today.'

'Then our kids will probably meet today as well. It's a small school.'

Carrie smiles that shy smile, and Della warms to her. She is so different to Tash, gentle and calm, but there is a steadiness in her that feels reassuring. It's a compelling combination. Della feels she can breathe for the first time in a week.

'Are you married, or . . .' Della lets the question hang.

Carrie shakes her head. 'No. It's just me and Jude. We're making a fresh start together.'

'Like me and Alex,' says Della, thinking about the strange symmetry that exists between them. Two women, each in opposite halves of a house. Their teenage children without a parent. She is not alone, then. This woman's life is a strange reflection of hers.

Chapter Twenty

Della and Carrie talk for two hours. Della tries to call Alex, several times. She resorts to texting to tell her about Marmite, to ask what time she is coming home, but it is clear she is being ignored. Somehow, this doesn't cut as deeply as it would have done this morning, because she is here, in this room full of boxes that contain the most extraordinary things, talking with a woman who makes her feel interesting.

Over the course of the afternoon, she understands that Carrie is a listener. She asks gentle questions in such a way that Della wants to answer them. Carrie asks, quietly, if Della would like to talk about Leo. The way she says this, in a casual tone, unburdened by drama and pity, makes Della want to. All of the conversations concerning Leo in the past week have been strained with worry. But now, she lets the good memories of him blossom in this room, a strange mirror of her own lounge. It is like being in a parallel universe where she is allowed to be happy. She talks about the things she loved about her husband, what made him a good father to Alex. The way he made them both feel they were the centre of his life. Carrie listens, her eyes never leaving Della's. She nods in all the right places. She has a soft laugh that reaches her pale blue eyes, a wide smile that comes easily as the afternoon progresses. The shyness Della noticed when they first met seems to melt away. But, behind the smile, Della thinks she sees sadness. Della recognises it because she carries it herself.

So Della stops talking. 'Enough of me,' she says. 'Tell me what brought you here.'

Carrie looks wistful for a moment. 'Well, there's not much to tell. I was with a man who got a better offer. He's in Australia doing his dream job. He's always wanted to work there. Jude and I couldn't compete.'

'You didn't want to go with him?'

'I couldn't, really. We weren't married and I didn't want to get married. There were visa issues. And, really, I wanted Jude to grow up here, in the country he was born in.'

'Was he Jude's father?' asks Della tentatively, wondering if Carrie minds the question.

Carrie shakes her head and answers quickly. 'No, no. Jude's father was out of the picture before he was born.'

'Oh, I'm sorry.'

Carrie gives a bright smile. 'We weren't right together. Jude and I have a good life. We get on well.'

Della puts her tea glass down on a polished wooden side table next to her covered in delicate fretwork. 'We're not so dissimilar, are we? We're both in mourning, in a way.'

Carrie's face softens. 'I wouldn't put myself in your category. You must be . . .' She pauses, unable to articulate. 'How are you doing? You and Alex?'

Della gives a bitter laugh. 'Badly. I'm finding out some things about myself I don't like very much.'

'What things?' asks Carrie.

'I let Leo do too much for me,' she admits. 'I'm struggling to get a grip on our finances. He was an IT consultant and specialised in security for small businesses. So his own computer is impossible to get into, and I can't find his phone.'

'His phone? Do you have one of those find-my-phone apps? Maybe it would show up.'

Della shakes her head. 'He never wanted stuff like that on his phone because he said it could be hacked.' Della wonders whether to tell Carrie about her past. 'My brother is . . .' She wonders how to describe Ethan. 'He's very problematic,' she says, careful not to scare Carrie. 'Leo was always very careful about personal information and how it got shared. But it's backfired now because he never shared his passwords with me and I'm locked out of everything.'

'Is there another way?' Carrie says with concern.

'I think now I have the death certificate it will be easier to transfer everything over. But . . .'

'But what?'

'That's not really the point,' Della sighs. 'I think Leo hid things from me. Things I may never get to the bottom of.'

'Plenty of people don't share passwords with their spouse because they don't believe they will die like Leo did. It's not something we like to think about.'

'I suppose . . .' acknowledges Della.

'We all have an interior life, and that's OK, isn't it? We don't have to share everything with everyone.'

'I guess. It seems so simple when you put it like that.'

'That's because you can choose to make it simple,' Carrie says, shrugging.

The sound of a key in the lock echoes through the house and Della hears the door opening and closing.

'Mum?'

'It's Jude,' Carrie says to Della. 'In here, Jude,' she calls. 'We have a visitor.'

A tall boy with a shock of dark, curly hair comes into the room. His eyes are a cool blue, like Carrie's, which looks striking against such dark hair and pale skin. His eyelashes are black, as if they have been inked by a fine brush.

'This is my son,' says Carrie. 'Jude, this is Della, our new next-door neighbour.'

Jude stands awkwardly.

'Did you meet my daughter at school today? Alex? She's your age,' says Della, giving him a big smile.

'Yeah. Um, actually, I spent the afternoon with her in the village.' Jude looks uncomfortable and glances at his mum. He raises his hand to rake through his curls and as the cuff of his shirt drops away, Della notices a tattoo, an intricate design laced around his wrist. She wonders who did this, if it hurt, and if Carrie minded.

'Everything OK?' Carrie asks him.

'Uh, well, we were in the village, and she got a message about her dog. So she decided to go and see him at the vet's. I went with her,' he begins.

'That was nice of you, thank you for doing that,' says Della, feeling absurdly grateful to this awkward boy.

'Um, but when we got there her dog had died. She's pretty upset.'

Della looks at her phone and sees she missed a call from the vet when she was trying to call Alex. All the calm she felt for the past two hours disintegrates. 'Where is she?' she asks, standing up, unplugging her phone and pocketing it.

'I just dropped her off, next door. The vet said it was peaceful. He just . . . fell asleep and didn't wake up.'

'Della—' says Carrie.

'Thanks for the tea,' Della says, trying to keep her voice from breaking. She only just makes it out of the house before she begins to sob.

Chapter Twenty-One

Alex has left the front door open. Whether in defiance of the security precautions that Leo and Della drummed into her, or whether it was because she didn't want to have to open the door to her mother, Della can't tell. She runs into the kitchen, but Alex isn't there, so she takes the stairs two at a time and finds her, in a ball, on her bed.

'Jude just told me,' Della says, sitting down next to her. She touches her daughter's back, tentatively, gives it a little stroke, as if she is an animal she is trying to tame.

'I know,' Alex says in an icy voice. 'I asked him to.'

'What happened?'

'I was too late. Just like with Dad. I'm always too late.'

Della feels helpless in the face of Alex's grief. Her own tears are stopped by the sight of her child, curled up like a baby in utero. 'It's not your fault,' she whispers, desperately. 'None of this is your fault.'

'Go away,' Alex says quietly, raising her head from her knees. Her eyes are glassy and black. Her face has no expression. And Della sees a flash of something that stops her in her tracks as she recalls that phrase, *a bad seed*, and wonders if there is something inside Alex that has the potential to grow crooked, to mutate into something else, should the worst conditions transpire. Alex has only ever known light, nourishment and warmth. But now, her daughter is in darkness, and it is the same darkness that descended on Della and Ethan.

To be left alone is what Alex wants, Della can see that. It is the only good thing she can do for her daughter. So she leaves Alex's bedroom and goes into the kitchen, where she stands in the middle of the floor, not knowing what to do. Eventually, she kneels at Marmite's bed and curls herself into it as best she can. The smell of him, embedded in the blankets, is heady and beautiful.

She closes her eyes and remembers the day Leo brought him home. She remembers the warmth of his young body, the soft weight of it, in the cup of her hands. The pads on his paws that were a delicate, untouched pink. Even when he was a puppy there was something very grown-up, very human in the way he looked at you: with hope, humour, disappointment, regret. She misses him already with a hollow longing, knowing she will never again feel his nose impatiently nudge the back of her leg, never feel his muscular body brush by her in the woods, never hear him groan with contentment in front of a fire after a good meal. She won't feel the heavy warmth of his head resting in her hands, or look deep into his eyes and allow herself to be enveloped in his gentle gaze.

She knows it is inappropriate, to grieve in this way for a dog who had a long and lovely life, but Della feels the depth of it. More profound, perhaps, than her grief for Leo. She tries to understand it and realises it is because Marmite was the one innocent thing in her life, the one member of the family who treated her with absolute honesty. He looked at her with undiluted love, always. Something she has not felt for a while, she realises. Leo had been so distant this past year, the lack of closeness between them happening by degrees. Now, without Marmite, her only ally, she feels truly, terribly alone.

A well of despair opens up within her and she recalls this feeling, experienced once before, when she was about sixteen, waking up in the middle of the night, a strange, flickering light in her room, a feeling of hot pain at her feet. There was a small fire, burning in a neat circle, at the foot of her bed. The sight of it was so extraordinary she did nothing for a moment, thinking she was dreaming, before the pain forced her to throw the blanket over it to smother it out. She looked around, wildly, in the darkness, the smell of lighter fluid and singed wool filling her bedroom.

'I know you're thinking of leaving.' Ethan's voice sounded quietly from the corner of her room. A metallic scraping cut through the darkness and the lighter he was holding gave out a flame, illuminating his face. 'Just so you know, I will find you, anywhere you go. It's my job to look after you. To keep this family together. If you leave, I will come for you.'

The next morning was the first and only time she discussed what was going on in that house with her mother.

'He's just doing his best, Della,' her mother said helplessly. 'It just comes out in a funny way, that's all. He's so young, still. He doesn't know how he comes across.'

That afternoon, her mother had given Della a flimsy lock for her door. Della took it out of the palm of her hands and a slow, sad realisation spread over her, like smoke. Her mother could never do anything to stop Ethan, she didn't have it in her. She was as powerless as Della.

Finally, Della gets up out of Marmite's bed, reaches for the box of tissues on the kitchen table and blows her nose. Her eyes are swollen and sore, but it doesn't matter because she is done, she realises. It is a decision she can make, to stop giving in to grief, to do something instead. She makes a call to the vet, who assures her that Marmite died of natural causes. Then she climbs the stairs once more to Alex's room, the sharp, cool feeling of intent coursing through her body.

'Get up,' she says to Alex, who still has her back to her.

At the tone of Della's voice, Alex stiffens and rolls over to look at her.

'Get up,' repeats Della. 'We're going to do this properly. Together.'

'What?' asks Alex, up on her elbow, now, looking uncertain.

'We're going to go to the vet, and we are going to bring Marmite home. Then we're going to dig for him, in the woods, and give that dog the burial he deserves. I'm not leaving him in that place for a moment longer.'

Alex sits up in bed, an unfamiliar expression on her face, and swings her feet round to the floor. 'Let's do it,' she says, resolute, tying her hair back with a scrunchie from her wrist.

Della locks the house up and they climb into the car, slamming the doors in unison. It is dark, now, and the shadows of the trees wave and reach out over their heads as their lights illuminate the forest from below. They drive in silence to the vet, who is keeping the building open for them, but the silence is different to the one that existed between them before. Using the picnic blanket that Carrie lent her, they wrap Marmite carefully and carry his body to the boot of the car. Then, still in silence, they drive home, and together they bring him into the house, lying him carefully in his bed, arranging his blankets around him, making sure his tail is wrapped around his body, just the way he liked. He looks peaceful, as if he is asleep. They stare at him for a moment, and then Alex turns to her mother.

'What do we do now?' she whispers.

'Now we dig,' says Della, her voice firm.

Chapter Twenty-Two

Della and Alex work together for hours. The ground is soft and pliant after the rain, but it is hard to find an area that is free from the roots of the trees. Finally, they find the perfect spot visible from the house and they dig through the night until it is done.

As they begin to cover his body, a robin's call cuts clearly through the dark air. Quietly at first, and then a little louder, the whistle of a blackbird joins in, echoed by another across the wood. Then the song thrushes chime in with their warbling, bubbling call. As the minutes tick by and the sun begins to light the sky, the first notes of the dawn chorus fall into an orchestra of sound, filling the air with a melody that becomes impossible to follow. When they finish covering Marmite's body they both stop to watch the sunrise, and Della cannot think of a more beautiful way to say goodbye.

'Bedtime, I think,' says Della, to Alex. 'But first, we need to clean up.' She takes Alex's spade from her mud-smeared hands. They are both filthy. Alex nods, compliant, and after a shower they go into their separate rooms and fall into a deep and dreamless sleep.

When Della wakes only a few hours later, it is late morning. She goes down the stairs and dreads entering the kitchen, knowing there will be a horrible space where Marmite's bed used to be. She spends the morning, aimless and fidgety, jittery from lack of sleep but too wound up to go back to bed. On impulse, she grabs Leo's house keys, lets herself out and knocks on Carrie's door.

Carrie's face creases with concern when she opens the door. 'How are you doing?' she asks.

'Better, actually,' replies Della. She explains what she and Alex did last night, how it began to heal something between them. 'It still feels fragile, but at least it's something.' She looks at Carrie. 'Thanks for looking after me yesterday. What you did for Marmite. I don't know how long I would have been in the wood if you hadn't been there.'

'What are neighbours for?' Carrie asks, smiling. She pushes her hair off her face and a large bruise appears from underneath her shirtsleeve that falls away when she reaches up.

'Ouch. That looks painful,' says Della, indicating the mark.

'It looks worse than it is. I think I told you I'm the clumsiest person alive. Not helpful when you're carrying boxes around and moving furniture all day.'

'Is Jude not here, then?' says Della, looking behind Carrie and into her house.

'He wanted to get stuck into school.'

Della sighs. 'I completely forgot about school. I should call them, I suppose, to explain where Alex is. How is Jude settling in?'

Carrie shrugs. 'I think his maths class covered a topic already that they didn't do in his last school, so he has to do most of the work himself. The exams are only a few weeks away.'

'Yeah, it's a difficult time to start a new school.' Della waits for Carrie to elaborate, but she doesn't so Della decides to ask. 'You mentioned you and Jude were having a fresh start?'

'I'm a big believer that a change is as good as a rest. We move around a lot.'

'Oh, I see. Where have you come from?'

Carrie smiles at Della. 'Let's go inside so we can talk. I should have invited you in earlier. Everything's at sixes and sevens in here. I think I left my brain in one of these boxes.' Her foot catches the corner of a box in the hallway. 'It's not just our possessions that are all over the place. Jude and I have a lot of work to do on the house.' Carrie picks the box up and stacks it carefully on top of another.

'What is he going to do when he finishes school?' asks Della, following her in.

'He's going to take some time out.' Carrie turns to her and smiles. Again, Della gets the impression there is a sadness behind that smile.

'Would you like a hand?' asks Della. 'I can unpack a few boxes with you.'

Carrie looks uncertain and then seems to make a decision. 'Sure,' she replies. 'That would be really great. How about we do the kitchen? I cleaned out some of the cupboards yesterday. You don't want to know what I found in there.'

They walk into the kitchen, which is still as Mrs Winters left it. The cabinets are solid wood but look dated and tired. 'I'm going to paint the cupboard doors in something cheerful when I have a moment,' says Carrie. 'Or Jude will, if he's not too busy with schoolwork. We're going to renovate the whole house together. We like a project.'

'Before you do much else, you should make sure the storm shutters are working. You might need them sooner than you think. It can get windy without much warning, and it affects us more than most. You don't want to deal with broken windows if you can avoid it.'

'I didn't think about high winds. How dangerous are they?'

'Only dangerous if you get caught outside. The house is solid. I can go through a few safety-do's-and-don'ts when you're settled in.'

Carrie flashes her a grateful smile. 'Thanks. That makes me feel better.'

Della is lifted by the notion of having a new friend, someone that needs her help. It's been so long since she needed anyone else in her life. Tash, Robin, Alex and Leo seemed enough. But being with Carrie, it feels good to talk to somebody unconnected to her past or her family. A friend she can call her own. Carrie asks her questions about the workings of the house, and she likes the way it feels, to be looked up to by this woman.

'Does Jude have any siblings?' asks Della, opening a box of glassware, wondering if there are older children who have already left home.

'No,' replies Carrie, kneeling on the floor to clean out a cupboard. 'Jude's enough for me. How about you? Does Alex have a brother or a sister?'

'No, unfortunately. We would have liked another, but Alex's birth was tricky so . . .' Della lets the sentence fall away, surprised at the emotion she feels when she remembers the day she was told that Alex would be their only child.

'I'm sorry.' Carrie's face is full of sympathy.

'Don't be. Alex was a wonderful surprise. Leo was the happiest I've ever seen him. He couldn't wait to be a dad. I'm just sorry I couldn't give him another. It would have been nice for Alex to have a sibling.'

'You have a brother, don't you? I think you mentioned something yesterday.'

'Yes, but . . . I don't actually get on with my brother.' Della is aware of her tongue running away with her. She hadn't meant to talk about such personal sorrows, but Carrie seems to coax it out of her, effortlessly. Della takes a breath. 'I think I told you yesterday that my brother, Ethan, was problematic.'

'Yes, you mentioned something about that.' Carrie stops what she is doing. She sits back on her haunches on the floor. 'Sounds tricky.'

Della sighs.

'Is your brother ill?'

'I think so, yes. Our father died when we were young, and that affected him. I wondered if it was genetic, though, and that it might be somewhere in my DNA, too . . . and Alex's,' she finishes quietly, hardly able to believe she is voicing her deepest thoughts.

Carrie says nothing. She waits for Della to continue.

Della looks at Carrie, straight into those cool, blue eyes. 'I know that it's mainly nurture, not nature, that shapes a child. But sometimes, now that her dad is gone, I wonder about Alex's reaction to it. She's so angry.'

'She's allowed to be angry, Della,' Carrie says thoughtfully. 'It's a cruel thing that's happened to her. To both of you.'

Della lowers her eyes. 'I'm afraid of it. I learned to run away from anger. I hate it. I can't cope with Alex dealing with Leo's death like this. Sometimes, I look at her, and there's a flash of Ethan there. It worries me.'

'Have you talked to her about it? Explained how you feel?'

'God no!' exclaims Della, inwardly berating herself for talking this much. 'She doesn't know about Ethan, so I'd appreciate it if you didn't mention it to Jude or Alex. Leo and I decided it was best to protect her from him. He turns up, occasionally, and we didn't want her worrying about that. It's only really me he wants to see.' The memory unfolds, of Ethan in the woods, appearing from behind the trees. She shuts it down, smiles at Carrie.

'Doesn't Alex suspect something is going on?' Carrie queries. 'When your brother comes to the house?'

'She's usually been at school when it's happened. But also, we sometimes get strangers knocking on the door thinking the house is a café or a hostel, so she knows we can get a few oddballs out here. She thinks that's why we're so security conscious.' Della smiles what she hopes is a reassuring smile. 'Anyway, that is my problem, not yours. And please don't worry about him causing trouble for you. He doesn't come here very often. Threatening to call the police usually does the trick.'

'I'm not worried, Della, but you look as if you are. I assume it was easier to deal with him when Leo was around.'

Suddenly Della wonders if she has said too much. There is something about being in this house that she finds liberating. Carrie isn't like Tash. When she speaks to Carrie it feels as if she is being given space to form her own thoughts. With Tash those thoughts need to be ready-made and hardened off to withstand the power of Tash's opinion. But Carrie gives them the freedom to unfold. 'If you could just not say anything to Jude about Ethan . . .' she asserts, fighting down a feeling of panic.

Carrie holds her hands up. 'Of course. It's your story to tell. It's none of our business. I won't discuss it with Jude, I promise. I'm very good at keeping secrets.'

Della believes her. Then Della's phone rings, making them both jump. Carrie fumbles and drops a delicate patterned teacup on to the stone floor. It shatters into tiny pieces.

'Oh, well,' she says, ruefully. 'Time for a break, I think. You answer that and I'll get the kettle on.' With effort, she heaves herself up off the floor.

Della pulls her phone out of her pocket, wondering if it is Alex, but it's a number she does not recognise. Perhaps the funeral parlour, firming up arrangements for Friday.

'Hello?' she answers. 'Della speaking.'

'Mrs Harkin? I'm calling from Woodside Hospital Trust. You came here on Sunday to pick up your husband's belongings and you reported that his mobile phone was missing.'

'Yes, that's right.'

'Well, we've located it. Somebody handed it in. It's ready for you to collect whenever you want.'

The idea of driving to the hospital, after the night she has had, makes her hesitate. She and Alex need to finalise the readings for the funeral today.

'I'll come and pick it up tomorrow morning,' she says, wondering if the contents of Leo's phone will be as elusive as what's on his computer. Even though she is desperate to get hold of it, a part of her wonders what else she might find, what other secrets he has hidden, what lies he has told.

Chapter Twenty-Three

When Della drives away from the hospital, she hopes it will be the last time she ever has to go there. Leo's phone is charging in the car and is already beginning to light up, a list of notifications pinging on the screen. When she stops at a traffic light near the village, she cannot help herself. She scrolls through the list, but it is a combination of news headlines and calendar alerts. The phone is protected by a fingerprint, but it can be circumvented by putting in a code. Della has already locked herself out of the phone for ten minutes for trying the wrong code too many times.

The traffic lights change to green and, instead of turning right to reach the woods, Della decides to carry on towards the village. Mo might be able to help her unlock the phone. He said he was better with phones than he was with computers. She drives, still glancing at the phone as it delivers several days' worth of unread messages. And then she sees the funeral parlour she has asked to take care of the service on Friday and, instinctively, swerves and parks up outside.

Since they buried Marmite things have been a little easier between Della and Alex. Last night, they went through readings and poems together, trying to choose something appropriate for Leo's service.

'He wasn't really a poemy person,' said Della, rejecting the more sentimental suggestions from a book that Alex had brought home from the library. 'He was more head than heart.' They had both laughed when Alex pointed out that updating security software was far more interesting to her father than poems. It was the first time they had laughed since Leo's death. It was progress in a sad sort of way.

Della pushes the door to the funeral parlour open and a discreet buzzing sounds in the back of the building. Very soon, a man dressed in a dark suit comes out; he extends his hand and knows her name. 'Mrs Harkin. How are you?'

She has a vague memory of meeting this man, still in the raw pit of grief, when Leo's death wasn't something she had come to terms with. She's impressed he has remembered her and then she supposes that people are the core of his business. Remembering their names is the least he can do.

'Um, I was just passing,' Della begins. 'Alex and I decided on some readings for Leo's funeral last night, but I'm not sure if we give them to you or to the person taking the service. We aren't sure if we'll be able to do it on the day, so . . .'

'That's fine. You can decide last minute what you want to do. Mr Harkin's service is on Friday at the crematorium, yes? They're very good there. Very flexible and relaxed about last-minute changes. I can pass them on, if you like, so they have a copy should you need someone else to read it.'

'Oh,' says Della, feeling foolish. 'I don't have them with me.'

'You can send them to me via email, or drop in. Whichever is easiest,' says the man.

'Thanks.'

'Is there anything else I can do for you? Do you want to see your husband?'

Della is taken aback. 'See him? Now?'

'Yes. We have a viewing room. Some relatives like to come and spend time with their loved one before the service. They find it helpful.' He takes in Della's expression. 'Of course, you don't have to. Whatever you feel comfortable doing.'

Della is in a quandary. 'I didn't realise . . .'

He gestures to the comfortable-looking chairs in the waiting room. 'Would you like to have a think? You can sit here if you like. There's no hurry.'

Della doesn't need long to decide. 'Actually, yes. I'd like that. I'd like that very much.'

'Wait here. I'll be a few minutes.' He disappears through a door with a keypad, punching in a four-digit code that releases a lock before he can go through. Della sits on the nearest chair, too fidgety to look through the selection of bland magazines spread on the low table beside her. Eventually, after several minutes, he opens the door and gestures for her to follow him, indicating a different door with a number screwed into the wood. 'Number three. Mr Harkin is in room three. Take as long as you like, Mrs Harkin. Take as long as you need.'

She enters the room. It is an ordinary room, simply furnished, dimly lit. There is a vase of good-quality fake flowers on a polished side table. It is an unremarkable space were it not for the fact that her dead husband is lying in the centre of it. He is in the coffin that she cannot remember choosing, the lid of it hidden away. Leo is wearing the suit he wore to their wedding, one of their happiest days together. It was a source of pride for him that he still fitted into it. She imagines the undertaker dressing Leo like this, pulling his arms into the shirt, knotting his tie as if he were a boy on his first day at school. Leo looks different to the last time she saw him in the hospital, in the room they had tried to resuscitate him in. His eyes and lips look slightly unnatural, and she wonders if they have been glued shut. Della reaches out, slowly, and touches his forehead, the grey curls on his head. His skin is very cold. She looks for signs of her husband, and after searching this man's face, she understands there are none, that Leo is truly gone.

'Alex and I have picked out some readings for you,' she murmurs, feeling self-conscious. 'I hope you like them.' Then she leans over him, kisses his cool cheek. She stares at his face for a long time, wondering what she should say to him, knowing it is the last time she will talk to him when he is physically there. 'I wish you'd been a bit more open with me,' she eventually whispers. 'I wish we'd had more time together.' Della steps back, shoves her hands in her pockets. 'I love you,' she concludes. 'Alex and I both love you. You know that. And we'll miss you. More than you will ever know.'

Della shivers; the room is cool. Wrapping her coat around her body, she feels her phone vibrate. Pulling it out, she realises she has brought Leo's phone out of the car. She has unplugged it, unconsciously, assuming it was hers.

A reminder about a meeting he should be attending in five minutes flashes up. Della wonders if Robin has told them he won't be coming as she pockets the phone. She knows it is time to leave, but cannot resist touching Leo once more. Taking his left hand, she notices the dent his wedding ring has left behind and brushes her fingertips over it, cupping his hand in between hers. But it is not the same. His fingers are icy. She looks for the last time at his elegant hands, the nails trimmed, the cuticles neat. Everything is just right, even though it is all wrong.

It only occurs to her, then, what she must do, and as she pulls Leo's phone out of her pocket once more, she wonders if her subconscious led her here, that she is cleverer than she thinks.

Della gently pushes the phone against Leo's fingertip, hardly believing it could be this easy. When it doesn't work, she tries his thumb. Then she tries the fingers on his other hand. Feeling cheated, she straightens his cuffs and puts the phone back into her pocket. She is still flustered when she exits the room.

'Can I do anything else for you, Mrs Harkin?' The funeral director is waiting for her in the foyer.

Della feels like a thief. 'No, I mean, yes. I don't know.' She looks at this man with his kind expression, tells herself she will never see him again after Friday, and what's the harm in asking? She brings Leo's phone out of her pocket, not sure how to phrase her question.

An expression of understanding crosses the man's face. 'Is that your husband's phone?'

Della nods, uncertain.

'The fingerprint technology doesn't work after death,' he explains kindly. 'I believe it works by an electrical charge which dies with the deceased.'

'How did you know I was going to ask?'

'It's a much more common dilemma than you think. People see it in movies. They come here and it doesn't work. They don't understand why. We get the police here, sometimes, asking. Even they don't seem to know.'

'Oh,' says Della, feeling a bit better.

'Is it an iPhone?' he asks.

'Yes,' she replies.

'Do you know if Mr Harkin added you as a legacy contact?'

'What's that?'

'You can name a person to inherit your data. If Mr Harkin did that and named you as a legacy contact, you just need the code and his death certificate.'

'Thanks,' says Della, feeling dejected as she leaves the funeral parlour. 'I'll look into it.'

Della gets back into her car, knowing that she will search Leo's belongings for a legacy contact code, certain she will not find anything. Leo was the most thorough person she knew. He would have set her up as a legacy contact if he had wanted to, he would have told her about it in the same way he explained the tweaks he'd made on their house insurance every year. She plugs his phone back into the car charger, wondering what is in there that he wants to keep her away from, determined somehow to get it.

Chapter Twenty-Four

Friday settles on them like a shroud. The house is quiet as they both get dressed for Leo's funeral, each in their own private bubble of heartache. It is not practical to get a hearse down the track that leads to the house, so Della and Alex decide to drive themselves to the crematorium instead. But as they prepare to leave the house, there is a knock on the door and Carrie and Jude are there, dressed soberly, looking awkward.

'Alex asked Jude to come with her,' Carrie explains.

'Did she?' says Della, surprised and pleased Alex has asked a friend.

'I thought we could drive you both there. Give you some support. Is that the wrong thing to do? I wasn't sure.'

Della feels a flood of gratitude and relief. She had been dreading the journey there, just her and Alex in the car. 'Alex?' she calls into the house. 'Carrie and Jude said they would drive us.'

Alex appears dressed in a short black dress, her hair loose around her shoulders. 'Hi,' she says, smiling at Jude and Carrie. 'That would be great.'

'OK then,' says Jude, pulling out a set of car keys. 'Ready when you are.'

'You passed your test already?' asks Alex, impressed.

Jude grins. 'Yeah, I took it as soon as I could. Mum doesn't like driving.'

'You picked a strange place to live if you don't like driving,' remarks Della, getting into their car.

'Jude loves to drive,' Carrie replies. 'It's a good arrangement. And there are taxis if I get really stuck.'

The atmosphere in the car is jovial, an unexpected relief. Della lets Alex sit in the front so she and Jude can talk together. 'How are you holding up?' asks Carrie quietly, as Jude navigates the dirt track.

Della swallows, hard, and nods. 'Pretty good. We just need to get this day over and then we can start to come to terms with everything. This is a big help. Thank you. It's a nice gesture.'

'I always think funerals are more about the living than the dead,' says Carrie. 'I'm glad we could help.'

An unnatural calm overcomes Della when they arrive. She has imagined this day so many times over the past week, and each time she thought she would crumble in the face of it. But something has happened to her and Alex since they buried Marmite in the woods. Like the papery spathes on a daffodil bud protecting it from early frost, something has enveloped them both, defending them from the worst of their grief. Now this dreaded day has arrived, it feels like a relief. Even the sight of Robin doesn't faze her. She allows herself to be hugged by him, allows herself to be led into the chapel by him. He acts as if their last conversation never took place. Tash takes Alex's arm and all four of them walk in together as if they are family, leaving Carrie and Jude to find their places among the guests.

Della glances at Alex, covertly, during the service, not wanting to make her feel she is being spied upon, and although she can see Alex still has tears to shed, she is as self-possessed as Della feels, and she manages to walk up to the lectern at the front of the room, face the small congregation and speak, with a steady voice, to tell the audience what Leo meant to her. When it is Della's turn, she is ready.

'I had lost my parents by the time we met,' Della begins. 'I think it was that loss that drew us together. Leo was very close with his own parents and had a strong sense of family. He knew he wanted to build his own and I will forever be grateful to him for choosing me to be the person he built that family with.' As she speaks, Della looks around the room at the many friends and colleagues Leo has made in the past. Robin and Tash sit in the front row, next to Alex, who is red-eyed but composed. She looks for Carrie and Jude, who melted away as soon as Tash and Robin found them. She spots them in the middle row of the congregation with an elderly aunt of Leo's.

Della's eye is drawn to the back of the room, where a latecomer sits swiftly down on the back pew. As his head breaches a shaft of sunlight slanting from the tall windows, she sees his face before a long sweep of dark brown hair obscures it.

She is sure it is Ethan.

For a moment, Della cannot speak. The words dry up in her throat. She hesitates, hands trembling, and looks at her notes, which blur and scatter into meaningless letters. She looks to Tash for help, who nods her head encouragingly. Della searches the back of the chapel in vain, trying to find the seat where she is sure he sat down, but her view is obscured. Della mumbles her thanks for the support she and Alex have been given and then she descends the few small steps to the congregation, a sick feeling in her stomach. As she walks to her seat she rakes the back of the crowd for his face, but she can't relocate where he is. Several times during the service, she turns around, but her gaze is only met by a sea of sympathetic faces. When it is time to stand and leave the building, she has to stop herself from racing down the aisle to find him. Instead, she is forced by convention to move to the exit and greet every guest as they come out with Alex and Tash and Robin. Eventually, the crowd leaves the room.

'Is that everybody?' asks Della, craning her neck back into the chapel.

'I think so,' says Tash. 'Robin can go and look if you like?'

'No,' says Della, 'I'll do it.'

She walks back inside the chapel, and she can see the room is empty, but still she steps, slowly, looking in between the pews to check if Ethan is crouched there, waiting for her. She does this, her head moving right to left, until she reaches the end of the room. The entrance door is wide open, letting the thin sunshine warm the stone floor.

'Della, is everything OK?' calls Tash, who has come to find her.

Della spins around and smiles her most reassuring smile. 'I'm just making sure nobody left anything.'

'No, you're not,' counters Tash. 'You look upset. Tell me. I thought something happened when you were reading that eulogy, suddenly you seemed to fall apart.'

'I thought I saw Ethan,' says Della, a desperate note in her voice.

Tash looks around cautiously. 'Ethan? Here?'

'In the back of the chapel. A man came in and, when he sat down, he looked just like him. He didn't come out with everyone else.'

'Could it have been someone at the wrong funeral?'

'No. It looked just like him,' Della repeats. 'Apart from he was wearing a suit.'

'Well, it doesn't sound like Ethan. He hardly likes to dress for an occasion, does he? And I'm willing to bet he doesn't own a suit.'

'I was so sure . . .'

Tash puts her arm around Della. 'Well, if you think about it, these places have loads of different chapels and it's easy to go into the wrong one. Perhaps it happened with this chap?'

'I suppose,' says Della, unconvinced.

Tash squeezes Della's shoulders. 'Why would Ethan come to Leo's funeral? How would he even know he's dead?'

'I don't know,' replies Della, feeling stupid.

Tash links her arm through Della's and walks her down the aisle back to the thinning crowd. 'Even if Ethan knew, he'd have to know when the funeral was going to be held and where. It's a bit of a stretch.'

Suddenly, Della is not so sure of what she saw. 'Yeah, I guess so,' she says vaguely, wanting the conversation over.

'Come on. Let's go to the pub. I need something to eat, and so do you and Alex. Is she still only eating toast?'

Della smiles. 'She's moved on to other things, thank goodness. She let me make her scrambled eggs the other day. And I saw her heat up a can of soup last night.'

'Good,' declares Tash, loudly.

The guests gather in the pub and the speeches become more and more alcohol-fuelled and sentimental. Della feels she is sleepwalking through the afternoon. Her mind wanders, unable to focus on the memory of Leo, and the legacy he left. It keeps returning to the man in the chapel, and the certainty that Tash demolished begins to build itself up again. By the time she is ready for bed, she replays the moment he sat down, analysing the way the sunlight struck his face.

As she gets into bed and turns off the light, uncomfortable thoughts surround her in the darkness. Maybe Leo was paying Ethan off, after all, and now the money has stopped Ethan has come to find her.

She replays the conversation she had with Tash in the chapel. It was a surprise that Tash discounted her fears so quickly when Della voiced them to her. Della thinks about the detail that Robin knows about their finances, the feeling he was hiding something from her when she asked about the missing money.

Della is familiar with paranoia. She grew up with it, like a smell in the air that never went away. She knows she must control her paranoia where Ethan is concerned, but today she cannot help it.

What if Tash and Robin know about the missing money? What if it is connected to Ethan somehow?

And then another thought resolves itself in the darkness, like a ghost.

What if there is nobody I can trust?

Chapter Twenty-Five

The darkness is so absolute in the winter it is a comfort to be woken by birdsong in the gloom, knowing it will be twilight soon, that the sun will rise within the hour. Della feels she has overcome a hurdle by getting through the funeral yesterday. It has been a point in the week that Alex and she had to endure, time and effort spent on preparations neither of them wanted to make.

She hears the bathroom light-pull click off. 'Alex?' she calls, frowning. 'Are you OK?'

Alex pokes her head around the door.

'How come you're up so early?' Della asks, sitting up in bed.

'I just needed the loo. I'm going back to bed now. Sorry if I woke you.'

'You didn't. I was awake.'

Alex comes over and sits on the edge of the bed and sighs.

'Everything OK?' asks Della, moving her legs over to make room. Leo's side remains untouched. It is neat and smooth, the pillows plumped. Neither of them mentions it, but nobody is ready to occupy that space.

'It just feels like a big fat anticlimax. I thought it might be different after the funeral. But it's not.'

'It's going to take time. It's only been nine days.' *Though it feels like a year,* she does not say. She is two different people. Pre and post Leo. The loss is something she will contend with for the rest of her life, adjusting herself to fit into a new shape every day.

'Did you get anywhere with the bank stuff yet?' asks Alex.

'Robin's dealing with it.' Then Della remembers the conversation she had with the funeral director. 'Listen. Did Dad ever talk to you about being a legacy contact for his data?'

'What's that?'

Della explains, pleased she is telling Alex something she doesn't know about technology. Then she confesses she tried to unlock the phone at the funeral parlour.

'Oh my God, Mum, that's insane. Like something out of a movie.'

'Yeah, apart from it works in the movies, not in real life. I'm still locked out of his phone.'

'Can't you just use the code?'

'I don't know what it is.'

'Isn't it his grandparents' wedding date or something? Whatever that number is on that ring he wore?'

'What? Why didn't you tell me this before?'

Alex looks sheepish. 'You didn't ask me.'

'I *did*. I asked you about his computer ages ago!'

'That's different. I don't know how to get into that.'

Della lets out a noise of frustration. 'How do you know about his phone?'

'When he set me up with my phone security code he said it was better to use a long number that was hard to figure out for a thief but easy for me to remember. He said he used his grandparents' wedding date because it was inscribed on that horrible ring he inherited from Grandad. So he always had it on him if he forgot. It was eight digits long.'

'You mean the signet ring?' says Della, nudging her out of the way, leaping out of bed.

Alex shrugs. 'I don't know what you call it. It was grim, anyway. A big fat gold thing.'

Leo's rings, removed by the hospital at her request so she could keep something personal of his and pass them to Alex, are in a small bag in her underwear drawer. She opens the drawer and tips the contents out on to the duvet. His wedding ring, a plain gold band, clatters out with that of his father's and his grandfather's signet ring. All three rings have dates inscribed on them. It was a running joke in Leo's family that there would be no excuse to forget a wedding anniversary if the date was on their wedding bands. She turns the signet ring over and tips it towards the bedside lamp. Faintly, she makes out a date. She reaches for Leo's phone, which is charging next to her bed, unplugs it and punches the eight-digit number in. It opens like magic.

'Unbelievable,' sighs Della.

'I'm going back to bed,' yawns Alex. She shuffles out of the room and Della hears her bedroom door shut.

Della cannot wait to start. She begins methodically and goes through his text messages, but they are infuriatingly shallow. Most of them are between Leo and her, letting her know what time he is coming home. Her replies are so bland she could scream. She wants to yell at the two people she sees on the screen: *Why don't you say anything that actually matters? Don't you know how little time you have left together?*

Della goes back months, then years, over discussions about what is for dinner, requests to pick up milk, little affections and exclamations that seemed trivial at the time but mean so much now it touches her in a profound and beautiful way. She reads these exchanges until her appetite for the minutiae of their relationship is sated. Then she searches for other people he texted, gorges herself on the back and forth between him and Robin, cheering for Leo when Robin suggested going out together on an evening Leo knew Della had planned something special.

Can't you tell her something's come up at work? We haven't had a lads' night out for ages.

No mate, sorry, Leo responds. I promised Della. Let's get a date in the diary.

It is not the only message of this type. Robin often texts Leo to try and tempt him out. Sometimes, Leo agrees, but if he has planned anything with her or Alex, he will not be persuaded. Leo's loyalty, his absolute devotion to his family in the face of Robin's guilt-tripping and wheedling, rings out in these messages. The comfort they bring Della is something she knows she will seek out again and again.

The emails are harder to go through. There are so many to do with work she doesn't really understand which ones she should look at and which ones she should leave. She decides to forward on the ones that look like they might be useful to her own email account. She has a look through Leo's apps and tries to open the banking apps, but they need a fingerprint to access them, or a code she doesn't have. She knows that eventually they will be open to her, so she makes a note of each bank to ensure she has access to everything.

Scrolling through his contacts means nothing to her. The names she doesn't recognise seem to be work contacts with companies in brackets. There is nothing unusual or out of the ordinary. She is just about to put the phone back on charge when she remembers to check his call history. It goes back for years. Calls to her, calls to Alex, Robin and Tash, calls to the same people with company names in brackets that she has just seen in his contacts list. And then a few random numbers that don't have names. But one in particular catches her attention. It appears often, almost every week. Della scrolls down, down, through the months. Every week that number appears for almost a year. Before that, nothing.

Della scrolls forwards in time, noting the pattern of the call. Around twelve months ago, Leo received a call from this number. Then there was a flurry of calls, which peter out to a weekly call, always generated by Leo, never by the mystery number. Della thinks. If he called this person so often, why weren't they in his contacts list? For a whole year he had regular contact with this number, yet he didn't think it was important enough to store in his contacts list. Or was he trying to hide it from her?

Della thinks back to what was happening twelve months ago. Leo's father died around that time. It might account for the beginning of the calls, but not how they carried on until ten days ago, a whole year after the death of his father. She looks out of the window, through the budding branches of the trees. Is it tied up with the inheritance, then? And the disappearing money? The timeline fits. Again, Della goes over the face of the man she saw at the back of the chapel. She was so sure it was Ethan. If it was, everything makes sense and this is Ethan's number.

She looks at her watch. It is just after eight. Early enough to catch someone at home, late enough that they might be awake. Her heart swoops like a bird in her chest as she presses the number and puts the phone to her ear. It rings once, twice, three times. She waits, drumming her fingers on the duvet. It rings a fourth, a fifth time, and then it goes to voicemail on the sixth. Just like Leo's phone, the voice taking the message is a generic male voice, telling her the owner is unavailable. Della hadn't figured on voicemail. She kills the call and drops the phone on the duvet. Then, almost immediately, she picks it up again, looking at the screen. Then she presses the number once more and waits for the voicemail to kick in.

'Hello?' she says into an empty void. 'This is Della. Call me back.'

Chapter Twenty-Six

Della spends the day in the studio, fulfilling orders. She works into the afternoon, trimming a set of plates a local restaurant has commissioned, fixing them back on to the wheel now they are leather hard, smoothing their surfaces down as they spin, paring away imperfections until she is satisfied they are ready to be bisque fired before they are glazed. The hours tick by, unnoticed by Della, who submerges herself totally in the task at hand. It is only when she feels the waning light dimming the studio that she thinks about Alex. Della looks at her watch and then she wipes her hands and takes out her phone. There is no message. Frowning, Della locks up the studio and returns to the house, which is in darkness. As she unlocks the back door, she can see a half-eaten piece of toast on a plate on the kitchen table. She shouts up the stairs. Alex doesn't answer because she isn't there. Then, from next door, she hears the distinctive laugh of her daughter, joined by Carrie and Jude. Della listens, frozen to the spot, feeling like an interloper in her own house. She cannot help herself, she creeps in the darkness to the adjoining wall in the hallway and she presses her ear flat against it. Their voices are muffled and indistinct, but there is no doubting the emotion she can feel coming through the walls. Happiness. Jollity. There is something raucous and conspiratorial about the way they are all speaking together. She can hear the beat of music, pulsing through the brickwork. Della thinks about the past few days. It is only now that she realises Alex has spent a lot of time next door, more time with them than she has with her. Della feels a pinch of jealousy, and before she can have a word with herself, she hears Carrie's front door close and her own door rattle to the sound of Alex's key in the lock.

'I was wondering where you were,' says Della, trying not to sound like a harridan.

'Why are you standing here in the dark?' asks Alex, clearly still amused about whatever was happening next door.

'I only just came in from the studio,' replies Della. 'How come you didn't text me to say where you were? I was worried about you.'

'I was only next door,' scoffs Alex.

'Yes, but I didn't know that,' says Della, realising how fussy she sounds. 'What are you doing over there?'

'I'm going to help Jude and Carrie renovate their house,' says Alex as she hangs her keys on the hook in the hallway. 'It's going to be amazing! Carrie has really awesome taste and she's going to let me paint one of the walls this crazy pink colour, like a really deep magenta. It's called Schiaparelli Pink, do you know what I mean?'

Della doesn't know. 'Your exams are beginning in two months. It doesn't sound like a very good time to start renovating a house,' says Della, doubtfully.

'I'm not even sure I want to go to university,' says Alex, pushing her way past Della into the kitchen. 'Jude isn't. He's taking a year out.'

Della follows Alex into the kitchen, where her daughter is rummaging in her schoolbag. 'Well, OK. It's all very well taking a year out, but you really need to get good grades, so you've got a university to go on to when you finish having time out.'

Alex pulls a face. 'I can always resit.'

Della feels a surge of annoyance. 'You haven't even sat them yet! Why are you talking about resitting?'

Alex tosses her hair back as she shoulders her bag. 'I'm just saying, I'm not really *feeling* them, you know? Going to university is really expensive. It doesn't make sense to go somewhere I don't really want to be, if it costs that much.'

Della feels sidelined. 'But I thought you wanted to go to university?'

'*You* want me to go to university. I never said that.' She pulls a band from her wrist and twists her hair into a messy ponytail.

'But we spent all of those weekends doing those uni open days. We spent a weekend in Edinburgh last month. I thought you were really excited about going.'

'Things have changed. Carrie and Jude are showing me a different way. I don't have to do what you and Dad wanted. I need to think about what I want. It's my life.'

Della feels helpless in the face of Alex's conviction. 'But Alex . . .'

Alex makes a noise of frustration. 'This is the first time I've been excited about anything for ages. Jude is a really amazing carpenter, he's learned all of these cool skills in the other houses they've lived in and done up. I could do that too. He said he would teach me. He's so creative. Look what he can do with wood.' Alex reaches into her pocket and pulls out what looks like a small wooden ball.

When Alex drops it into her palm, Della doesn't look at it. She clenches it into her fist and swallows down her anger. 'Alex, you've known him for five minutes. And now you're changing your whole outlook on life?'

Alex shrugs, unconcerned. 'Whatever my outlook on life was, it changed when Dad died. Exams are just a piece of paper. We don't know how long we've got left on this earth and it's important to embrace life and live it to its fullest.'

'That sounds like Carrie talking, not you,' says Della bitterly.

'Carrie talks a lot of sense,' Alex says with a belligerent tone as she pushes past Della once more and goes up the stairs to her room.

'Don't you want to eat?' asks Della, following her into the hallway, calling up to her as she disappears.

'I ate at Carrie and Jude's,' calls down Alex. 'She made sushi.'

'Sushi?' echoes Della weakly.

Alex's head appears over the banister. 'Yeah. We ate with chopsticks. It was really cool. We all sat on the floor, Japanese style.'

Alex disappears into her room, leaving Della standing in the dark. She opens her palm, aware her fingers are still wrapped around the little wooden ball. But when she opens them and examines what Jude has made, she is mesmerised. She switches on the hall light to get a better look. It is a little rabbit sitting with its back rounded, its ears flattened against its flank, chubby and well fed. It is astonishingly detailed and beautiful. There are light score marks all over its body to depict fur, and the texture moves around the contours of it, making it look alive. Della cannot help herself. She strokes it. Its paws are curled under its chin and its eyes are closed as if it is contemplating something important. There is something wise and nourishing about it. As Della turns it this way and that, examining the animal from every angle, she immerses herself in the feeling of deep satisfaction this little object gives her, and she considers the boy who produced this. This little carving is filled with the kind of emotional intelligence that can only be acquired with age, yet Jude is not a man, he is a boy who has been unable to put down any roots. A boy who has grown up without a father, just like her own brother. She turns the rabbit over, looking for flaws, something incomplete, careless or unfinished. But she finds only perfection. She thinks of Ethan at Jude's age, filled with rage, and she wonders how adversity makes some people want to destroy things, and some people want to create.

The squeak of Alex's door opening sounds above her. Alex's head appears over the banister once more. 'I forgot,' she says. 'Carrie said this came for you, but it was posted through her door by mistake.'

Alex drops an envelope over the banister and it flutters to the floor. Della bends down to pick it up and before she has opened it she sees the name of the funeral home, detailed in elegant script on the back of the cream envelope. With a sense of foreboding, she opens the envelope, carefully, as if to avoid upsetting the contents. When she unfolds the thick paper, she sees the total cost of Leo's funeral printed at the bottom of the page. It is a huge amount, more than she thought possible. She feels a little weak, steadies herself in the hallway against the sideboard, and places the envelope with the growing pile of bills.

She only has a few weeks to make a decision. If she can't earn some money soon, she will have to sell this house. And if she does that, Alex will never forgive her.

Chapter Twenty-Seven

The woods keep to their own time, sometimes slow and dragging, where changes move like molasses, but sometimes, after a sunny day, a transformation occurs. Change breaks out urgently, violently. The wood anemones that carpet the forest floor, their buds tightly fisted, are suddenly open, spread wide as if they have always been there, glowing like stars in the shade. It is the same with grief. Time stretches and contracts and grief announces itself in the least likely of places.

After Leo died, she felt as if time had slowed. Each day seemed like three, yet Della has no memory of what she did with those hours. Now, time begins to speed up, as if nature is telling her she must move with her grief, she must incorporate it into her life, or she will be overtaken by it.

The budding kinship she felt with the woman next door has slowed in the past week after the funeral. Carrie and Jude are well underway with the house renovations and Alex has been absorbed into their project. Della wonders if she is less interesting now the funeral is past, or perhaps Carrie is aware of her disapproval over Alex's involvement. Several times she has knocked on the door next to hers, and Carrie has opened a window above her head, a paintbrush in her hand, or a drill, to say she can't come down. It is a sign that everybody is moving forward and so must she.

Leo's phone, still plugged into the wall socket in her bedroom, has not received a call from the mystery number. Della has googled it, and it is not a company. She dials it at different times of the day and never gets a reply. She has called the number using her own phone. It goes straight to voicemail. Today, Della decides it is time to stop. For a moment, the unfamiliar sensation of optimism spreads its wings over her. She picks up her phone and calls Tash.

'Well, this is a surprise,' says Tash. 'It's usually me chasing you.'

'I just called to say hi. And to thank you for the support you've given me over the past couple of weeks. You've been amazing. As always.'

'You are absolutely welcome. What's brought this on?'

'I don't know, really. I suppose I've decided to stop worrying about what Leo was up to. There's only so many times I can dial that stupid number on his phone.'

'Good girl. Have you thought about selling the house? Moving closer to me and Robin?'

Della pictures the bills that have come to the house over the past two weeks. Envelopes Leo would have picked up and taken care of without involving her. A reminder to renew the car insurance came yesterday, along with a letter informing her the mortgage payments will only pause for a few weeks before beginning again in earnest. She doesn't have long to turn their finances around, but the idea of selling and facing Alex's wrath is too much. She has to try something else before she does that. She hesitates before telling Tash about the idea that has been forming in her head, but eventually Della takes a breath and blurts it out.

'I'm going to give it a go here first. I'm thinking about setting up a pottery school, actually.'

'A school?' Tash sounds sceptical.

'Well, not a school,' says Della, backtracking. 'More of an after-school-club-type thing for kids.'

'Why?' asks Tash.

'I think I might be good at it. Do you remember the pottery teacher at school? Miss Abramovich?'

'That old crone. She was bonkers.'

'She wasn't bonkers,' says Della, feeling irked. 'Anyway. I need to set up another income stream and this might be it.'

'Don't you have to have a teaching qualification to do that? I don't think you can set up a school without a lot of faffing around.'

Della begins to feel uncertain. The idea she had brewing in her mind over the past few days now feels weak and unworkable. 'It's just a thought,' she says. 'I can't see any evidence of a savings or investment account using Frank's money. Robin hasn't found anything either, so I have to assume the money is gone and it's up to me to figure out how to pay the mortgage. I can't sit around and wait for the house to be repossessed.'

'Then sell it. It's an asset.'

'Alex would never forgive me.' She doesn't say she has had paranoid visions of Alex moving in with Carrie and Jude if she ever sold their house. 'Prices in the village are expensive. I wouldn't be able to afford anything with a big garden, let alone a studio. I need to find a way of earning enough to pay the mortgage or I need to find out what's happened to that money.'

Tash clicks her tongue in thought. 'Leo must have paid Ethan off with his father's money. It makes sense if he told you he saw him shortly before he died.'

'I suppose so,' Della says. 'But I can't see Leo giving away such a huge sum unless it came with a promise never to come back. And then he would have told me. It would be a cause for celebration, wouldn't it? Not a big secret.'

'But it makes sense that Ethan hasn't shown up here,' Tash persists. 'Leo probably told him to get lost for good. Maybe that was what he was doing the day he died. And he was going to tell you that evening?' Tash warms to her idea. 'Maybe he was in the village picking out a nice bunch of flowers or something to surprise you with the good news?'

But Della can't make herself believe it. 'What about the funeral? I thought I saw Ethan, remember?'

'Believe me, if Ethan was at Leo's funeral, he would have approached you. He wouldn't have been able to resist. That man wasn't Ethan.'

Della feels her certainty crumble once more. She doesn't know what to believe. All she knows is that the money is gone and she is powerless to get it back.

'Listen, Della, Robin's calling me. But come over for dinner soon, OK? You and Alex. We can have a look at Rightmove. See if we can't persuade you to come into the village.'

Della ends the call feeling annoyed. Every time she suggests something to Tash, she bats it away or talks it down. Why shouldn't she set up a school here? Why shouldn't she try to make it work? She doesn't need Tash and Robin looking after her. She can look after herself.

In that moment, she yearns for Leo, for him to be here, giving her his reassurance. But then she reminds herself that he is the cause of this. That if he'd paid the mortgage off like he said he would, she wouldn't have to worry about losing the house. She looks under the kitchen table, searching for Marmite, wanting to go for a walk, before she realises he isn't there anymore. Then she gets up and goes to the back door, trying not to let misery overwhelm her.

If you want to walk in the woods, you can do it alone, she scolds herself.

Della puts on a coat, checks her phone is charged up and texts Alex, who is next door again, telling her she will be back in an hour. As she walks through the trees, Tash calls again and she kills the call, not wanting to be pulled into another conversation about what she should and shouldn't do.

She wonders if there is something wrong with her, something lacking. She is so used to defining herself as Ethan's sister, Tash's friend, Leo's wife, Alex's mother. Who would she have become without all of these people shaping her, telling her what to do?

'Would the real Della please step forward,' she mumbles under her breath.

Her phone buzzes again, a text from Tash, a big red heart next to a sad face.

Her relationship with Tash has become complicated. Tash is now more loyal to Robin than to her, and while that was manageable when she had Leo onside, now she is alone, Tash is not the ally she needs. Not for the first time, she wonders if Tash and Robin know exactly where the money has gone, and if it is a truth they do not want to share with her.

Della wanders, aimlessly, enjoying the damp air, the cool breeze, the smell of lichen and wet wood. Eventually, she reaches a clearing and turns around to orient herself. She has walked a wide and wandering circle through the woods. She can see the house from here and she notices the piece of blue fabric, still attached to the branches of the beech tree. She looks around for the oak tree she found Marmite lying near when he collapsed. She had meant to come back here to see if she could find anything that might have poisoned him, but after the vet told her he had died of natural causes the thought went out of her mind. She looks for signs of vomit around the base of the tree. There hasn't been any rainfall since Marmite was here, and the high winds that have been talked about on the weather forecast have come to nothing. Della toes the leaves, wondering if there are any poisonous mushrooms growing here. She scours the area, and after a while she concludes the vet wasn't just being kind, he was telling the truth. Marmite died of old age.

Feeling wobbly at the thought of him, Della sinks down and sits on the damp earth, her back against the bark of the oak.

If only we could spend our lives running through the woods with people who love us and then go to sleep for ever, she thinks. Life was so simple for Marmite. Her hands sweep the earth around her legs. There are tree roots here that are older than she can imagine. They dig into the ground like claws. She feels their scaly texture with her fingers. Everything here is older than she is. Everything here will live on, long after she is dead. And there is something hopeful and beautiful about that thought.

Her fingertips catch on a texture that is not wood, not leaf mulch. It is a folded piece of paper stuffed into a crevice in the roots of the tree. Della turns on to her knees and tries to lever out the paper, but it is wedged into the wood with such force she thinks she will end up ripping the paper before she gets it out. She scratches at the earth around it, freeing it from its housing. Then she has a moment of shame. She remembers the stories that Leo told her, the confessions the villagers gave to the tree. She looks up at the oak. It is old, very old. It must have been the same one Leo and his schoolfriends used to wish to for girlfriends. Should she be reading other people's secrets? It is not her place to interfere. She looks at the folded paper, knowing she cannot resist. She reasons with herself that if she takes it, anyone looking for it might think their confession has been swallowed up and absolved, their wish granted.

Slowly, she unfolds the dirty paper. It is clean inside, the paper is not that old and the weather has been kind. The writing is small, the letters are shaky. But the form of them is as familiar to her as her own reflection. This is Leo's writing.

I killed him. Forgive me.

Della looks at the letters, trying to make sense of what she sees. At first, she thinks the note refers to Marmite, before she realises Marmite died after Leo did. She cannot believe that the meaning is literal, that Leo has actually killed a person. Surely this is some kind of joke. But as she thinks back over the last week of Leo's life, her brain stumbles from one memory to another in a terrifying dot-to-dot. His low mood. The yawning gap between them. She thinks of the injuries on his face. The car going straight to the garage. Then, with a nauseating lurch in her stomach, she remembers his words at the hospital.

I saw Ethan.

Della drops the note.

All my fault. I wrote it down.

Then she understands.

He's in the woods.

Chapter Twenty-Eight

Things happen all the time, unnoticed. Rivers of sap run through unseen channels, pushed by invisible forces through trunk and branch. The wood itself creeps like a thick, sluggish liquid, dripping over obstacles, filling corners like melting wax. It is always in motion, on a relentless march of survival. The biggest things, though, they move the slowest, with patient stealth.

It is the same with secrets.

Since Leo died, the ground has shifted beneath Della's feet. But before that, the quiet creep of deception changed the nature of her husband, colouring her life with a man she thought she knew.

She has spent the night staring into the dark, trying to redefine her husband's memory. The missing money, the mystery number – she was dealing with that in the best way she could. But to take a life, her brother's life . . . that's the kind of secret that rots a man from within. Della questions everything she knew about Leo, everything he said to her in the week leading up to his death. She thought he was taken over by grief at the anniversary of his father's death. But he had turned from a loving husband and father into a murderer, a killer. It is huge, overwhelming, this knowledge that she carries inside her. It presses her to the bed in the darkness.

She picks apart their relationship, from the time she met Leo to the last few minutes of garbled conversation in a hospital waiting room.

Leo was a good man, wasn't he?

On the surface, yes, Della thinks to herself. She felt safe, loved, secure. But like an upturned stone in the depths of the wood, there were things underneath she should have looked at more closely. Things starved of light, writhing in the dark. Della wonders about the woman she would have become if she hadn't met Leo. The life she would have led, if she had met someone unconstrained by an aversion to risk. And then she wonders if that is why she likes being with Carrie, if that's why talking to her feels like floating freely in a spring breeze. Because she is the woman Della would have liked to become. Hers is the house she would have wanted to live in, had she not run from Ethan into a life governed by Leo.

Her mother showed her what marriage looked like. Wives deferred, husbands led. How was she to know, age twenty-three and pregnant, that it could be different for her? And if she had known, she thinks to herself, would she really have wanted anyone else?

At breakfast, she receives a phone call from the crematorium to remind her she hasn't picked up Leo's ashes yet. She ignores a text from Tash. She fields random, horrible thoughts, hardly able to believe what she knows must be true. Now she understands why Leo was so insistent she didn't sell the house. What has he done with Ethan's body?

He's in the woods.

She looks up, wondering if there are cameras somewhere filming her reaction, it is so beyond her comprehension.

And Alex.

Della can't bear to think about her daughter finding out. She must never, ever know.

Della's mind spools frantically from the past to the future and back to the past again. Occasionally, developers come knocking, asking her to sell off some of the land. That can't ever happen. She thinks back to the few occasions they have had to call the police. It will be on record that Ethan was trouble for her. Could she be implicated too if it ever came to light? The only silver lining is that Ethan will not be missed. He was so suspicious of authority he took himself away from society. Della doubts he will be missed by anyone but her.

She weeps, then, at the thought of the young boy who soaped her hair, who held her hand to cross the road, who dropped a bar of chocolate into her lap. But she is not sorry that the man who occasionally appeared between the trees, a lighter in his hand, has gone.

For now, Della is certain she will never find Ethan's body. The area is too big, and Leo would have done a good and thorough job of covering his tracks. He will have been careful, of that she is sure. But what if she can't pay the mortgage? What then?

Now, her fear is replaced by confusion as she wonders if the money wasn't used to pay off Ethan after all. Della runs upstairs to find the bank book to look at the dates. The last of the money was drawn out the day before Leo died. It cannot have been used to pay Ethan off, because he was dead by then.

A muffled thump can be heard behind Alex's door as her daughter wakes up. Della cannot face her. She needs more time to process what she knows, to normalise it. To squash it so far down it can never, ever surface. Della quietly tiptoes down the stairs. She writes Alex a note, snatches up her car keys and drives to the crematorium to pick up Leo's ashes.

Half an hour later, after a journey she cannot remember driving, she is handed a cardboard box with Leo's dates written on a sticker on the front and climbs back into her car, but when she reaches for the ignition key she cannot turn it. She doesn't have the strength. Looking to the passenger seat where Leo's ashes sit, she takes the box on to her knee and opens it. Inside is a clear plastic bag, half filled with grey ash, the top folded over and stuck down with another sticker containing Leo's details. She supposes they do this because it's possible the wrong ashes can go into the wrong box.

Della peels back the sticker and opens the bag, carefully, rolling the plastic back down on itself so she can get a better look. She bends her head and draws a deep breath through her nose. There is no smell. She can detect a faint whiff of incense, possibly, but she is not sure if she is smelling Leo, the box he is in, or the remnants of Alex's perfume in the car.

She stares at the grey, granular dust, remembering the time, aged nineteen and freshly orphaned, she returned to the newsagent's after she was released from hospital. She had spent the night under observation, grateful she was on a female ward. She had no idea where Ethan was until the police came to talk to her. It was obvious they didn't realise he was responsible for the fire. They were treating it as an accident. She wondered, for a moment, if it was. But then she went through every incident between her and Ethan since their father died, from the first time he singed her hair, to the fire at the foot of her bed.

'I could take everything away from you in a heartbeat,' he'd said to her the night before, as he struck match after match, flicking the charred remains on to the floor between them. He had learned to burn a whole match through without dropping it. That, or he burned himself so much practising he didn't feel it anymore. 'If I find that portfolio, Della, it will become dust. Your place is with me.'

She had suffered the past three years in the shop, with Ethan. She missed school, particularly the feeling of clay under her hands. Sometimes she dreamed about throwing pots, her fingers remembering the texture of the clay, her hands knowing just where to push and pull. She had kept up her sketching, as Miss Abramovich had advised; it was the only creative connection she had with her old life. And then, completely out of the blue, she had bumped into her old teacher in the street.

'They are taking applications for art college, Della,' she had said. 'You should apply.'

'I don't know how to,' replied Della. Her old life seemed so long ago.

But Miss Abramovich wasn't to be denied. 'I will do the application for you. But you need a portfolio.'

'I haven't thrown a pot for three years,' Della said.

'But I have photographs of every pot you made, and believe me, they are better than most. You still sketch, yes?' Miss Abramovich had looked at her and Della felt as though she had seen right inside her, to her soul. Sketching was the only thing in her life that brought her solace.

'Then it is decided. On Monday, you come to the school, four p.m. I give you clay. You can hand-build at home. You don't need a wheel.'

'I don't know how to hand-build.'

'Then I give you book, and you read it. Simple.'

Della felt swept along by the force of her, a sensation she had missed. It felt like an aching hunger had been sated just by talking to her, just by being the subject of her gaze.

'OK,' Della said, slowly, wondering how she would escape the shop without Ethan knowing where she was going, not knowing how she would hand-build without him seeing.

But she had done it. Every vessel she made, she gave it to Miss Abramovich, who photographed it for her portfolio and mounted the large glossy prints on to card. The portfolio had been kept at school for weeks leading up to the fire. Della had only brought it home that afternoon to finalise everything. The submission date for college was the next day. All she had to do was get it back to Miss Abramovich without Ethan seeing. But he must have found out where she had hidden it, because the police told her they thought the fire had started in the stockroom at the newsagent's, underneath their flat. As soon as she heard that, she knew she wasn't going back. Her mother was dead, Tash had left for university months ago. She had nobody.

Miss Abramovich showed up like a genie, just as Della was being discharged. Della left the hospital with her and allowed herself to be bundled into her car, still in shock from the death of her mother, the loss of her home. Miss Abramovich drove like she was in the only car on the road. 'You stay with me,' she said to Della, weaving in and out of traffic. 'For as long as you like.'

Neither of them spoke about Ethan. In the silence, in between their words, Della understood she was being protected from him, that she shouldn't contact him. That Miss Abramovich's house would be a safe house, as long as it stayed that way.

It had been explained to her, gently, that there was nothing left of her old life, but when Della questioned it, Miss Abramovich nodded and swerved the car across the street in a fearless U-turn. Della could smell the burning before she saw what was left of her home. They both got out of the car, and they stood together, looking at the catastrophe before them, the stench of smoke still polluting the air. Miss Abramovich allowed Della to take it all in. 'Take your time,' she said. 'You need to look, to see it has happened, to see that there is nothing left. Only then can you begin to accept it.'

At the time Della thought she was just being wise. Years later, Della wondered if she, too, had suffered a similar loss, that perhaps it was the reason why she had found herself teaching in a nondescript town in England. That she, too, had had to run away.

Della stayed for a couple of weeks with Miss Abramovich before Tash tracked her down. She had heard about the fire and then did the one thing that bound them both together for the rest of their lives. The thing that Della has been repaying through her loyalty ever since. Tash gave Della an escape: her floor, rent free, for as long as she needed. Tash had gone to a university more than two hundred miles away. It seemed like a delicious distance she could put between herself and Ethan, who by now was released from hospital and looking for her. It had been an adventure, living in a hall of residence, but she was in limbo, an interloper who could never really fit in with the people who had a reason to be there.

That feeling changed when she met Leo. From the very first day Tash introduced them, and he heard her story, he became her protector. She felt like they were fated to meet, that all the injustice and loss she had suffered had been part of an elaborate journey that led into his arms. Leo was everything that Ethan was not. Even after they split up, after she had told him she couldn't be with him anymore, he had rescued her once more with a house in a wood, and a marriage proposal.

And now this terrible knowledge she has. It is Leo's legacy. A lasting protection for her and Alex. She cannot feel happy about it, it is too raw, too close to home. But she can imagine a day when she might feel differently.

As Della stares at what is left of her husband, it feels so pedestrian that a man like Leo should be turned into a grey, formless dust. But as she does so, an idea forms in her mind. The moon jar she was making for their anniversary. It needs glazing. Bone ash is often used to glaze pottery. If she could put some of Leo's ashes into the glaze for the moon jar, it would be a way of honouring him while keeping him close. She doesn't know who the man she married really was. Maybe this will be a way of giving her more time to figure him out.

Chapter Twenty-Nine

Alex is in the kitchen, idly tapping at her laptop, when Della returns with Leo's ashes. She puts them carefully on the kitchen table, watching Alex close the laptop and touch the box. She moves her fingertips over the sticker, before she opens the lid, slowly.

'Did you do this?' she asks when she sees the bag has already been opened.

'Yes,' confesses Della. 'I was curious. Do you want to see as well?'

Alex nods, and Della wonders if she is grateful to be given permission, to be told it's OK.

'There's a lot, isn't there?' Alex observes. 'Do you really think it's him?'

'Yes, I do,' says Della. Then she tells Alex of her glazing idea.

'That's cool. That's a very cool idea.' Alex nods, thoughtfully. 'But I had kind of imagined scattering him on Marmite's grave.'

Della thinks. 'We can do both,' she concludes. 'I won't need much ash, and I'll have to sieve it out to make it fine, so it mixes with the glaze. The rest we can scatter.'

'What will the jar look like when it's done?' asks Alex.

Della feels a flush of pleasure. Alex has never shown any interest in her work before. 'It's probably easier if I show you,' she says. 'Open up your laptop.'

Della tells her what to look for. They scroll through several examples of Korean-style moon jars, and then Della directs her to look for specific glaze images to give her an idea what the surface of Leo's jar will look like. There are endless blogs about glazing and the chemistry involved.

'Wow,' Alex murmurs. 'I had no idea the pottery community was so nerdy. Some of these people are fanatical.' She clicks on a YouTube channel. 'This guy has, like, nearly a million views.'

Della leans closer. 'Oh, him. He's a master at raku, that's probably why. I had no idea he had his own TV show, though.'

Alex snorts. 'It's not TV, Mum. It's YouTube. You know him?' she asks, looking interested.

'Not personally. I have a couple of books by him, and I used to run into him at different shows. I got really interested in raku before you were born.'

'What's raku?'

'It's a firing process. You don't just put the pot in a kiln after it's glazed, you set light to it and the flames give the glaze a particular quality and colour. It's volatile, unstable.' Even now, to talk about it, Della feels herself heating up with enthusiasm. Alex listens to her without interruption.

They both turn back to the screen to watch a green glazed pot, still hot from the kiln, being lowered into a firebox full of wood shavings. The hot vessel sets the shavings ablaze and everything is temporarily devoured by fire. The pot is then moved into a large bucket of cold water and then it is wiped clean to reveal a transformation. The surface has completely changed colour. The green has transformed into a coppery metallic hue, swirled with bright blue.

'That's incredible,' says Alex. 'Beautiful. You used to do this? Set fire to your pots?'

Della laughs uncomfortably. 'Yes. All the time. I developed a little obsession, I think.'

'Can I see them?' asks Alex. 'Are they in the studio?' She has a look on her face Della hasn't seen before. Respect.

'I sold them years ago,' replies Della. 'I don't have any left.'

'Who did you sell them to?'

'Friends. There was one guy, though. I can't remember his name. He owned an art gallery somewhere.'

'OK, I can work with that,' says Alex, punching at the keyboard.

'What are you doing?' asks Della.

'I'm searching for your work. There might be pictures.'

'Oh, I doubt that—' begins Della. But then, after a few different searches, Alex puts in Della's maiden name and the most incredible thing happens. The screen on Alex's laptop loads up an image of a raku-fired pot she made, years ago. One of her last and most beautiful. The colour sings out, racing around the elegant shape of her vessel, rising from a metallic copper at the base through blazing green and blue, finishing in saturated pinks and oranges. The intensity of her work leaps out of the screen and, for a moment, Della can smell the flames that made these colours come alive. She leans closer to the laptop to see where the image came from. It is a Facebook page from an art gallery in New York. She cannot believe her pot has travelled so far away from her. She reads the text underneath the image. *Raku-fired vessel by Della Locke.* Alex scrolls through the close-ups, and Della sees the little mark she makes on the base of each piece that comes out of her studio. A capital *D* with an *L* intertwined through it. She looks at the surface of her vase and remembers making it, the weight of it in her hands, the feel of the blackened paper peeling off, revealing the colour she can see here.

'Wow,' breathes Alex. 'Look how much it's going for.'

Della looks at the price and draws in a sharp breath. 'That's insane.'

'I take it that's not what you sold it for?' asks Alex, sounding impressed.

Della stares at the whopping four-figure sum. 'No. I don't understand.'

Alex scrolls down the page. 'Mum, look at the comments underneath.'

Della looks.

Beautiful.

Incredible mastery of raku. Only a few pieces of hers on the market. Very rare.

Why?

She stopped making about fifteen years ago. Unbelievable talent. Such a shame.

What happened to her?

She must have died. No online presence.

Alex turns to Della with a look on her face. 'You're famous. Sort of. In a very niche way.'

'How old is that article?' Della asks.

Alex glances at the screen. 'They posted it a few years ago. I wonder how much that pot would fetch now?'

Della re-reads the comments. It is a strange feeling, observing the discussion about her life and work. And her possible death.

'This looks nothing like the work you do now. The colour is incredible. Why did you stop doing it?' Alex asks her. 'Why do you churn out grey dinner plates all day long?'

Della tries not to feel the sting of the comment because she knows it is true. As the years have passed, she has lost the creativity in her work and given in to repetition. It wasn't a conscious choice, it just happened. 'You were toddling around,' Della replies. 'Raku has to be done outdoors. The fire is unpredictable and hard to control. It was too dangerous to do it when you started walking.' She doesn't tell Alex about the argument she had with Leo.

I don't like you doing it, Della. I don't like the look on your face.

'You should do it again,' says Alex. 'You might be able to pay the mortgage if you can sell more stuff like this.'

'Huh,' says Della, lost in the past.

'Anyway,' says Alex, snapping the laptop shut, breaking Della's reverie, 'I need to leave.'

Della wants to offer Alex something in return for what she has just given her. 'Shall we invite Carrie and Jude over?' she asks her. 'It's Saturday, so they should both be around. We can do lunch or an evening meal for them.'

But Alex's face immediately shuts down. 'No. I said I'd go and help with the painting today. Jude's put together a playlist and everything.'

'But you need to eat,' pleads Della.

Alex looks awkward. 'I don't want to invite them here,' she confesses.

'Why?' says Della, looking around. 'What's wrong with our house? Everyone says how swish it is.' She immediately regrets using the word *swish*. It sounds so parochial.

'It's got no soul. You've ripped out all the old details. It looks like a showroom. Everything in Carrie's house has a story. Everything is there for a reason. Everything in our house is there because it's *new* and *safe*.' Alex hooks her fingers into parentheses in the air as she says these words.

'Well, that's your dad's influence, not mine,' says Della feeling wounded. 'I never wanted all those old architectural details removing.'

'Then why did you go along with it if you didn't like it? You should have said something. Just like you should have carried on making those pots.'

Della is lost for words. Because Alex is right. She should have said something, she should have picked up the raku firing again when Alex went to school, but she never did. In her mind's eye, whenever she thought about disagreeing with Leo on something important, she would anticipate the look of disappointment on his face.

I thought we were a team, Della, he would say, shaking his head, sadly.

But it's not just that, she admits to herself. She was afraid of how much she loved those flames. Leo saw it. Neither of them spoke about it.

'Your dad wasn't keen,' she says, simply. 'He worried about the fire.'

'I know you think I idolised him, but Dad wasn't always right. You should have ignored him.' Then, Alex smiles at a memory. 'Dad and I always said you were such a pushover.' She laughs as she gets ready to leave the house.

'I'm not a pushover,' says Della, amused and indignant.

'Don't you remember when I got my first phone, and I told you I hadn't downloaded any social media apps? And you *totally* believed me. It was Dad who realised I'd hidden them away from the home screen. You *are* an absolute pushover. And you should have said no to Dad a bit more if you didn't like some of his decisions. He would have been fine with it, you know.'

As Alex runs upstairs to retrieve something from her room, Della remains in the kitchen, memories materialising like a mist around her, and she recalls these little in-jokes that Leo and Alex used to have with one another, little asides that were often gentle digs at her. Della had tried to fight the sense she was being ganged up on. She'd had the same feeling when Leo, Robin and Tash got together and started talking about their uni days. The sense she could never quite fit in, that she wasn't one of them. And then she wonders how much of her feelings were her own fault, how much responsibility she should have taken to pursue the things she wanted, regardless of what her friends and family thought.

When Alex bangs shut the front door of the house, too hard, Della can hear the voices of Carrie and Jude welcoming her in. As the sound of music vibrates through the floor, she feels left behind. A small surge of annoyance heats her face. The idea of honouring Leo with a special glaze on her moon jar seems silly and trite now. She goes upstairs, feeling tired. As she sits on her bed, wondering if it is acceptable to have a nap at this time of day, she sees Leo's phone, still plugged in, still unlocked. She unplugs it and begins to search through it once more. She reads new emails and text messages sent by people who still don't realise he is dead. She answers as many as she can, telling them gently why they haven't heard from him. When she has finished, she opens his apps, one by one, idly, not really knowing what she wants to see. She opens a navigation app, something he used in the car, she supposes. And there, before her, is an address she doesn't recognise, visited weekly for the past year.

Della looks it up, assuming it is the drop-in centre Leo volunteered at. But it isn't in Tilberry. Tilberry is in the opposite direction. Then, with a sickening realisation, she sees dates next to this address. Dates this address was visited. Every date corresponds to a Wednesday afternoon, when Leo was supposed to be volunteering at the centre.

Della takes her own phone, looks up the number for the centre and calls it.

'Hello, Digital Drop In?' says a voice, a middle-aged man.

'Oh hello,' says Della, feeling as if she is in a crime drama. 'I was wondering if I could speak to someone who worked with Leo Harkin.'

'Leo Harkin?' repeats the man.

'Yes. I believe he volunteers there on Wednesday afternoons. Well, he did.'

'I'm the only bloke who volunteers here, and I can assure you my name's not Leo.' The man chuckles to himself.

'This is the digital drop-in centre in Tilberry, yes? In the village hall by the church?'

'It is,' says the voice carefully. 'But nobody of that name volunteers here. There's only three of us.'

Della rings off, astounded. Leo used to tell her stories about the people who came in to ask for his help. The little old ladies and the little old men who couldn't work their laptops and phones. The boxes of biscuits they brought in to say thank you. Once again, she feels the slick, oily feeling of stupidity sloshing around inside her stomach.

Della turns to the navigation app and tries to see what the address is, where it is precisely, but it is hard to zoom in on a small phone screen. She can't really tell. It looks like the middle of nowhere. And then she wonders if this is the point. Maybe she isn't looking at an address. Maybe she is looking at a good meeting point for two people who don't want to be discovered.

Della looks at her watch. There is plenty of the day left. Alex is occupied next door. She is not needed. She clicks the address coordinates once more and then the button underneath it that says *Go.*

Chapter Thirty

It is a forty-five-minute drive to the coordinates on the navigation app, and it feels good to be out of the house, away from Alex and the laughter next door. Della keeps going over the conversation she had with the volunteer at the drop-in centre. The only reason Leo would lie to her is a bad one. He hid parts of his life from her because in his eyes she couldn't be trusted with the truth. Was she really that weak, that vulnerable?

The villages peter out into country roads, fields and forests. She hasn't been to this area before and she wonders if that is why Leo chose to come here almost every week in the past year. The last few hundred metres are a long, straight, open road leading out of a village called Culbrook. As she nears the coordinates in the navigation app, Della can see where she is supposed to be. It is a large, smart pub called The Beehive. She pulls into the car park, looking at the building, trying to figure out the significance of it. She hasn't been here before, she hasn't been to the village of Culbrook, she is sure of it. Della has a moment of uncertainty, an urge to turn back, hating the feeling of being alone and, as if she has been conjured up, Tash calls.

Before she can say anything, Della interrupts her. 'Listen, Tash. Have you ever heard of a pub called The Beehive just outside the village of Culbrook?'

Tash hums to herself as she thinks. 'Is it a posh-looking gastropub? Is the sign bright yellow on a tall mast?'

'Yes,' replies Della, glancing up once more through the windscreen.

'I've driven past a couple of times on the way to Robin's mother's house, but I've never been in. Why?'

'I found out that Leo used to come here every week. So I thought I'd investigate.'

'Without asking me?' says Tash with indignation.

'It was a spur-of-the-moment thing,' says Della, feeling guilty.

'Why does it need investigating, anyway?'

Della feels torn. She hadn't been sure whether to trust Tash, but now Carrie is busy with the renovation, she feels the pull of her old friend. 'Do you remember he used to volunteer at the digital drop-in centre in Tilberry?' she says, deciding to confide in her.

'Vaguely,' says Tash.

'Well, it turns out he lied about that. He was coming here, instead. Presumably to meet someone. I don't know who, though. Do you have any ideas?'

'No!' shrieks Tash, loudly. 'Oh my God. That's so weird.'

'I know.'

'Hang on. You mean, he never volunteered? At *all?* He lied that he was doing it?'

'Yeah. That's about the crux of it. I called the centre, and they'd never heard of him.'

'Why didn't you tell me about this?'

Tash's fury soothes her, and she grins to herself, despite how she's feeling. 'I only just found out. Literally an hour ago.'

'But I mean . . . I could have come with you today. Why didn't you call?' Tash says reproachfully.

Della believes Tash knows secrets about Leo, but the strength of her indignation tells her Tash didn't know this one.

'I wanted to call,' Della begins, feeling contrite. 'But I needed to get some facts straight first.'

'Hang on, who told you about this?' asks Tash, a note of suspicion in her voice.

'Nobody. I found out from Leo's phone,' Della explains. She looks at the pub in front of her. It is smart, the window frames painted a trendy shade of sage green. There are large stone planters on either side of the door, filled with elegant-looking holly trees that have been cut neatly into symmetrical, twisted shapes. 'It's so weird, Tash. I feel like Leo's turning into someone I didn't know. The missing money, and now this.'

'I thought we agreed he'd spent the missing money on Ethan?'

Della hesitates, her mouth open. But she isn't ready to tell Tash about the discovery she made in the wood. Tash would tell Robin. God knows what Robin would do with the information, but she guesses he might hold it over her somehow to get what he wants. She shudders. Nobody must ever know, if Alex is to be protected.

'Well, they could be linked, I suppose,' Della says, thinking fast. 'Perhaps he'd been meeting Ethan here to hand the money over.'

'It's possible he was meeting someone who worked there. Ethan might have a job there, I suppose. Have you been inside yet?' Tash asks, invested.

'No. I'm about to go in. I don't really know what I'm looking for.'

'Ask for the manager. Ask them if they know Ethan or Leo. Or if they have some kind of weekly meeting there.'

'Like what?'

'Gamblers Anonymous springs to mind. And take a photo.'

'Of what?'

'Of Leo, you idiot. They might be able to identify him if he was a regular.'

'You're a genius, Tash, thanks,' says Della, smiling.

'I wish I was with you to help.'

'You *are* a help.'

'Della . . . are you OK? It might be nothing, you know. There might be an innocent explanation for all of this.'

'I don't know what I think anymore. He lied to me, Tash. Why did he do that? What was he doing here every week?' Della can't bring herself to tell her she doesn't even know who her husband really was. What kind of a man kills another and keeps it a secret? What kind of a man digs a grave in the woods and tells his wife she can never sell their house? She needs to know everything now. Finding Leo's confession has tripped a switch. She has to know everything about who Leo was.

Tash breathes into the phone. 'Darling, I know it's hard. But I think you should put your big-girl pants on and go into that pub and find out. You need evidence. Incontrovertible evidence.'

Della gets out of the car and walks into the pub. It is a nice building with high ceilings and large windows overlooking a stretch of green at the back that slopes down to a lake. Della approaches the bartender, who is restocking the fridge.

'Can I help?' he asks, standing up and wiping his hands on a tea towel slung over his shoulder. He's young. Not more than twenty.

Della opens her phone and shows him a picture of Leo. 'I was wondering if you've seen this man. He's my husband. I think he came here every Wednesday afternoon.'

The barman shakes his head. 'I can't recall, sorry. It's a big pub. We have several staff.'

'Can you just take another look? Just to be sure?'

The bartender looks at her with a strange expression, wondering what to make of her.

'Do you have any groups that meet here on a Wednesday?'

'No. The only groups we host are mums and babies on a Monday and a life-drawing class on a Thursday night.'

Della feels herself grasping at straws. 'What about another man. Tall, skinny. Dishevelled-looking, with long, straggly brown hair. A tattoo on his neck that says *Love Burns.*'

'I'm sure I'd remember someone like that. No. Sorry.'

'Can I ask anyone else who might know?'

'You can ask the manager, I suppose.'

The bartender gets the manager and Della gets the same reaction. No, they don't remember Leo coming in every week; no, they don't recall a tall skinny man with long brown hair. In desperation, she brings up pictures of Tash and Robin, but there is no recognition. With a sinking feeling, Della has to conclude there is nothing linking the pub to Leo, or Ethan, or the disappearance of hundreds of thousands of pounds.

Della returns to her car and drives home, trying to unpick the mess Leo has left her in. Unexplained absences, every week. The missing money. And what about where he was found when he collapsed? He was picked up by the ambulance on the high street on the other side of the village from his office. He always took a packed lunch in. There was no reason for him to be there that afternoon. She doesn't accept Tash's idea that he was buying something for her to celebrate Ethan being out of their lives. Not now she knows Ethan is dead.

Della grips the steering wheel, tightly, as the same nasty idea that has been blowing around her head for the past couple of weeks finally reasserts itself.

Was Leo having an affair?

Was the purchase of the silver birch a salve for his conscience? An extravagant gift for her to distract her from a betrayal? She remembers the expression of sadness that sometimes shadowed his face when he thought she wasn't looking. She thought it was grief, but now she wonders if it was guilt.

Chapter Thirty-One

In an attempt to avoid torturing herself with the unknown, Della spends the next morning in the studio, sifting Leo's ashes. Alex is excited by the idea of using them for the moon jar and Della has decided this is something she must see through, or she risks disappointing her daughter again. There are delicate fragments of bone in the mesh of the sieve, and she wonders, with a dark fascination, what part of Leo's body these shards are from. Surprisingly, she is not repelled by the process, as she thought she might be. The uniform grey of him has reduced Leo to something two-dimensional. There is a strange intimacy, though, an awareness that this is a body she is handling.

Della is always conscious that when she enters the studio it is important to come with a positive frame of mind. She was never as superstitious as Miss Abramovich, but a part of her thinks the kiln gods might not look kindly on her if she brings negativity into her workspace. Leo has fallen from the pedestal she put him on and now she must reassess the relationship she had with him, reconcile herself to the man he became.

Instead of recriminations, she talks to her husband, telling him about Carrie moving in next door, the friendship that Alex has struck up with Jude. The finest ash is put aside, measured out and mixed into a white glaze she has devised for Leo's moon jar. She tips the rest into a lidded pot that she made years ago, and she wonders about her younger self making this elegant pot and its lid, oblivious to what this vessel would eventually turn into.

She thinks back to the Facebook page of the gallery in New York, the price her work demanded. As a child, she focused on mastering the clay, quenching the desire she had to exert control over something in her life. As an adult, she became more interested in glazing, how capricious it could be. Throwing pots was something she became good at through practice. But glazing, she had a knack for that. When she discovered raku, she could predict what the fire would do, how far to push it, how to get it to submit to her. She recalls a saying: *fire makes a good servant but a bad master.* That was the difference between her and Ethan. He could never control fire the way she could, he was always at its mercy. He loved it like an abusive lover. She respected it as an equal.

Glazing the moon jar is a tricky business because it is large and heavy. She has measured the size of the bucket that the glaze is in, to make sure it will fit the moon jar with space on either side. It is important the jar doesn't touch anything when it is dipped, otherwise the glaze will remember and bear the mark. After coating the inside of the jar with glaze, and pouring it out into the bucket, she grips the foot of the vessel, turns it upside down and lowers it quickly into the liquid in the bucket, making sure she is holding the pot level, so the tide mark of the glaze stops at the foot, making a perfect horizontal mark. The muscles in her arms burn and complain as she rotates the pot to make sure there are no air bubbles preventing the colour from leaching evenly into the clay. Finally, when she thinks she might drop it, she pulls it out, waits for the drips to stop and puts her hand inside the lip, where nobody will see her fingerprints. With both hands, she tips the moon jar the right way and sets it on its unglazed foot. She looks at the powdery surface, knowing it will not look anything like this when it is fired, and as she notes the milkiness of the glaze against the clay, she sees little specks of Leo's ash swirling around the surface of the globe, making it look like a far-flung planet. She has no idea how the ash will react with the glaze in the high temperature of the kiln. According to her reference books, glazes containing bone ash tend to make the glaze more opaque, and can cause the surface to blister, making the vessel highly textured. But Della doesn't know, really, how this particular piece will look after it has been fired. That is one of the reasons she loves doing this, the way she must give herself over, completely, to the kiln gods.

Alex opens the door to the studio, just as Della finishes clearing up. 'Ready?'

'I guess so,' Alex says, eyeing the freshly glazed pot. She hovers at the doorframe, looking uncertain. 'Are we going to do it on Marmite's grave?'

'Yes, I think Dad would like that.'

'And Marmite would too,' Alex says optimistically.

Her daughter looks so young. Too young to be confronted by two big deaths in her life so close together. 'Dad would have been so proud of you,' says Della. 'The way you're dealing with everything.' She wants to cross the room to envelop her in a hug, but the void between them seems too big to close.

'I don't feel I've done very much,' mumbles Alex, looking self-conscious.

'Going back to school, forming a friendship with Jude, showing him around, when you are within your rights to retreat into your room and not come out again for the next month . . .'

'Well, I guess this is a good time to tell you how awful my marks were in my mocks.'

Della gives her brightest smile and sends her an encouraging look. 'That's to be expected, Alex. When you do the final exams in eight weeks, you'll be back on track.'

'I don't think I'm going to do them, though.'

Della tries to control the surge of panic she feels. 'Leaving school two months before your final exams is madness, Alex. You've come this far. You're grieving. You'll feel differently about going to uni in September. It's six months away.' She gets up eventually, crosses the floor, wanting to give her daughter a hug.

Alex groans, turning away from her. 'I told you. I'm not going away in September. I'm not sure I'm going to sit the exams. When are you going to accept that?'

'You can't just . . . do nothing.' Della's arms dangle uselessly by her side.

'I'm not going to *do nothing*. I'm going to work for myself.'

'Doing what? You're not qualified to do anything.' She is so aware of her own lack of qualifications, she doesn't want Alex to be caught in a similar trap in the future.

'I'm learning right now, with Jude and Carrie. They're teaching me how to renovate their house and, when I'm done, I'll be able to advertise and do up other people's houses.'

'You've been helping them for a week!'

'I feel *happy* for the first time in ages.'

'Alex,' Della ventures, trying to save the situation, trying to get to the crux of the issue a different way. 'Are you sure you don't have feelings for Jude? That maybe because he's new and interesting it's colouring the way you think about things?'

Alex lets out a noise of frustration. 'Why do you have to assume I like something because of a boy? Why can't you give me credit for wanting to do something because I like it?'

'I don't . . .' Della feels everything slip away from her. The calm of her studio torn open with resentment.

'You're so controlling! You want me to do all the things you couldn't do yourself. What about what I want?'

'That's not fair, Alex . . .'

Alex throws her arms into the air. 'Yes, it is! The only reason you want me to go away in September is because you never went to uni and for some reason it makes you feel bad about yourself. It's not my job to make you feel better. If you wanted to go to university, you should have done it. You could have done it ages ago as a mature student, nobody is stopping you. You can take *my* place in September for all I care. But it's not what I want to do.'

As Della tries to reason with Alex, an army of doubts rises up and shoots down every argument before she can say anything. Is she really controlling? And why *hasn't* she gone back to university? What stopped her? The way Alex puts things, it seems so straightforward and simple. The confidence Alex has in herself and her own capabilities is astounding. Then she recalls the words she has just flung at her daughter. *You're not qualified to do anything.* The kind of words that Ethan used to throw at her, and she feels a horrible combination of dread and shame. The tight knot of confusion inside her chest feels hard to unravel, and the moment of spreading Leo's ashes, which should have brought them together, is carried out in a stony silence.

'Do you want to say something?' asks Della, tentatively, as they stand by Marmite's grave.

Alex scatters her handful of Leo's ashes and turns to leave. 'I'll do it later, by myself.'

Alex marches off, but Della is rooted to the spot. She stands there for some time, a fistful of dirt in her hands, not sure if she is supposed to throw it over ashes, or if that's just what you do at a burial.

Leo told her once that one teaspoon of soil contains more living organisms than there are people in the world. She looks at the lump of wet brown earth, a whole planet in the palm of her hand. And then Carrie's voice calls softly through the trees.

'Della? Are you OK? I just bumped into Alex. She seemed upset.'

In that moment, Della wants Carrie to leave her alone. After all, she is part of the reason Alex doesn't care about her exams. But the concern on her face, the hug she gives Della; it feels so easy to yield to the warmth of Carrie's friendship. 'I can't do anything right,' confesses Della, miserably. 'As soon as we seem to be getting on well, it just all just disintegrates.'

Carrie stands close to her and nods towards the mound that covers Marmite. The small pile of Leo's ashes is being lifted up and levelled by the wind. 'I see you scattered them then.'

'Yeah, but it didn't go according to plan.'

'What happened?'

'I wanted it to be nice,' says Della quietly. 'And then we just ended up rowing about her not wanting to do her exams or go to university. It just came out of nowhere. She said I was controlling.'

Carrie snorts. 'You seem fine to me. You just need a bit of distance.'

'What do you mean?'

'When something awful happens, everything gets heightened. And then when you gain a bit of distance, those feelings aren't as sharp or painful. Give it time.'

'It just seems like such a waste. Her exams will be over by the end of June. She worked really hard up until Leo died, and now it's all falling apart.' Della has promised herself she will not shed any more tears over Leo, but this is Alex, so she bows her head and lets her tears fall on to the earth.

Carrie puts her arm around Della and gives her a squeeze. 'She's young. She's an August baby, like Jude, not even eighteen yet. In fact, if she'd been born when she was supposed to, she wouldn't even be in this academic year at school. She'd be in the year below.'

Della nods. It is true. Alex was three weeks premature. If she'd been full term, she would have been born in September and doing her final exams next year instead.

'Fancy a cuppa?' asks Carrie. 'Or something to eat? You look pale.'

'No, thanks,' says Della, still feeling raw. 'I just want to stay here for a bit.'

'OK, I'll leave you to it,' Carrie says, turning towards the house. 'My door is open, just knock.'

As Della stands looking at Marmite's grave, and the pile of ash on the top of it, she wonders if this is what rock bottom feels like. She wonders when she will begin to climb out of the pit she seems to have found herself in. She never believed in luck, but when she met Leo all of that changed. For a short while, she led a charmed life. A beautiful home, a healthy daughter, a caring husband. As she tracks through the years of her life with Leo and Alex, she goes back to Alex's birth. She had come earlier than planned, but Della wasn't worried. She knew that everything would be alright. That sense of right had lasted until Leo's death, and now her conviction feels as fragile as an eggshell.

Della stops, looks up, and then towards the path that Carrie has taken. Did she mention to Carrie that Alex was premature? She can't recall doing it. Maybe Alex mentioned it. It was never really a big deal because she was allowed home after a few days. Della thinks hard, wondering when she mentioned Alex's birth to her new neighbour. It's not something she would normally share, but spending time with Carrie is so soothing, so easy, Della has felt herself open up and say things she wouldn't ordinarily. Della sifts through her conversations with Carrie, her brain churning. She remembers telling Carrie that Alex's birth was tricky, but no more than that. Carrie knows many details about her own life and the life of her daughter. But Della is none the wiser about Carrie. Now she thinks about it, every time she has asked Carrie about an intimate detail of her life, the conversation has been quickly, deftly, steered back towards Della.

Della opens the palm of her hand, allowing the earth to fall back where it came from. She pulls her phone out of her pocket and calls Alex. To her relief, Alex picks up. 'I'm sorry about what I said earlier,' she says in a rush. 'I didn't mean to be . . . controlling.'

'It's OK,' Alex replies.

'Are you in the house?'

'Yeah. But I'm going over to Jude's soon. To help with the renovation,' she says pointedly.

'Are you alone now?' Della asks.

'Yeah, why?'

'Nothing really, just . . . did you mention to Jude or Carrie that you were premature?'

Alex scoffs. 'Why would I do that? I'm not a total freak.'

Della massages her forehead with her fingertips, digging them in, hard. 'Forget it, it's nothing.'

'You're so weird sometimes, Mum, you know that?'

Della forces a laugh out. 'Yeah, I know. Ignore me.' She ends the call, replacing the phone in her pocket, and feels a chill wind blow through the trees. Another layer of Leo's ashes rises into the air and disappears into the woods.

Chapter Thirty-Two

On Monday morning at first light, Della sets the driest wood and kindles the fire. The glaze on the moon jar has dried overnight and she has packed it into the kiln with the other pieces. As she stands back and watches the flames grow, she cannot help but think of Ethan and, in this private moment, she contemplates his fascination with fire.

It wasn't long after their father died that Della saw what fire did to her brother. He never liked school. The shop became his territory, and he didn't like leaving it. She can't remember him being bullied exactly because their paths didn't cross much. But even so, she sensed he was an outcast, someone people avoided. But one day he came home unusually animated.

'Della, look at this,' he said when she found him in the kitchen. She slung her schoolbag down on the floor. He had found a tea light and with their father's lighter he lit the wick. The flame grew from a full stop to an exclamation mark.

'So?' Della said, unimpressed.

'Watch this.' He took a tall glass and lowered it over the flame. It burned for a few seconds and then it began to shrink and die. Ethan raised the glass a little, letting in oxygen. The flame rose once more and burned brightly. 'I can control it, see?' He repeated the process, over and over, the flame rising and shrinking as it gasped for oxygen. Della watched him, his changing expression as he looked upon the flame. His face became soft, his mouth slack, his eyes liquid with desire. She didn't realise it then, but later, when she was old enough, she understood what that look meant. He was falling in love.

When his experiments moved into the garden, where there was an old brazier that swallowed all the packaging from the shop deliveries, Della often joined Ethan when he lit a fire. She could understand why he loved it so much. It was the one thing in his life that seemed to do his bidding. Like the clay that yielded under Della's hands, fire bent to Ethan's will in those early days, before he lost control.

Now, Della looks at her own fire taking hold in the kiln. Fire is beautiful when it is contained like this, and she feels a connection she cannot explain. She can predict what the flames will do, how the fire will behave, before she sees it happen. It was like this with raku firing before Leo put a stop to it. She instinctively knew what would work.

The flames falter, hidden underneath the wood, as if they are shy and unsure of themselves. Della watches them slowly reach out and up, exploring the space around them. Then they take a grip on the wood, finding the right mix of oxygen and fuel, gathering in confidence until they begin to roar, giddy with their own power. The kiln should reach the correct temperature by this evening if she keeps feeding the fire. Then, overnight, it will begin the slow process of cooling down. By Wednesday morning, two days from now, she will be able to open the door and see what the fire has done.

Despite hinting that she might not complete her school year, Alex is up when Della enters the kitchen. She is wearing a pair of ripped denim shorts over a pair of laddered black tights. On top she has a large, knitted jumper that is too big for her, so it falls off her shoulder, exposing her bra strap. Della suspects the jumper is Leo's but says nothing.

'Are you going into school today?' Della looks at her watch. 'You're cutting it fine, aren't you?'

'Jude's giving me a lift. We're going to the builders' merchants afterwards, so I'll be back late.'

'OK.' Della shrugs, stepping to one side as Alex shoulders her bag and races out of the house, a piece of buttered toast in her mouth.

Della listens to Jude greet Alex outside, the car doors open then close, the engine start, and finally, as the car moves beyond her earshot, she listens to the silence of the house, the constant chatter of the woods beyond.

Della glances to where Marmite's bed used to be, at the space where his water bowl sat. She still steps to one side to avoid it, and she doesn't think that reflex is going to disappear any time soon. Too distracted and full of questions to open the studio, she knows she isn't in the right frame of mind to tap into her creativity and begin new pieces.

Her conversation with Carrie yesterday is still unresolved. She would have taken Marmite out for a walk in a moment like this, to blow the cobwebs away, to think things through. Instead, she snatches up her cardigan, and she knocks on Carrie's door.

'Hi, I hope it's not too early,' she says as Carrie opens the door.

'Not at all, I'm an early riser,' replies Carrie, letting her in. 'Jude can't get out of bed anyway without me waking him up, and I've got mountains to do here.'

'I thought you might need some help,' says Della, looking around. She doesn't know what she is looking for exactly, but she's determined to get to the bottom of who Carrie is. The thought has kept her up for most of the night.

Carrie hesitates, and then she nods her head. 'Actually, you could help me set up my wardrobe. It had to be dismantled for the move, and I don't think I can put it back together on my own.'

'Great, let's do that then.'

'Let me just tidy up a bit first. My stuff is all over the floor and I don't want you to think I'm a complete slob. Wait here.' Carrie climbs the stairs, slowly, gripping the banister.

'Are you OK?' asks Della. She can't work out if Carrie is hiding something, being deliberately slow.

'Just stiff from all the painting we did yesterday,' Carrie complains. 'I don't think I can spend another day squatting on the floor. My legs are killing me. Wardrobe assembly will be a welcome distraction. Go and have a look in the sitting room. It's pretty much done. Alex has done a wonderful job with the Schiaparelli Pink.'

Della walks through to the sitting room, and it looks stunning. The walls are a deep, rich magenta, not a colour she would have chosen herself, but it looks warm and exciting in this room. The furniture has been moved into its final position; all of Carrie's possessions are on display. Although the styles are mixed – she sees Japanese netsukes next to Indonesian wood carvings and German pottery – it all hangs together somehow. Della walks around the room, picking up some of the mementoes to get a better look, admiring the way the Murano glassware is positioned in a place where the sunlight strikes it, electrifying the colour.

'You like what we've done, or is it too much?' Carrie's voice is full of humour when she comes back into the room.

'You've transformed it,' says Della, remembering how it looked when Mrs Winters owned it. 'I can see why Alex loves spending time here,' she tells Carrie. 'It's going to be a beautiful space when it's finished.'

'Alex has been a huge help. I hope it's OK she's spent so much time here. She and Jude seem to get on well.'

'That's nice,' says Della, trying to disguise her hurt.

'It's none of my business, but Jude has spoken to me about Alex. He's not planning on making any moves on her. It's platonic.'

'Oh, I didn't think . . .' Della feels her face turning red. She hadn't come here to make demands.

'Well, I just wanted to reassure you. There's nothing going on. I think everybody knows it would be a terrible idea for them to start dating when they live next door to one another. But I don't think they fancy one another anyway, which makes things less complicated.'

'I hadn't really . . . I suppose I hadn't really thought about it.' As soon as the words leave Della's mouth, she realises she isn't being entirely honest. She had hoped it was a passing infatuation that Alex was having with Jude. The fact it is platonic, that it is a serious friendship, makes things seem more permanent, more serious somehow, which feels worse because of the way things usually work out with Alex's friends. Della shakes her head, trying to banish the thought. 'I'm happy she's found a friend. Someone her own age,' Della says, feeling defeated. 'Did you find these pieces when you were travelling?'

'Some. I travelled a bit before Jude was born, but most of this stuff is picked up from flea markets and charity shops. The little wooden carvings are Jude's. He makes them in his spare time.'

Della walks over to the netsukes. 'I thought these were the real deal. I thought they were Japanese.'

'Inspired by,' replies Carrie with a smile. 'He became obsessed with them when we took a trip to Japan when he was around ten or eleven. I bought him some carving tools and he learned how to make them.'

Della thinks about the little rabbit, still sitting in their hallway. She picks up each netsuke and turns it around in her hands. They are all animals – a crouching dog, a fish with large lips, a winged beetle. They all have the same magnetic pull. 'They're extraordinary,' she tells Carrie. 'He's so talented.'

'He puts the work in. He practises at something until he gets really good at it. Like a dog with a bone. I'm not sure if it's natural talent or hard graft.'

'It unusual to see that in someone so young.'

'I don't think young people are given the space to be creative these days. It's all maths and science at school. I try to encourage it as much as possible at home.'

Della wonders if there is a hidden barb in Carrie's comment, that she knows how Della feels about Alex coming here instead of revising. Then Della notices something. Her own house is covered in pictures of her and Leo, of Leo and Alex, of Marmite. Leo was forever printing off pictures and framing them. 'You don't have many photos. Of you, I mean. Family photos, that sort of thing.'

'Well, it was just me for most of the time. I inherited photos of my parents in old-fashioned albums. I suppose I should put them on display.' Carrie looks at the mantelpiece, which is covered in beach finds.

'What about your partner?' Della asks, adding a little more pressure.

'He was the one who took pictures, not me. So I guess he took them all to Australia with him.'

'You don't have any photos of him? I'm curious.'

Carrie looks surprised. 'I can find one, if you're desperate to see him,' she laughs, uncertain. Della knows she is acting strangely, but she cannot help it. Something is not right with Carrie. Perhaps it is the lack of detail, the lack of clarity and personal information, when she is so keen to get details of Della's own life. Whatever it is, Della wants to catch her in a lie.

After a short while, Carrie returns with a picture of her, Jude and a man Della has never seen before at a party of some sort. 'That's Shaun.' Carrie points to the man.

Shaun has his arm flung around Carrie and it is obvious from the look they are giving one another that they are a couple. When she hands the picture back to Carrie, Della realises she had half expected Carrie's ex to be Leo. She feels like an idiot.

'Let's go and sort that wardrobe out, shall we?' Carrie asks, looking at her with barely disguised curiosity.

'Yes,' says Della, giving herself a little shake. 'Let's do it.'

They climb up the stairs, and Carrie's room is indeed a mess, but there are framed pictures of Jude and Shaun on the windowsill, making Della feel even more stupid. Of course Carrie would have her pictures of her family here, in her private space. Not everyone has to display them in the living room for all to see.

They spend the morning putting together the wardrobe. Carrie has an impressive array of tools, including two electric screwdriver sets, which make everything easier. 'I can see why Alex likes coming here,' says Della, surveying the fully built wardrobe. She has a sense of satisfaction at something completed, something built with her own hands; it feels similar to working in the studio.

'I think we need a break,' says Carrie, snapping the toolbox shut. 'I'll put some tea on, shall I?'

'Yeah. I'll just hang a few clothes up for you and come down in a minute,' replies Della.

Carrie makes her way down the stairs and Della hears her filling the kettle up, lighting the gas on the hob. Then she is overcome by the need to snoop. Quickly, she looks around Carrie's room, opens her bedside cabinet, but there is nothing there apart from some essential oils and books on yoga and meditation. The contents of her wardrobe are all over the bed so she assumes there is nothing sensitive there or Carrie would have hidden it. The only other rooms up here are the bathroom and Jude's bedroom, which is right by the top of the stairs. Carrie reasons she can go to the bathroom later, so she opts to take a look inside Jude's bedroom first. She pokes her head in, the door is open, and she is shocked by how neat the room is, in contrast to Alex's, which is in a permanent state of chaos. She tries to look methodically, not really knowing what it is she is hoping to find. There is nothing out of the ordinary, apart from the tidiness. She quickly tiptoes over and surveys his bedside table. There is a tattered paperback that looks as if it has been dropped in the bath, an old inhaler, some half-eaten packs of chewing gum and TicTacs. Quietly, she opens the drawer, which has a few charging cables and old gig tickets scattered about. Then she sees a little wrap of tissue. It's not a crumpled wad, as if he has blown his nose on it, it is neatly folded around something hard. With clumsy hands, she unfolds the paper, and into the palm of her hand drops a pair of gold cufflinks. It is a strange thing for a seventeen-year-old to have, a pair of cufflinks like this. Teenagers don't seem to wear them anymore. But Della isn't shocked because of that discrepancy. She stares at them, heart beating hard, turning them over in her hands, because she knows these cufflinks very well.

She is transported back to a little jewellery shop in Venice, a romantic weekend away before Alex was born. They had gone in because she'd seen something she liked in the window, but while they were in there, the shopkeeper had overheard them talking.

'Your name is Leo?' he asked in English. 'That means lion, yes? *Leone.*' He pronounced the Italian slowly for them in his native tongue.

When they both nodded, the shopkeeper had beckoned them over. 'See?' he said, as he rolled out a velvet cloth on to the glass counter. 'This must be for you.' His hands reached into the counter below and he pulled out a pair of gold cufflinks. Each cufflink depicted a beautifully detailed winged lion. 'The lion of San Marco, you have seen in the square, yes?' the shopkeeper said.

'Yes,' Leo echoed, obviously charmed by this man and his winning smile. 'There are lions all over Venice.'

The shopkeeper grinned knowingly. 'Is a very powerful symbol for Venezia. And very old.'

'Leo, I think those cufflinks should come home with us,' laughed Della, already knowing Leo had no intention of leaving without them. He had worn them ever since, insisting on buying shirts that had cuff holes, just so he could wear them all the time.

As Della stands in Jude's bedroom, turning the little golden lions over in the palm of her hand, she still remembers the weight of them in the shop, the first time she held them. A weight she has become very familiar with, every time she takes them out of Leo's shirtsleeves. She remembers handling them the day before Leo died. Granted, she stopped looking at them so closely, but these are Leo's cufflinks, she knows it. How have they found their way to this side of the house?

Chapter Thirty-Three

Della finishes her tea and makes an excuse to leave Carrie's house as quickly as she can. She lets herself in to her own house and goes straight to her bedroom where the bag of clothes Leo wore on the day he died is still sitting in her side of the wardrobe. Pulling the shirt out, Della feels the cotton sleeves slip through her fingers until the fabric runs through her fist and she grips the cuff. Both sets of buttonholes are empty. Della tips out the bag just to check the cufflinks haven't fallen out, but she knows they won't be there because they are next door, in Jude's bedside cabinet, neatly wrapped in a piece of tissue.

It had taken all her strength to wrap them up again and leave them there, but if she took them back it would advertise what she knew. After checking the kiln and adding more wood, Della gets into her car and drives to Tash's house, calling her on the way to check she is there before she arrives.

'You look like death, Della,' Tash says as she lets her in. 'What's going on?'

'Is Robin here?' asks Della, looking around; she doesn't want Robin overhearing any of this.

'No. He's with clients all day, and then dinner meetings, I think. I'm just eating lunch, do you want some?'

Della doesn't feel like eating but she accepts a bowl of soup and a piece of toast to be polite. They sit opposite one another at the kitchen table.

'Is this something to do with Saturday, when you went to that pub?'

It seems like an age since she drove to The Beehive. 'I don't know,' she replies. 'I honestly don't know what's happening to me.'

'Tell me,' urges Tash. Suddenly, Della is transported back to the playground at school, spilling her troubles and being soothed by Tash's absolute conviction of what to do next.

So Della tells her everything, from Carrie's habit of not talking about herself, to her knowledge that Alex was premature, finishing with the discovery of the cufflinks. The only thing she omits is the certain and terrible knowledge that this cannot be anything to do with Ethan.

Tash leans back on her chair and blows her curly fringe out of her eyes. 'Well, OK, if I'm playing devil's advocate, I'd say there are plenty of people who find their neighbours more interesting than talking about themselves. Also, you're grieving, Della, she's bound to not want to talk about herself. She was probably being nice. And Alex. You can't remember clearly exactly what you said about her birth so it's possible you told her. The cufflinks . . . well . . . it's a massive coincidence if Jude has the same pair, but it's possible, I suppose, if I'm being generous. If it isn't a coincidence, it's Jude you need to worry about. Did he steal them from you? Is that what we're saying?'

'I suppose Jude could have got into our house and taken them.' Della's certainty is deflated by Tash's analysis of the situation. 'But they were in such an obscure place. It's not like I left them lying around.'

'Alex then. She likes Jude, you said. Does she like him enough to give him her father's cufflinks?'

Della thinks about the cardigan she has rarely taken off, the oversized sweater she wore to school this morning. 'No. I think Alex would want them for herself. I don't think she would give something like that to a virtual stranger, no matter how much she liked them.'

'Del, there is another thing.'

'What?'

Tash leans across the table and reaches for her hand. 'Leo's only been dead a few weeks. And Marmite. You've been through it. And I bet you're not sleeping well, or eating well, are you?'

'No,' says Della, feeling small.

'I'm not saying you're completely wrong. I'm just saying you need more evidence. Is it possible those cufflinks aren't exactly the same? I mean, how much did you really look at them, when you took them off Leo's shirts? You bought them years ago.'

Della feels uncertain about many things; it is why she is so willing to be told she is wrong by Tash. But she is certain about those cufflinks.

Tash runs her hands through her hair. 'Do you know when Jude was born? Is he a Leo, by any chance?'

Della raises her head. 'Yes. Carrie said he was an August baby, like Alex.'

'So Jude and Alex have probably been discussing their upcoming eighteenth in August, which means Alex might well have mentioned she was born three weeks early, despite what she told you. Jude's birth sign is Leo. Teenage boys are a nightmare to buy gifts for; I'm willing to bet he was bought or inherited those cufflinks by a relative and he's saving them for when he needs to wear a suit.'

Della squeezes her eyes shut. 'Where are Leo's cufflinks, then, if they aren't in Jude's bedside table?'

'My bet is they were nicked in the hospital, or they were removed or lost when they were dealing with him. His phone disappeared, didn't it? Why not a nice gold pair of cufflinks?' Tash looks pleased with this analysis. She nods her head to herself, and gets up to make coffee, putting an end to the discussion.

Della eats her bowl of soup and leaves Tash's house feeling alone and unsupported. Why does Tash always have to play devil's advocate? Why can't she just believe her? Those cufflinks are Leo's. They have to be.

When she returns home, Alex's schoolbag is in the hall, and she can hear her opening the fridge in the kitchen. 'I thought you were off to the builders' merchants?' Della calls as she takes her jacket off in the hallway and hangs it up.

'We are,' answers Alex from the kitchen. 'We decided we were starving. I'm just having a bite to eat. Then I'm gone.'

The doorbell rings and Della answers it. Jude is standing outside. Della remembers rooting through his bedroom earlier and tries to control a blush. She wants to blurt out questions she needs answers to, but she agrees with Tash. She needs more evidence.

'She's coming,' says Della with forced cheer. 'She's just raiding the fridge. Come in.'

'That's OK. I'll wait in the car. Oh, and I wanted to drop off these.' He hands Della a small bunch of keys.

'What's this?' asks Della.

'They're for Alex. I have to take Mum to an appointment tomorrow at lunchtime and Alex wanted to make a start on the bathroom. Mum said she could let herself in when she got home from school.'

'OK, just leave them here on the hook,' says Della, indicating the place she and Alex hang their house keys. Jude does as he's told and then Alex appears, putting on a battered leather jacket and pulling her hair out from underneath the collar.

'Let's go,' her daughter says.

'Are you back for dinner?' asks Della.

'I just ate,' replies Alex, walking through the front door.

'What did you eat? Toast?' Della calls out after her, but the door slams and she is left, once more, in an empty house, by people who have something much more exciting to do. Della looks at herself in the hall mirror. She is pale and there are dark circles under her eyes. Her blonde hair looks muddy and unwashed.

Tash is right, she thinks to herself. *I'm dealing with a lot and it's taking its toll. I need to stop being so hard on myself.* But then, the pile of unpaid bills on the hall table catches her eye. She doesn't have time to wallow. Things need to happen *now.*

What would Leo do? He would *do* something, put himself out there to save the house, to rescue his relationship with his daughter. He wouldn't wait around until something turned up. Her mind turns to the gallery in New York, selling her pot for thousands of pounds. She had been unprepared for the pull she felt to those deep, saturated colours. She had forgotten how much she had missed working with that kind of glaze.

Her hands act before she really processes what she is thinking. They reach for her phone and in a few clicks and swipes, she is calling the number of the gallery, glancing at her watch. It will be mid-morning in Manhattan.

'Lexington Gallery,' declares the voice. The New York accent sounds refined.

'Hello?' Della enquires, realising she has not prepared what she is going to say. 'Is there somebody there I can talk to about a raku-fired pot you sold a few years ago by an artist called Della Locke?'

'Well, you can talk to me, I'm Yelena Lexington. How can I help?'

'Oh. Are you the gallery owner?'

'Yes, I am, and I remember the vessel you are talking about.'

Della is astounded. 'You *do*?'

'Raku-fired ceramics are a passion of mine, and Della Locke developed a particularly fine style. If you're looking for more pieces by her, I can tell you they rarely come on the market.'

Della hesitates, unsure how to proceed. 'What if I had something to sell? Is her work still in demand?' It seems ridiculous, to talk about herself like this, in the third person, but if this woman tells her there is no appetite for her work anymore, it will be easier to hear it this way.

'Her work is very much in demand.' She pauses. 'I'm sorry, I didn't catch your name.'

Della bites her lip. 'It's Della. Della Locke.' Her maiden name comes out easily, without thought. As if it has been waiting, under the surface, knowing it wasn't done with just yet.

There is a small silence as the information transmits itself over the Atlantic. 'Are you kidding me?' says Yelena softly.

'No. I came across your Facebook page and saw my work. I—'

Della hears a breath blown out, from across the ocean. 'My, my. Where have you been, Della Locke?'

For reasons she cannot understand, the question brings tears to her eyes. There is something about this woman's voice. The warmth in it, the respect. The intimacy. It is like she knows her.

'I . . . that's a hard question to answer,' Della replies. Where has she been? Living another life to the one this woman imagines.

'We thought you were dead.'

Della remembers the Facebook comments. 'I'm not. I'm very much alive.'

Yelena says something to herself that Della doesn't catch. And then, 'This is unbelievable. Are you still making? Where are you calling from?'

'Yes.' Then, in a burst of honesty, Della tells her, 'I am making. But not the kind of pieces you sold. More commercial.'

'Why?' Yelena asks, bluntly. 'You're an artist. You have so much talent. So much passion.'

'It's hard to explain.'

'You don't have to explain.' She says something to herself again that Della doesn't understand. Then, like a ray of sunshine breaking out from a cloud, she suddenly thinks she does. This woman is speaking another language to herself. A language Della cannot speak, but the cadence is so familiar, so welcome, she feels lifted up by it. 'We know how difficult things were for you,' Yelena says, in English.

Della is too stunned to say anything for a moment. 'Who are you?' she asks, carefully.

'We haven't met. I'm Yelena. My Aunt Valentina knew you very well. Valentina Abramovich. She taught you at school, I think.'

'Miss Abramovich.' To say her name out loud is like uttering an incantation. She feels herself warming up, her body straightening, her mouth pulled up into a smile. 'Is she . . .'

'I'm sorry, she passed away several years ago. You didn't know, I guess. She said we wouldn't find you and she asked me not to try.'

'No.' Della's shoulders slump at the news. She had suspected Miss Abramovich might be dead, but to have it confirmed so soon after finding her seems doubly sad. 'Where did she . . . ?'

'She moved here to New York to be with her sister, my mother. She helped me and my husband set up the gallery and introduced me to your work. She was so proud of you. She always said you were her protégée.'

Della feels choked by emotion. 'She saw my work?'

'She loved the style you developed. There were only a few pieces on the market, but they caused quite a stir. Nobody could reach you, though. I know your family circumstances were difficult. Valentina was worried we would put you in danger by trying to find you.'

‘She . . . she told you about my brother?’

Yelena sighs. ‘He was partly why Valentina moved here. She was the last person to see you before you disappeared. He made her life difficult, so she came here.’

‘What did he do?’ Dellas asks, not wanting to know the answer but needing to face the truth.

‘He burnt her car out and then posted a note through her letterbox, threatening to do the same to her house if she didn’t tell him where you were.’

‘I’m so sorry. I didn’t know. I feel responsible.’ She squeezes her eyes shut to blot out the vision of Miss Abramovich’s car.

‘Then you were responsible for the best decision of her life. She was very happy in New York. She died surrounded by people who loved her. She had a good life here, and a good death.’

‘Did she carry on teaching?’

‘Of course. But she made and sold pieces too. Not for the prices that your work demanded. She got a kick out of that, by the way.’ Yelena clears her throat. ‘It’s a pity she’s not here, but she’d be so happy we connected like this. There’s appetite for your work, Della, if you have anything you’d like me to sell?’

Della’s mind is whirring. ‘I don’t have anything for you. I was just calling to see . . .’

‘But you’re still working, yes?’ Yelena presses.

‘Yes, I have a studio, but—’

‘Then I’d like to place a commission, if you have the time.’

Chapter Thirty-Four

The draw to the studio has never been so strong. Since her call with Yelena, Della sees a way forward that doesn't rely on her husband. The notion that she can begin to clear the bills without the help of Leo, Tash or Robin buoys her up. Yelena offered a down payment on her first commission.

There will be many more of these, I know it. Be prepared.

Her words revolve around the echo chamber of Della's mind.

But the feeling something isn't right with the family next door does not go away. It is a hurdle she must overcome before she can clear her head and focus on her partnership with Yelena. When she came down for breakfast this morning and waved goodbye to Alex, her eyes were drawn to Carrie's house key, which is still hanging on the hook. When Jude comes to pick Carrie up, at lunchtime, there will be a small window of opportunity when their house will be empty and there will be nobody to stop her going inside.

Della spends the morning lurking in the kitchen in case she misunderstood the conversation she had yesterday with Jude. He and Alex left for school, as usual. When the house is quiet she feels jumpy and unsettled. She has already been out several times to check the temperature of the kiln, and it is beginning to climb down. The moon jar is waiting, packed alongside her other commercial pieces. Soon the wood will burn itself out, the fire will slowly die and turn to embers and the kiln will cool enough that she can open it and see what she has created. She likes to be near the kiln when it is doing its work. She knows she cannot alter anything that is going on in there, apart from the temperature, but she needs the proximity, to be close to the alchemy that is happening. This is the reason potters refer to the kiln gods, the unseen forces that decide if a vessel makes it out in one piece or not. Even the most experienced, the most careful, suffer losses that they cannot comprehend. Things break and shatter in extreme heat – if air has not been expelled, or the clay is not dry enough, or if handles and spouts have not been attached with sufficient care. She will never fully understand the complex chemical reactions that occur in the blistering heat with each particular piece.

Things break when the kiln gods are angry, Miss Abramovich used to say. *They detest sloppy work, and they smite your laziness.*

But sometimes, when a piece comes out and its beauty surpasses all imagination, that something truly special has happened behind a closed door, it is human instinct to acknowledge forces outside your control, the makers of the magic. A moment of thanks that they looked kindly on your creations and allowed them to bloom in the heat. When Della closed the kiln door on Leo's moon jar, she had a moment of self-doubt, that it would not survive the fire. The urge to be near is strong, like an anxious mother, hovering outside a room where her daughter is giving birth.

Tash has never understood why Della is drawn to pottery, a craft so dependent on fire. She doesn't understand how she could bear to be reminded of the thing that took her possessions away and killed her mother. Della finds it hard to explain, too. For her, fire has become a friend. It is something that creates, not destroys. It is something that Tash has never understood.

Della ignores the urge to go to the studio, choosing, instead, to clean so she can hear Jude returning from school. She wipes surfaces free of dust, strangely aware these are the last of Leo's skin cells she is erasing from the house. She vacuums carpets and rugs, puts a wash on, unstacks the dishwasher. It is distracting, to be immersed in physical labour, so much so that when she hears the low rumble of a car idling outside the house, it takes a minute to register that Jude is here to pick up Carrie.

Della watches from behind a curtain as Carrie locks her house up. Jude gets out of the driver's seat and opens the passenger door for his mother, touching her shoulder gently as she climbs into the car. This act of kindness is at odds with how she has thought about him for the past twenty-four hours, as a thief and a liar. As the car disappears down the dirt track and is swallowed by the woods, she tells herself it is right, what she is about to do, that she can clear all of this doubt away in a single afternoon.

Taking the key off the hook, noting the time, she will give herself an hour. The house is not large, and she supposes any secrets will be kept upstairs, in the bedrooms. She remembers Carrie's willingness to have her downstairs, her hesitation before she decided to let her help build the wardrobe, the quick run upstairs to tidy before Della was allowed to follow.

The key slides willingly into the lock and turns as if it has been recently oiled. The house looks tidy downstairs now the boxes have been removed. She walks past the living room, the door to the kitchen, and tiptoes up the stairs straight into Jude's bedroom. Opening the bedside cabinet once more, she notes the cufflinks have not been moved. She feels about in the same spaces, to make sure she didn't miss anything, before looking in his drawers, moving her fingers around his clothes, feeling for anything hard, any other objects that she might recognise as her husband's. But there is nothing.

She goes into Carrie's room with a sense of desperation, opens the wardrobe cautiously, knowing there are no hidey-holes here, that she built it herself only yesterday. But she is running out of options. There is nothing to see but a row of patterned dresses and colourful harem pants shuddering in the light. She pulls out dresser drawers, feels around with her fingertips, examines the chaos of a jewellery box that contains nothing remotely familiar; everything is uniquely Carrie. Della rakes through finds from flea markets and charity shops, nothing that looks expensive or discreet like her own jewellery box, so she turns to the bedside table once again. She remembers the meditation and yoga books, but this time she removes them from the drawer so she can get a better look inside. A lip salve and a vial of essential oil roll together in the empty space. Della puts the books back, one by one, and sees that there is one book that is not a book. It is a diary. She hesitates, drawing in a breath. It's a huge breach of confidence, but she doesn't have a choice. Della takes a moment to walk to the window and check there is no car coming down the dirt track before she opens the book and begins to read.

There are no inner secrets, no declarations of betrayal. It is just used for appointments. It seems that Carrie has many; there are recurring names. A Mr Avasti pops up quite a lot; there are also weekly appointments with a woman called Flora who seems to be a masseur. Her business card flutters out of the book and on to the floor as Della turns the pages. Most of the book is blank because they are only three months into the year. The recurring names reveal nothing that helps Della in any way. There are appointments to do with the purchase of the house, appointments to do with Jude moving school. But nothing that raises a red flag. Until she notices a little motif, scribbled with regularity over the past three months, since the beginning of January. It looks like a series of circles that appear every Wednesday afternoon. When Della peers more closely, the image reveals itself to be a bee in flight. Della's mouth feels dry as she tries to swallow. Is this another coincidence? Or was it

Carrie who was meeting Leo at The Beehive every Wednesday? She looks up out of the window and thinks hard, her heart hammering. Della's birthday occurred at the end of January this year. She remembers it was on a Wednesday because Leo insisted on taking the afternoon off from the drop-in centre so they could go and have lunch together instead. Della turns the pages, slowly, not knowing what it is she wants to see. She wants to feel she is not going mad, that there is something going on with this woman that she doesn't understand, but at the same time she wants everything in this diary to be innocent, for Carrie to be her friend.

Della turns the pages all the way back to January, to the date of her birthday. There is a bee motif the week before, and the week after. On the date of her birthday the page is blank.

Chapter Thirty-Five

Even with the evidence staring at her, Della cannot allow herself to believe that Leo cheated on her. Like a rabbit in a trap, her brain scrabbles about for an alternative explanation. But it's too much of a coincidence, too overwhelming. She takes pictures of the diary pages with her phone, the scribbled bee motif, and lets herself out of the house, checking to make sure she has left everything as she found it. It is only when she opens her own front door and closes it behind her that she realises she has been holding her breath, and lets it out in a gasp. When her heart stills, and the sick excitement of rummaging through Carrie's things subsides, she is left with a heavy feeling of suspicion. Questions swirl around in her head like leaves in the wind. They scatter and fragment, only to form themselves once more into problems she must now confront. Was Leo having an affair with Carrie? Is that why they met every week at The Beehive? Della turns it over in her head. If two people are having an affair, surely they'd book a hotel, or go to one another's house? It doesn't seem right. She thinks about confronting Carrie, but what does she have, really? Photographs of a diary with a bee motif and a pair of cufflinks that she can't prove are Leo's. With a sick feeling she realises she can't prove anything. It will only make her look like a madwoman who broke into Carrie's house and looked through her stuff.

There is a logical explanation for this, she knows there must be. She just has to think. Sitting at the kitchen table, Della makes a list of all the things she cannot understand.

The missing money.

Who was Leo meeting every Wednesday?

Why was Leo in the village when he collapsed and who was he with?

Whose number has he been calling?

Does Carrie or Jude have anything to do with this?

Cufflinks?

Diary??

She looks at the list, everything seemingly unconnected. The person she really needs to talk to is Leo. He is the only one who can answer all of these questions. Della's brain begins to whirr, like a clockwork toy that has been wound up. It begins to march forward from one point of logic to another. With Leo gone, Robin is the next best person to talk to. She already suspects he knows more than he is letting on and he is not telling her because Robin puts himself first at every turn. Della bites her lip. She knows things about Robin that he would rather Tash didn't know. Is she willing to risk her friendship to get what she wants? Della thinks hard about the repercussions of what she is about to do, and grabs her car keys.

Robin doesn't deserve to be warned. She doesn't want to give him any time to think before she turns up at his office.

The receptionist at the front desk buzzes her through, and Della walks into Robin's office, feeling sick with nerves.

'I thought you didn't want to see me anymore?' he asks, looking up from a pile of paperwork, clearly puzzled.

His office has walls of dark, polished wood. She has not been in here before, and as she feels the ownership of this room, Robin's dominance, she shrinks a little from the task at hand. He sits behind a long desk carved from a huge chunk of black veined marble with awards for financial services lined up on a bespoke shelving unit that Della knows Robin commissioned from a local carpenter. She imagines him standing in this office, hands in pockets, making the poor man measure each award so they could be displayed at their best in purpose-built cubbyholes lined with smoked mirror glass, softly illuminated by hidden lights. There is a view over parkland behind him, through a huge window that occupies most of the wall. Della hopes it makes him cold in the winter, that the glass is draughty, but she suspects it is triple glazed and expertly fitted.

'I needed to ask you something,' she says, sitting down on a very comfortable leather padded chair opposite him.

'Ask away, I'm at your disposal.' Robin leans back and folds his hands in his lap, looking at her intently. She has purposely dressed well for this meeting, she has even put some make-up on. Power dressing, they used to call it. She's not feeling powerful.

'I've been thinking about what you said the last time we met. I thought at that time, that Leo was faithful, a good husband. But since then, I've found out a few things and I've had to revise my opinion of him.'

Robin leans forwards, his attention piqued.

'I think Leo has been hiding something from me. Something financial. I also think . . . I think he was having an affair.'

'An affair?' Robin echoes, not breaking her gaze.

The fact Robin doesn't deny it destroys something inside Della. A last vestige of hope that she was wrong. Clearing her throat, she asks outright, 'Do you know anything about Leo having an affair?'

Robin's answer is quick. 'No. Nothing.'

'And the missing money? Do you know where that went?'

'I don't,' Robin replies. 'I'm still looking.' But Della knows him well enough to see a small hesitation.

'Well, anyway,' she continues, refusing to be put off, 'it's made me think. The last twenty years, Leo wasn't the man I thought he was.'

She has his full and undivided attention now.

She swallows and says quietly, 'I've always known how you felt about me, you've always been very honest about that. But my loyalty to Leo meant more than anything else, so I never acted upon it.'

'Oh, come on, Della. I can think of at least one occasion . . .'

'I was very drunk.'

'And *very* sexy.'

Della feels the conversation slipping in a direction she isn't prepared to follow, but she smiles her best smile at him. 'Robin, did you mean what you said to me after Leo died? About leaving Tash if you could have me?'

For a moment, Robin looks vulnerable. He looks so happy, like a little boy who is about to have all his birthdays come at once. 'Seriously?'

'Seriously. I've been thinking about it. Did you mean it?'

Robin nods, and this is not what she wants. She needs him to say it.

'You said you wanted to look after Alex and me. That you'd leave Tash if I said the word.'

'What's brought this on?'

'Honestly? I'm angry. And lonely. Why should Leo have all the fun? Robin . . .' Her voice cracks when she says this, and it makes her seem as if she is full of authenticity. She is so impressed by the urgency in it she almost smiles. 'I think we could be good together. We've known each other for years. It would work. I know it would.'

'And what about Tash?' he asks, warily. 'She's your best friend.'

'It doesn't need to affect her if she doesn't know about it. We're both good at keeping secrets, aren't we? We can be careful.'

'Yes,' Robin nods, eagerly. 'We can.'

Della leans forward, holding him in her gaze, hardly able to believe he is falling for this, that his ego is really this big. 'The night you came and found me working in that bar, after I'd broken up with Leo. I often think about that night and wonder what might have happened between us.'

Robin looks confused. 'But you've always pushed me away when I suggested anything more.'

'That was before I found out Leo was a cheat and a liar.' It almost kills her to say it. To voice it out loud is an admission of her own part in this – the part of her that never asked questions. The part that trusted Leo blindly like a child trusts a parent. But she knows these are the words that Robin wants her to say. The idea of besting Leo is like catnip to him.

Robin gets up from behind his desk and for a moment she thinks he is going to kiss her, but his office door is made of glass, and there are people outside.

He leans over her chair, gripping each arm with his hands until his knuckles turn white. 'I would have you here, right now, if I could, Della,' he murmurs, close to her cheek.

'We have to do this properly,' Della murmurs back. 'We need to be discreet.'

Robin lets go of the chair arms as he thinks. 'I know a place,' he says. 'A nice hotel. About an hour's drive from here. We can spend the whole weekend in bed. I've used it before.'

This is news to Della, but not a surprise. She wonders if Tash knows about Robin's infidelity and turns a blind eye, or if it would end their marriage if she found out. 'OK. Let me know,' says Della, sliding out of her chair, desperate to leave.

Robin lets her out of his office with a rapacious look on his face. She has to stop herself from running out of there.

As soon as she is in the car, she pulls out her phone from the top pocket of her jacket and makes sure everything has been recorded. Then she calls Robin.

'Hi,' he says, his voice liquid and low. 'Missing me already?'

'Mmm, not really,' replies Della, her stomach contracting. 'I just recorded our conversation and I'm going to play it to Tash unless you tell me what Leo has been up to.'

'What? You little—'

'Sorry. But I couldn't think of another way to do it.'

'You wouldn't dare play that to Tash. You value her friendship too much.'

'You're right, I do,' Della concedes. 'But I'm so sick of being lied to, I'm prepared to risk it. I've thought very hard about this, Robin. If you don't tell me what you know, I will tell Tash, and she will have her pound of flesh from you. I think my relationship with her might survive over time. But yours won't.'

For a moment, Della feels sorry for him. Her voice softens. 'Where did the money go, Robin? I know you know. Leo's dead. You're keeping secrets for someone who doesn't care anymore.'

Robin sighs, loudly, down the phone. There is a long pause. Eventually, Robin capitulates. 'Leo used it to help someone.'

'Who? Ethan?'

'Ethan? Why would he help Ethan?' The surprise in Robin's voice is genuine.

'Who was it then, Robin?'

She hears Robin take a breath. 'Your new neighbour. Carrie.'

Della feels winded. 'Carrie? Was he having an affair with her?'

'He didn't say. They've known one another since they were kids, apparently. She's from around here. He was helping her out.'

'Helping her out to the tune of thousands of pounds? Come on, Robin, there's more to it than that.'

‘I don’t know all the details. He was pretty cagey about it, said she got into some financial difficulty, and he owed her.’

‘What did he owe her?’

‘How should I know?’ says Robin, sulkily.

‘Because he told you everything.’

‘Not everything,’ Robin admits. ‘Leo kept secrets from us all, even me.’

Chapter Thirty-Six

When Della returns to the house, Carrie's car is parked outside, and it takes an enormous amount of willpower not to go to Carrie's side of the house to have it out with her. But there is too much that still doesn't make sense and she needs some time to think about it before she can gather her feelings and confront her neighbour. Why would she move here, next door to Leo's family, if she was having an affair with him? Even if she wanted to, they would both risk being found out. Leo might be callous enough not to care about Della's feelings, but he always put Alex first. Della sits in her car, still gripping the steering wheel, trying to figure out the truth. The phone rings, and it is Tash. For a horrible moment Della wonders if Robin has told her what happened between them this morning, but Robin never owns up to anything if he can help it, so Della decides it is safe to answer.

'Tash?' she answers with a questioning voice.

'I'm just checking in. How are you doing?'

Della wonders how much to tell her. She isn't sure what Robin has told his wife about Leo's relationship with Carrie, but she guesses Tash is as clueless as she is. To tell Tash what she knows is to tell her she has had a run-in with Robin, though, and the less Tash knows about that, the better. When she has evidence, incontrovertible evidence, she will bring it to Tash, and Tash will help her come to terms with it. But now, she just needs to hear her friend's voice.

'I'm fine,' Della replies, trying to sound breezy. 'I'm going to open up the kiln this morning to get my orders out. And a gallery has been in touch about commissioning some new work. I think I may be able to get myself on track, financially.'

'Good girl. I'm glad you're getting on with work. How's Alex?'

Della brightens, glad to think about something other than Leo and Robin. 'Well, I wish she *would* get on with work. She seems more interested in painting Carrie's house than doing her revision.'

'She's probably in love with that boy,' says Tash. 'What's his name? Jude?'

'I was coming to that conclusion, but according to Carrie, Jude isn't interested, it's just platonic.'

'Pull the other one. Any hot-blooded male would have to have the willpower of Batman to ignore Alex. She's gorgeous.'

'You think?'

'Don't you?'

'All that stuff she wears. The eyeliner, the ripped-up clothes. The baggy jumpers.'

'She could go round in a bin bag and still look like a supermodel.'

Della grins to herself. Tash's unwavering love of Alex has made her the perfect godmother. For a moment she feels a pang of regret for doing what she did to Robin. But it is fleeting.

Tash continues to think out loud. 'Jude would have to have a heart of stone not to fancy Alex. Or maybe he's into men? That would explain why Carrie's so certain he's not interested. Maybe she thinks it's not her story to tell?'

'True.' Della looks to Carrie's side of the house. There is no sign of her or Jude, even though she knows they must both be in there. 'I better go, Alex will be home soon,' she says, 'and I need to get on with things.'

'Call me if you need anything, OK?'

Della puts her phone into her pocket and goes around her side of the house to the studio. When she has unlocked the door and left it open, she walks around the building to the back to the kiln, touching the brick walls to feel how much heat is in them. The fire has died down to ash and the external temperature gauge tells her it is safe to unlock. Holding her breath, she turns the handle on the door and pulls gently to see what has happened in the last forty-eight hours.

It is dark inside, but the open door lets in light. Della ignores the sets of mugs, plates and bowls she knows have fired correctly; she's done them a million times. There are no shards of pottery on the floor to tell her things have gone wrong. The kiln gods have been kind. With two hands she gently lifts the moon jar. It still contains some residual heat and is warm and comforting to touch, like a pregnant belly. Della purposefully averts her gaze. She wants to see it in the studio, under the windows, on a revolving pedestal, so she can inspect it safely from all angles.

She walks with deliberate care through the studio door and positions the moon jar on the pedestal. She can hardly see the join between the top and bottom halves. Gently, she touches the curve of the vessel, slowly sweeping her fingertips over the glaze, turning the pedestal this way and that to see how the light catches the colour. The glaze is uneven, milky and flecked, with a transparent aspect that makes the jar seem ethereal and mysterious. In some areas the white thickens and blooms across the surface like smoke, making the face of the jar appear as if it is in perpetual motion. Fine cracks and fissures run over the glaze like a web, and their delicacy is beautiful. As Della leans in to look more closely, she has the feeling she is omniscient, looking down from a great height on to meandering rivers and well-trodden paths. She can't quite put her finger on it, but there is something timeless about it, this bringing together of the new and the very old.

It is their wedding anniversary tomorrow. They would have been married for eighteen years. She should be giving this to him, celebrating their life together, their future. Now all she sees are the hours she put into this vessel; the sourcing of the best porcelain clay, experimenting with different glazes, the logistics of throwing something much larger than she is used to, the difficult act of bringing together two halves. This vessel contains her sweat, and yes, her tears. All for a man who has lied to her, betrayed her and left her with a burden she cannot carry. She recalls the little speech she planned to make when she gave this to him. How their wedding date shared the vernal equinox, a time when the northern hemisphere tilts towards the sun. How she hoped the same would happen to them after a very dark year. Now, that speech seems deluded. The thought put into this gift seems filled with misguided self-importance. What kind of a mug did Leo think she was?

She acts on instinct before she can stop herself. She opens her palm and pushes the jar to the ground. Even before it hits the concrete floor, she regrets what she has done. As the vessel falls through the air, time slows and she can measure out each emotion as it passes through her, like sand in an hourglass. Spite, first. There is something pure and clean in spiting Leo, and spiting herself. The sensation feels like a hot knife slicing through her. It doesn't make her feel better, it just converts the pain into anger. As the jar hits the floor it splits into three equal pieces, and she sees her family in those pieces, torn apart. The remorse overwhelms her, like nausea.

She doesn't hear Alex enter the studio, back from school. She doesn't know how long Alex has been standing there, until her daughter cries out. 'That's Dad's present! His *ashes* are in there. Why would you do that?' Alex elbows Della out of the way to gather up the pieces. Della tries to help. 'Don't touch it,' warns Alex in a tearful voice. 'Don't you dare.' Alex finds a cardboard box while Della sinks to the floor, frozen, unable to move. Alex carefully places the pieces together before taking the box out of the studio, leaving Della behind, blinking back tears.

The shock comes a few seconds later, when silence replaces the sound of destruction. Then Della weeps on the floor, and she cannot tell if the tears she cries are regret for what she has done, anger at Leo's deceit, or fear, for the person she has become.

Chapter Thirty-Seven

It is not clear to Della how long she stays like this, kneeling on the concrete floor, but the ache in her knees is beginning to make itself known when she hears Carrie's voice behind her.

'Della? Are you alright?'

Della turns. Carrie is walking towards her, on her phone, talking to Jude. 'It's OK, she's here in the studio. You keep Alex at ours and I'll take Della back to her house.'

Carrie puts her phone into the pocket of her cardigan and helps Della up. 'Are you alright?' she repeats. 'We heard Alex . . . Jude's with her. Are you hurt?'

Della looks at her hands, which are dusty from the floor. Her palms have tiny shards of glittery glaze embedded into the surface of her skin. She wipes them on her thighs. 'I'm fine. It was a . . . it was an accident.'

'Alex said something about a present for Leo?'

Della doesn't want Carrie here, in her space. Not when she doesn't understand if she is a friend or an enemy. She pushes her hands away and gets herself up, without help. Carrie grabs her elbow as she wobbles. The feeling of this woman's hands on her stirs up her anger. 'Don't touch me,' says Della, her voice ragged.

Carrie steps back, holding her palms up. 'Sorry. I . . .'

'What are you doing here?'

'Alex was upset, we wanted to help . . .'

'I don't mean *here*. I mean in my *life*. What are you and Jude doing here?' Della draws herself up and dusts herself off. The action of doing something gives her strength.

Carrie looks as if she has been slapped. 'I don't understand.'

'You knew Leo, and you said *nothing*.' Then Della has a realisation. 'Oh God, is that why you offered to drive us to his funeral? So you could be there to say goodbye without arousing suspicion?'

Carrie looks horrified. 'Della . . . this is insane—'

Della speaks slowly, as if Carrie is very, very, stupid. 'You've known him since childhood. He's given you *money*. *Our* money.'

Carrie is staring with incredulity at Della. 'I don't know what just happened here, but—'

'You're denying it?'

'I'm sorry you've been having a hard time, you and Alex have been through a lot—'

Della groans. 'I'm so sick of people telling me what a hard time I've been going through! It doesn't mean I'm going mad, or I'm unhinged. Admit it!'

'Admit what, exactly?'

'That you and Leo were having an affair. You must think I'm such a mug.'

Carrie's face softens and for a moment Della wonders if she is going to cry. 'I don't think you're a mug. I think you're a lovely person and I'm lucky to have you as my neighbour. I swear on Jude's life I am not having an affair with your husband. Was. I wasn't having an affair.'

Della falters. The strength of her denial, the look on Carrie's face, both tell Della that Carrie is being truthful. But she can't be, because why would Robin tell her those things?

'How well do you know Robin?' Della asks.

'Robin who?' answers Carrie, looking confused.

'Robin, Leo's friend from university. He was Leo's financial adviser. Lives here, in the village.'

'I don't know anyone called Robin.' Carrie's expression has an air of desperation, and it crosses Della's mind she is a little bit afraid of her. *Good,* she thinks. *She needs to be.*

'I found a pair of Leo's cufflinks in your house.' Della blurts this out, knowing she is on shaky ground, knowing she had no right to go snooping in Jude's bedroom. Della swallows down the uncertainty as she waits for a response.

'Cufflinks?' Carrie repeats, shaking her head.

'Cufflinks. We bought them together in Venice. Gold cufflinks with lions on them.'

'Listen, Della, it's obvious to me you're feeling—'

'*Don't* patronise me,' spits Della.

Carrie starts backing away. 'I think I should go. I'll send Alex over when she's calmed down.' Carrie turns around and slowly begins to walk to the door of the studio.

'I also read your diary,' shouts Della after her, feeling desperate. The conversation has lost its balance, she can feel it tipping away from her, the weight of the truth slipping out of her reach.

Carrie stops walking and turns back towards Della, looking angry. 'You read my diary?'

Della juts her chin out in defiance. 'Yes. You've been meeting Leo.'

'How did you get hold of my diary?'

'I found it.' Della feels herself stepping into dangerous territory, but she has started down this path and she wants to get to the end. 'You've been regularly meeting my husband for the past year.'

'Oh, really?' Carrie folds her arms, tight across her chest. 'It's March. My diary begins in January, like any other diary. That's three months. Anyway, that's beside the point. You're . . .' She searches for the words. 'You need help, Della.'

Della begins to feel desperate as she sees the expression on Carrie's face. 'You've been with my husband every week,' she says, her voice rising.

'And how do you work that one out?'

'There's a bee motif drawn on every Wednesday afternoon.' As soon as the words leave her mouth she can feel the madness in them. She sounds deranged.

'A bee motif. Well, that explains everything, I suppose.' Carrie raises her arms and drops them helplessly by her sides.

'Yes,' Della ploughs on, regardless. 'Leo met you at The Beehive pub every Wednesday afternoon when he was supposed to be volunteering at a drop-in centre for technophobes.'

'A . . . what? A drop-in . . . what?'

'Never mind about that,' says Della, realising she is not focusing on her goal, which is getting Carrie to admit she knew Leo. 'You met him in a pub every Wednesday afternoon, for the past year apart from my birthday in January.' Della is babbling, she knows it, but now she is up to her neck in it, she may as well deliver all the evidence she has. The way things are going, it is unlikely they will ever speak again.

Carrie looks defiant. 'And who told you this? This *Robin* person?' She says the name with such derision.

'No, I—'

'So where are the witnesses? Maybe the pub landlord can testify to this steamy affair?'

Della is silent, knowing full well that nobody in that pub could testify to anything. She feels like crying again, and to her horror there are tears welling up in her eyes. 'And you told me Alex was premature—' finishes Della lamely.

'What's that got to do with anything?' says Carrie in exasperation.

'You said she was premature, and I don't . . . I don't think I told you that.' Della is fully crying now, there is snot threatening to pour out of her nose. She can feel her face heating up, becoming red and blotchy.

Carrie's face softens. 'Oh God, Della, you're really in a bad way, aren't you?' She strides across the room and envelops her in a hug. She smells faintly of a musky, amber, smoky perfume that reminds Della of a quiet moment in a beautiful church. It brings Della a deep, unfathomable comfort to be held like this, and then she realises she has just destroyed this budding friendship before it had a chance to blossom. That she may never get a second chance.

'I'm sorry,' she whispers into Carrie's hair. 'I'm really, really sorry. I don't know what's wrong with me.'

Carrie pulls her to arm's length and the compassion in her eyes makes Della weep all over again. 'You've lost the love of your life,' says Carrie with an expression of real concern. 'You've lost your beautiful dog. And you're at odds with your daughter, the only family you have left. There are plenty of things that are wrong. But none of it is your fault. It's just . . .' Carrie pulls her in again for a hug. 'One of those days, that's all. You're having a bad day.'

Della nods, allowing her back to be stroked, to be soothed like a baby. Eventually Carrie pulls back again and looks at her. 'Do you want me to come back to yours with you? I can make you tea, something to eat, perhaps. When was the last time you ate?'

Della can't remember. But she needs a moment to compose herself. She feels stupid, foolish and small. 'I just need to finish up a few things here. I'll be fine. I promise. I'm so sorry. I'm so sorry for what I said.'

Carrie smiles. 'It's fine. I'll send Alex over when she's feeling calmer and see if I can feed her if I can't feed you.'

'That would be great, thanks,' sniffs Della. She feels bone tired.

As Carrie walks towards the door, Della watches her, unable to believe she just accused this woman of having an affair with her dead husband, of stealing his cufflinks. The fact she has been forgiven so completely, so swiftly, is staggering. Most women would still be smarting. They wouldn't have comforted her like that. They would have stalked off and never spoken to her again. And then Della replays the last part of their conversation, the smile Carrie gave her just before she left. A pulse of adrenaline shoots through Della. Was that a smile of relief? Was Carrie so forgiving because Della was put off the scent? That she was pulled back from the brink of finding out the truth? Carrie's words come back to her. *And you're at odds with your daughter, the only family you have left.* How does Carrie know there is no family left?

The frantic scrabbling in her chest starts up again as Della tries to navigate a maze of misunderstanding. She thinks back to the list she drew up on the kitchen table in an effort to remember all the things she needed answers to. There is one thing she didn't confront Carrie with. In a flurry of activity, Della pats herself down and finds her phone. She hasn't called the unknown number for a while now. It always goes to voicemail.

Della runs out of the studio. Carrie's silhouette is not far away, walking slowly down the path towards the house. Unable to tear her eyes away, Della presses the number and, a second later, a ringing can be heard through the trees. She sees Carrie's phone light up through the fabric of her cardigan. As Carrie pulls it out, she looks to see who is calling.

This is when Carrie stops dead, turns around and meets Della's eyes.

Chapter Thirty-Eight

Della lets her arm drop to her side, her phone still calling Carrie's number. She has no strength left. They stand about twenty metres apart. Long enough for Carrie to get a head start, should she want to, but where would she go? Della knows where she lives.

'Don't lie to me,' Della says in a dangerous voice. 'I deserve to know the truth.'

Carrie's shoulders slump. She bows her head and nods. 'We'd better go to your place. I don't want Alex or Jude hearing any of this.'

Heart pounding in her chest, Della follows Carrie to the back door of her house and Carrie stands patiently while Della unlocks it, like a guest waiting to be invited in for tea.

'Sit,' orders Della as she gestures to the kitchen table. Della takes a seat opposite, and she can feel her whole body shiver uncontrollably. She would like to grip a warm mug of something, but she doesn't want to offer anything to this woman that would make her feel more comfortable.

'I wasn't having an affair with Leo,' begins Carrie. 'I just want you to know that before we get into this. We were not having an affair, OK?'

Della doesn't know what to believe. She doesn't know whether to believe anything that comes out of this woman's mouth. But she needs to hear what she has to say because some instinct tells her she might get nearer to the truth. 'I'm listening,' she says, her head swimming.

'I've known Leo since I was a kid,' says Carrie with a sigh. 'We went to the same school. The same school Jude and Alex go to, actually. We started dating when we were about sixteen.'

Della draws breath, and holds it there, unable to let it out.

'We were supposed to be a couple when he left for university, but we both knew it might not last. We had conversations about it, but nothing definite was decided. We wrote to each other quite regularly until, suddenly, his letters stopped coming, and I guessed it was probably because of a girl.' Carrie shifts slightly in her seat. Her hands are in front of her, resting on the tablecloth. Her fingers are bound by many rings, and she twists each ring on her left hand with her right as she considers what to say next. 'He came home for Easter and I knew as soon as I saw his face that it was serious. That he'd fallen in love. He was such a gentleman. He wanted to tell me himself, face to face.' Her voice is quiet, full of regret and sadness. She wipes away a tear that has begun to track its way down her cheek. Then another one appears, and another. She looks up at Della with a sad smile. 'It's actually a relief to be able to tell you this, to be able to cry about him. I know you've had a hard time, but it's been very difficult for me not to show how sad I am about his death.'

'So you did manipulate us into coming to the funeral,' concludes Della.

'Yes,' says Carrie quietly. 'I asked Jude to talk to Alex, make it sound like a favour. I knew Alex would want him to come. I wanted to say goodbye to Leo. I knew it would look weird if I just showed up without telling you.'

'Weren't you afraid of being recognised by people at the funeral? You said you grew up around here.'

‘I haven’t been back for ages. My parents moved away. There was no reason to come back. Especially when Leo . . .’ Her voice trails off.

Della makes herself sit more upright in her own chair. ‘Why are you living next door to me? To me and Alex? You must’ve bought the house when Leo was still alive. Are you still in love with him?’ Then a different, more sinister idea unfurls in her mind. ‘Are you stalking him?’

A weary look crosses Carrie’s face. ‘Let me just tell you from the beginning. It’s easier that way. Then you’ll understand.’ Carrie reaches for a tissue from the box on the kitchen table, blows her nose, balls the tissue up and puts it into her pocket. Then she runs her hands through her hair, and Della can tell she is thinking about what to say next.

‘I didn’t see much of Leo for the next year or so because he was busy at university, busy with you, I suppose. I think he got a job there because he didn’t come back over the summer.’

‘Yes,’ says Della. ‘He worked at a department store. We all did.’ She thinks back to that time, she and Tash, Robin and Leo working in different departments in the same store over a long, hot summer. She never once thought about the place that Leo came from, and he never talked about it. It was as if their lives only began when they all found one another. Any references to where they had come from seemed out of place and obsolete. Even she and Tash rarely discussed their hometown. So many bad things had happened there, Della was happy to forget all about it.

Carrie continues her narrative. ‘When Leo came back after he graduated, I was surprised. I thought he’d stay there, with you. And then I found out that you’d split up.’ Carrie gives Della a look from under her eyelashes. ‘Somebody told me you dumped him. He seemed miserable enough, so I guessed it was true. It was only a matter of time before we bumped into each other. You’ve seen how small this village is. It was even smaller back then. There was only one pub for a start, and I happened to be working in the kitchen.’

'So you got back together?' Della asks.

'On and off, until he disappeared one weekend, and then everything changed.' Carrie looks out of the window. The sun is beginning its descent. The light is muted and cool. 'Anyway,' she continues. 'When he came back, he had you in tow.' Carrie gives a hollow laugh. 'So maybe not such a gentleman after all.' She glances briefly at Della before looking to her hands, twisting her rings this way and that. 'I heard through the grapevine a few weeks later that he was going to buy the house next to Mrs Winters'. His parents were going to take care of the deposit. It looked like he had everything planned out. A perfect life.'

'Did he say anything to you? Did he explain?' asks Della.

'I didn't give him a chance. I quit as soon as I could, and left. My friend was setting up a yoga retreat in the Cotswolds and she needed somebody to cook. I didn't think twice.'

'Carrie . . .' No other words come to her. Della doesn't know what to say.

'I found out you were getting married not long after that. My mother called to tell me because the village gossips were scandalised. The word was Leo's bride-to-be was already pregnant. It was going to be a quick wedding.'

Della nods, remembering that time. 'Yes. We got married soon after we put an offer on the house.'

'It seemed like that chapter in my life was over. I was happy working at this yoga retreat. The woman running it talked about us becoming business partners. Leo was reunited with his true love, and I minded less about that every day. It seemed our relationship was finally over. Except . . .'

A cold finger of fear traces itself down Della's spine. 'Except what?'

'Except I was pregnant too. With Jude.'

Chapter Thirty-Nine

Suddenly, all the sympathy that Della was beginning to feel for Carrie evaporates as she tries to process the bombshell that has just exploded in her kitchen. For a shocking moment she feels like having a drink. 'Jude is Leo's son?' Della says, for no other reason than she can't think of anything else to say.

'Yes. Can't you tell? I thought maybe you would put two and two together when you saw him.'

Della thinks back to the boy she has barely spoken to. But yes, now she thinks about it, there is a look of Leo about him. The curly black hair. The same as Leo's before his went grey. His obsession with detail. For doing things properly, and something in his manner she can't quite put her finger on. Then doubts begin to upturn her thoughts.

'I can't just take your word for this,' she says. 'This could be another lie.' But as she says the words, she knows, deep down, it is not.

Carrie says gently, 'I have a paternity test. You're welcome to look at it. I insisted on having it done so Leo could be sure.'

'When?' says Della, feeling as if she has been cut adrift. 'When did this happen?' She imagines her husband changing Jude's nappies in secret visits. She imagines seventeen years of being lied to, and how that will alter all her memories of those years with Alex, when she thought it was just the three of them.

'Last year. Leo only found out last year.'

A wash of relief courses over Della, but the relief is momentary. 'You didn't have any contact with Leo until last year?' she clarifies.

'That's right,' replies Carrie, still twisting her rings.

'Why? Why didn't you tell him?'

'He had made his choice. He chose you. I don't like being second best.'

'So why did you wait for so long and then decide to tell him?' Della looks at her, and something unknowable clouds Carrie's expression.

'That's my business,' Carrie says after a pause, not looking at her. 'I was having a difficult time in my life, and I thought Jude should know his father. My partner had just left, everything felt, I don't know, impermanent, up in the air. I suppose I wanted something solid in my life, in Jude's. Leo and I were friends before it turned into something else. We loved each other.'

'But to move next door. That's insane.'

Carrie shrugs. 'It was cheap. I needed somewhere to live. Leo wanted to be near his son.'

The words slice through Della like a knife through butter. *His son.* The sibling for Alex they'd always wanted. Only, not like this.

'So Leo met Jude?'

'Several times.' Carrie looks cagey. 'Every Wednesday afternoon,' she relents. 'Leo wanted to maintain a relationship with him, but he wanted to do it slowly.'

Della imagines the three of them having lunch at The Beehive pub every Wednesday. The thought makes her stomach lurch.

Carrie says softly, 'The money was for Jude, and I didn't ask him for it. He wanted to make up for all the years he wasn't in his life. Leo wasn't perfect, but his morals were in the right place.'

Della gives a dry laugh. 'You think so?' she asks sarcastically. 'He kept this from me for a whole year.'

'It was a lot for him to process,' replies Carrie, 'and I think his father died at around the same time. Bad timing, I guess.'

Leo, crying in the bedroom. Leo staring out of the window, lost in his thoughts. *He was thinking about Jude, not his father,* realises Delia. *And I comforted him every time.*

'Neither of you thought to tell me? Or Alex?' Della groans when she thinks about Alex, who will now have another life-changing piece of news to deal with.

'Yes, eventually, Leo was planning on telling you. He wanted to establish a relationship with Jude first. But obviously neither of us figured he would die like this.'

Della puts her head in her hands. 'Alex. This is going to break Alex.' A familiar surge of anger wells up inside her at the injustice of it all.

'Alex and Jude get along fine. It's not like Leo was having an affair.'

How do I know that? Della thinks. *How do I know any of this is true?*

As if Carrie has just read her mind, she leans forward and touches Della's hand briefly. 'It was always you,' she says simply. 'You were his one true love. He loved me in a different way.'

But Della cannot believe it. 'Come on. Nobody moves next door to their ex-boyfriend, the father of their child, unless they want something more than friendship.'

'I moved next door out of necessity. I'm a pragmatic person. There really are no feelings between me and Leo apart from an old friendship that should've stayed that way when he came back from university. I'm very aware that Jude is the result of a rebound.'

'How much of his story does Jude know?' asks Della, her eyes narrowing.

'All of it. We have a very honest relationship.'

'Is that why you told me he would never be interested in Alex?'

'Yes. He knew the situation before we settled here.'

'But Alex . . . she knows nothing, and I'm not so sure she feels the same way. She's following him around like a duckling.'

'I have kept a close eye on them both. Don't forget she's spending all of her spare time with Jude at my house under my supervision.'

'How could he keep that kind of secret from her? He's only seventeen.'

'I asked him to keep quiet about it until I could figure out what to do. I wasn't expecting to have to deal with this by myself. We've been improvising since Leo died. The house sale was only finalised on the morning of his death. The timing couldn't have been worse.'

Della feels her jaw go slack. 'You were with him, weren't you, that morning?'

Carrie looks uncomfortable. 'Yes. He came with me to get the keys to the house from the estate agent.'

Della has a vision of them both, excited and full of anticipation, going into the estate agent's together to pick up the keys to their new home, when, all the time, Della thought Leo was hard at work in his office on the other side of the village. An understanding settles on her, like falling snow. She shivers. 'That's where the missing money went, isn't it? He bought that house for you.' The injustice of it, that he has paid for the house next door, but she is still paying for the mortgage on her half, feels like the deepest betrayal. To be valued so little, it's diminishing. She feels winded and worthless.

For the first time, Carrie looks contrite. 'I put in as much as I had. It wasn't enough. He wanted some kind of stability for Jude, and he said the house would be an investment for him, his way of saying sorry he hadn't been involved in his life. I went along with it because— of course I would, wouldn't I? I wanted the same thing for Jude. He's all that matters to me.'

'What about me?' Della says, her voice wavering. 'Don't I matter? What about Alex?'

'Leo didn't know he was going to die, Della. I'm sure he wouldn't have done it this way if he knew that. He thought he had years left. Years to sort this mess out.'

But Carrie's words are no comfort. She wants this woman out of her kitchen, far away from her house, but she also wants, desperately, to know about Leo's last day on this earth.

'Can you tell me what happened, when he collapsed?' she says in a flat voice.

'Like what, exactly?'

'I want to know everything. From when you met him that afternoon, to when he was taken away in the ambulance, because it was you, wasn't it? You were the one who called me that morning from his phone.'

Chapter Forty

Carrie tells Della as much as she can, from meeting him at the estate agent's to his collapse on the street.

'Did Robin know about the house?' asks Della, thinking about the meeting they had, the hesitation when she asked Robin about the money.

Carrie nods. 'Yes. Robin helped with the house purchase. He arranged the mortgage. But I never met him. Leo dealt with him.'

Another black mark against Robin's name. But Della knows she would have asked Tash to do the same if she had to. 'And when he collapsed? Was it sudden, or did he feel ill that morning?'

'It came out of the blue,' says Carrie. 'But he knew it was serious. He said he heard something in his head. He felt it. That's why he told me to call you. When you came round to my house that day and told me you were looking for his phone, I realised I still had it so I took it back to the hospital as soon as I could.'

'What about his cufflinks?' Della queries in a cold voice.

'Leo asked me to take them off before the ambulance arrived.' Carrie hesitates. 'For Jude.'

'I see.'

Carrie swallows. 'Look. If he had given them to me, I'd offer them back to you. But it's the only thing Jude has of him.'

'That and a house,' says Della in a caustic voice.

Carrie ignores her tone and gives her a small smile. 'I think he had a fantasy we would all be friends one day.'

Della snorts. 'Seriously? He was that deluded?'

'Family meant everything to him. He just wanted everyone to get along.'

'I feel like I'm part of an elaborate experiment,' Della mutters, darkly.

'What do you mean?'

'Leo has us all in this curated world, away from everyone else. He has us exactly where he wants us. I never saw him as a controlling person but, since he died, I really think he was.'

Carrie considers this. 'Yes, I suppose he could be controlling. He wanted to control the happiness. He wanted everyone to love him.'

'Then you're as deluded as he was. None of this has made me love him. The opposite, in fact.'

'It's a shock, for you. And it will be for Alex. But please try and think of it this way. He never cheated on you, he loved you more than he ever loved me.'

'What makes you say that? How can you know that?'

'Nothing happened between us, Della. We met every week for a whole year. There was no spark. It was Jude he wanted to see, not me. We were friends, good friends, nothing more.'

Della cannot help the twist of jealousy she feels about Jude. She imagines afternoons in The Beehive, father and son, with Carrie looking on. She cannot get over it. She doesn't know if she will ever get over it. Anger, something just bubbling under the surface in every emotion she has these days, boils up inside her.

'I don't have to accept this, you know,' Della snaps. 'I don't have to lie down and have you and Leo and Jude steamroller over me. Leo has behaved appallingly to me and to Alex. He's lied to us, he's given away our money. Alex's *inheritance*. I'm not just going to nod and accept you and Jude living next door to us because that's what Leo wanted.'

Carrie says quietly, 'We all have to accept things we cannot change.'

'What is that?' Della says in a mocking voice. 'The Serenity Prayer?'

'If you fight against the inevitable, nothing good will come of it.'

'There's nothing stopping me from selling this house and moving far away from both of you.' As the words form in her mouth she knows they aren't true. That Leo has compelled her to stay in this house. He must have realised Della would eventually find out about Carrie and Jude. He must have known, by burying Ethan here, in the woods, he would force her to become a family with them both. Carrie was right about one thing. Family meant everything to Leo.

Something in Carrie hardens. Her expression changes and her usual sympathetic demeanour is replaced by something that shocks Della.

'You think you're so perfect, don't you?' spits Carrie. 'Leo was just doing his best, making the best out of a difficult situation. I'm trying, too, you know. I didn't particularly want to live here, but I could see it would be good for Jude, good for Leo. And yes, good for Alex, too. But you just won't have it, will you? Everything hinges on your goodwill, and you're going to ruin it for all of us.'

Della regards her, filled with spite. 'I'm allowed to have an opinion. And I don't want to live next door to my husband's ex and his illegitimate son.' She regrets the words as soon as she says them, but she doesn't regret lashing out. She wants to hurt Carrie as much as she feels hurt right now.

Carrie laughs loudly. 'Because *your* standards are so fucking high?'

Della is stopped short by the swear word. She has never heard Carrie swear. She doesn't seem the type.

'What's that supposed to mean?' Della feels as if she has been slapped.

Carrie leans forward and looks at her with a dangerous expression. 'I think you know *exactly* what I mean. People make mistakes. People lie. Even you, perfect Della.'

The way she says it, Della can hardly believe that Carrie, of all people, would know. Not even Tash knows. Nobody knows. Nobody must ever, ever know.

'I don't know what you're talking about.' Della chokes on the words, her mouth dry, her heart hammering.

'Yes, you do,' says Carrie in a grim voice. 'I'll spell it out for you, shall I?'

And then she says it. The unthinkable lie that Della has kept buried for the past eighteen years.

'Alex isn't Leo's child. Not in the biological sense, anyway. What's the word, Della? Oh yes. *Illegitimate*.'

'You don't know what you're talking about,' Della says, desperately.

'Yes, I do. Very much so,' replies Carrie in a steady voice.

'You can't possibly . . . you can't possibly know that,' cries Della. 'How do you know that?'

'Leo found out, and he told me,' says Carrie in a regretful voice. 'I take no pleasure in telling you this. But you're being such a sanctimonious bitch . . .' She shakes her head, gives a dry laugh. 'This is why I know Leo is a good and honourable man. He knew all along that Alex wasn't his child. Yet he treated her as his own flesh and blood.'

'Get out,' says Della weakly. 'Get out of my house.'

Carrie rises slowly and with great dignity. 'I'm not here to judge you, Della, we all have to get along in life and do our best for our children. But you are so very quick to judge others, aren't you? I have tried hard to be friends with you, to be neighbourly, and to nurture a relationship between Jude and Alex. They can sleep together for all I care because I know they aren't related. But no, instead I pretend to Jude he has a sibling because it's the right thing to do. It's the only lie I've ever told him, and I did it for *you*, to keep the peace. You, on the other hand, you seem intent on destroying everything because we aren't the people you want us to be.' Carrie faces her and spreads her arms out wide. 'We are here. We exist. Leo loved us, just like he loved you and Alex. The sooner you get off your high horse, the better. For all of us.'

Chapter Forty-One

The feeling of wanting to get blind drunk and forget about that terrible conversation with Carrie is so strong Della has to muster every fibre of willpower she has to stop herself from leaping into her car and driving to the nearest off-licence. But that's what got her into trouble in the first place, and not touching alcohol has served her well over the years.

Della sits at the kitchen table, in the growing darkness, thinking about the secret she has carried inside her for eighteen years. The number of times she nearly blurted out the truth to Leo when Alex was a baby and she was sleep deprived. She wonders, now, if she had allowed herself to drink alcohol after Alex was born, that she might have told him everything in a moment of inebriation. That it might be Carrie, Leo and Jude living in this house, not her.

She has lied to herself, as well, she knows this. She never thinks about that time. Whenever something reminds her of it, she shuts it down and makes her brain move on. She's become so adept at forgetting, she stopped thinking of Alex as someone else's child. She was Leo's. It became as simple as water in a glass. But in darker moments, when she felt alone, or sad, she tortured herself with the truth, and how, if it hadn't been for Robin and a bottle of tequila, Alex would never have been conceived.

She regretted splitting up with Leo as soon as she did it, but she loved him more than she hated Ethan, so she thought she was setting him free. Her life was so complicated, so sad and fucked up, she didn't want to share it with someone as lovely as Leo.

Ethan traced her to Tash's university. Before he could sink his claws into her again, she left for a nondescript town with nothing to recommend itself to anyone, except for its proximity to a major motorway. It was the perfect place to hide out while she evaded Ethan and nursed a broken heart.

The bar she found work in was a riotous place. All of the staff were young, like her. Drop-outs and drifters, like her. She felt she had found her crowd. They drank while they were on the job, sneaking shots here and there as they worked, accepting drinks from customers whenever they were offered. After the bar shut, they had a lock-in most nights. Then bed, usually with each other or random hangers-on, until it all started again the next day. Della was just coming to the realisation that she couldn't go on like this, that the lifestyle she had cultivated couldn't be allowed to grow. She began to look for another job. She stopped sleeping around, but giving up alcohol was frighteningly difficult. And then, one night, Robin appeared like a ghost from a past so far back, he didn't seem real. He was a mirage from a time she cherished. A huge wave of nostalgia swept over her, helped by several shots of tequila that had been liberally shared out by one of the staff.

'Robin!' she screamed. 'Oh my GOD, how ARE YOU DOING??' It was a Friday night. Everyone was pleased to have the week behind them and the music had been cranked up in an effort to make the place look livelier than it was. Robin represented everything she missed: Leo, Tash, playing pool in the university bar. Eating chips from the paper in the kitchen they shared when they all stumbled home from a night out, dancing.

Robin, who looked like a fish out of water in that bar, registered how pleased he was to see her. His face lit up. And in that moment, a fresh tequila shot coursing through her veins, she felt the power she had over him.

'So this is where you ended up,' he said, his face full of wonder and – did she imagine it? Lust.

'Yeah. It's just temporary, though. Until I figure things out.' She felt grown-up, in charge of her own life. She was on good terms with everyone who worked there, and they let her chat with Robin, covering her area without complaint, amused she knew this guy who was dressed in a new suit and had his hair cut just so.

'What are you DOING here?' she shouted in his ear.

'It's a business meeting. A client. I'm leaving tomorrow.' Robin didn't take his eyes off her.

'Where are you STAYING?' she bellowed, leaning over to him so close she could smell him. With a jolt, she realised he wore the same aftershave as Leo. It was so familiar, so welcome, she fought the impulse to linger there, sniffing his neck. He named a hotel she had never been in to. Somewhere expensive that she couldn't possibly afford. 'You're doing well for yourself,' she remarked, giving him a wide smile.

The night passed in a blur. She and Robin talked non-stop about the old days, as if they had all stepped willingly away from one another, that Della hadn't dumped Leo, that it had been a mutual decision. She had to stop herself asking about Leo, even though she wanted to, desperately. So they talked about things they had in common that didn't really matter, until the bar shut, and she was left with him, wondering what was going to happen next.

'Come back for a nightcap,' he said. 'It's a nice hotel and the bar shuts late.'

She hesitated.

'I have an expense account. My treat.'

She had always wanted to see inside the hotel, but really there was something about Robin that was so intrinsically linked with Leo, she wasn't ready to let him go. To talk to him like this about old times was to have a piece of Leo, and the nourishment it gave her made her yearn for more.

She can't remember when the evening stopped being fun. She remembers having several drinks in the hotel bar and feeling sophisticated. But soon the conversation dried up and the bar staff started to stack the chairs and do the wipe down.

'You should see my room,' said Robin. 'It's on the top floor and it's got the most amazing view. They have these lights that change colour. It's so cool.'

Della followed him because she didn't have anything else to do. There was no one to go home to, there was no one waiting for her. And to talk to Robin was to talk to Leo, in a strange way. The last of the booze she had drunk in the hotel bar hit her in the lift on the way up. She began to feel dizzy.

'Sorry,' she slurred. 'I think I should go home.'

'You look like you need to lie down. I can't send you home in that state.'

'Maybe just for a minute,' she said. 'Then . . . then I'll get going.'

He lay down next to her on the bed, and they talked about the first time they met, the fun times they shared. Filled with nostalgia, the scent of Leo's aftershave thick in the air, she let him kiss her. She kissed him back. It was only a matter of minutes before she found herself, her skirt hoicked up, her underwear on the floor, wondering how she had got herself into this situation. She pictured Leo, and the fact that it was Leo she wanted, not Robin. She wondered if Robin might tell Leo about this, and realised it would matter to her, a great deal, if he did. It would matter so much it would tear her apart.

The shame of her terrible judgement, her inability to control her drinking, made her weep. She left as soon as she could, walking in the freezing cold all the way home until she found herself in her flat, the lights still on, a party in its final, drunken throes. As she picked her way across the sticky kitchen floor and climbed the stairs, strewn with human bodies, to her room on the first floor, she endured a barrage of knowing looks and jokes about what she had been up to with the man in the nice suit. It made her want to scream.

She woke up hungover and full of regret. It was only when she was halfway through a bowl of cornflakes that she remembered the drunken tearful message she had left for Leo in the early hours of the morning.

I miss you so much. I want to come back. I want things to go back to the way they were before.

She went to work feeling like a husk. She swore she would never drink again and, suddenly, the bar seemed like the worst place in the world, a place of destruction. She was walking around the floor collecting spent glasses, a tall stack of them extending from her outstretched arm to her shoulder, when she heard him.

'Need a hand with those?' The sound of his voice was like slipping into a bath of warm water. She turned, and it was all she could do to stop herself from dropping every single glass and running into his arms.

'Leo,' she breathed.

He looked at her, a smile on his face. 'I got your message. I've come to take you home.'

Chapter Forty-Two

She found out later that Robin had lied. He hadn't been there on business. It wasn't a coincidence. Tash had let slip to him where Della was working, and he had gone there with the intention of hooking up. Robin was still dating Tash, they were engaged. He had just as much reason to keep quiet about their liaison as she did. When Della returned and moved in with Leo, she made sure she was never left alone with Robin, but on the few occasions she was, neither of them referred to what had happened between them, and Della was grateful for his silence.

After Alex was born and Tash failed to get pregnant, Tash told Della their relationship had faltered when Robin refused to get tested at the fertility clinic. He told her he didn't want to have his manhood called into question, and didn't want children if it meant jumping through hoops. Robin's intransigence nearly drove them to divorce. Della couldn't give Tash the information that would have made everything clearer – that the medical fault didn't lie with Robin, it lay with her. She tried to be as supportive as possible and, every time she commiserated with Tash, she felt like a traitor. But to tell her the truth would be to expose her own treachery – not just to Tash but to Leo. She had lost Leo once. She wouldn't make the same mistake twice.

Around that time, Robin tried to rekindle whatever he thought he had with Della. She was an expert at evading Ethan, so Robin didn't present too much of a problem. They had the odd dinner as a foursome, the odd night out. She kept her relationship with Tash separate, encouraging girls' get-togethers and weekends away. It was Alex who presented the biggest problem for Della. She had something of Robin about her, none of Leo's curly hair. If Robin knew, he never let on. Della suspected he was too stupid to realise the consequences of his actions, nine months on, and when Alex grew into a woman he sometimes flirted with her inappropriately, which set Della's teeth on edge but reassured her he was clueless. As for Leo, he was so happy to have a healthy baby, he never questioned it. But now, after what Carrie had said, it seems like he had.

Since Leo died, she has had to re-evaluate his memory several times over. He has gone from perfection to a betrayer, to a man who has lovingly brought up his best friend's daughter without rancour. She wishes she could talk to him, ask for his forgiveness. She wishes she could find out how he felt. Before she knows what she is doing, she takes her phone and dials the number once more. And for the first time, it is answered.

'Hello,' Carrie says, sounding tired.

'How long did Leo know about Alex?'

Carrie sighs. 'He didn't give specifics, but I got the impression he did it when she was a young girl.'

'Did what?'

'He took a paternity test.'

Of course. Leo would want to be sure.

'Did he . . .' Della doesn't want to talk to Carrie like this, but she doesn't have an alternative. 'Did he think differently of me after he found out?' She feels needy, having to ask. 'Did he love me less?'

'If he did, he didn't tell me. I know he loved Alex through and through. He shined when he talked about her.'

'Why didn't he say anything to me? Didn't he want to know who the father was?'

'He knew who the father was,' says Carrie. 'He said it became more obvious to him the older Alex became. Which is why he did a test.'

Della feels winded. 'Did he talk to you about it?' she asks in a whisper, trying hard to voice the words.

'No,' Carrie replies. 'That's all he said.'

Della can tell that Carrie doesn't know the significance of this, that Leo has not discussed Robin with her. She reaches for an explanation for Leo's motivation in not confronting her, for not using it as a stick to beat her with.

Della recalls how close Leo and Alex were, sharing private jokes, common interests. She wonders if it was Leo's way of claiming her as his own. He was good at putting his own stamp on things. Then she remembers the conversation she had with Robin shortly after Leo died. *He liked to win.* Was getting close to Alex some sort of one-upmanship for Leo? To have the child Robin and Tash so desperately wanted? To forge an alliance with Alex that bested Della's own efforts?

'Can I say something?' Carrie asks, breaking into Della's thoughts.

'Go on,' says Della.

'All this soul-searching you're doing. This anger and regret you're holding, what's it for?'

'It's how I feel, I can't help it.'

'But how is it helping you? OK, so Leo wasn't the man you married. You weren't the woman he married either. But you had a happy marriage, didn't you?'

Della replies in a small voice. 'I wonder that the secrets he had, the secret I had, made it a sham.'

'Nobody is the same outside that they are inside. We aren't transparent. Everyone has secrets, and to respect that is a form of love.'

'How can you be so . . .'

'So what?'

'So . . . easy-going?'

'Life is short, Della,' Carrie says, bluntly. 'Shorter than we like to think. Now, if you don't mind. I'm tired.'

'One more thing,' Della pleads. 'Two more things, actually.'

'What?' asks Carrie.

'Does Robin know about Jude? Did Leo tell him?'

'I asked him not to. Leo said he wasn't planning on telling him anyway, because of your friendship with Robin's wife. Leo thought he wouldn't be able to keep something like that to himself.'

'OK. The second thing is, please don't tell Alex anything. I want to figure out the best way of telling her myself.'

'I wouldn't dream of telling her. It doesn't change anything in my eyes. As far as I'm concerned, she's family.'

Carrie ends the call, and Della is left with her own troubled thoughts. For some reason, she finds herself thinking about Miss Abramovich, in the early days when she began to allow Della a little more independence on the wheel. When Della first began to master the process, she found it hard bringing up the sides of a vessel without knocking the whole thing off balance. Her fingers could never seem to control the wobbles as the clay spun in front of her. The walls of her vessel bore the imprint of her inexperienced fingers, the uneven pressure she had exerted. Often, the structure was too thick. But she found that if she brought the neck of the vessel in so it was very narrow, nobody could see inside it. She became very good at perfecting the exterior instead, smoothing its contours, making it look perfect from the outside.

Miss Abramovich was having none of it. 'This belongs in bin, not in kiln,' she would say, waving her fingers dismissively at the wheel. 'I see what you are doing, Della. You cover up mistakes.'

Della sometimes thought she had a sixth sense for things like that, but still, she tried to defend her work.

Miss Abramovich would shake her head, sadly, and say, 'I know the walls of this vessel are too uneven. Why you want to save it? Why you spend time making this look pretty when is ugly as hell on the inside? Sure, it will look nice on a high shelf. But every time you pick it up, it will be heavy. Heavy with your mistakes. Make another, make it better.'

Make another, make it better. Della thinks about this advice. She tried to do this with her family, once. She left Ethan, she married Leo and had Alex. Now that family is falling apart. She knows Leo wants her to make a new family with Carrie and Jude, but it is Leo's wish, not hers.

Chapter Forty-Three

Alex came back late last night and left for school without talking to Della. She is still so angry about the smashed moon jar, and Della doesn't know where she has stored the pieces. As Della hears the front door close, too loudly, she knows she should start boxing up orders to send to customers, but the fact that Robin didn't tell her about being involved in Carrie's house purchase makes her wonder what else he hasn't said. She spends the morning prowling around the house before she settles down to some paperwork. But she cannot sit in her own skin until she makes the decision to go and find Robin once more in his office. It is approaching lunchtime; he might be available.

As she arrives in the car park close to Robin's place of work, she is thwarted by Tash, who is also getting out of her car.

'What are you doing here?' Tash asks, looking delighted. 'It's so good to see you. Why didn't you tell me you were coming?'

'There's a few loose ends I wanted to tie up to do with Leo's estate,' she says.

'We could have come to you to do that. You don't have to make the journey to his office.'

'It's OK, I was passing,' Della lies. 'I haven't made an appointment, I'm not even sure he'll be free.'

'Well, I can tell you he is. We're going out to lunch together. I should be working, but I wanted to try that new Thai place that just opened up on the high street. Come with us. I'm sure they can squeeze you in.'

'That's nice, but I've got a ton of orders to go through this afternoon. I haven't got much time.' She wonders if she is going to be able to get rid of Tash, if Tash will allow her and Robin to talk freely together, but as she realises this is unlikely, Della understands she can use the presence of Tash to her advantage. Robin, despite being threatened, has still withheld the truth from her, by not disclosing that he helped with Carrie's house purchase. If she adds Tash into the mix, it might bring him to heel. Plus she can find out how much Tash knows, how trustworthy she is.

They walk through the car park together and, as they enter the building, Tash greets the receptionist warmly and breezes straight through into Robin's office before he can be warned. Della walks slightly behind her and observes Robin's face as he sees first his wife, who he is expecting, and then Della, who he is not. He does a good job of composing himself, but Della can see he is rattled.

'Look who I picked up on the way,' proclaims Tash. 'I'm trying to persuade her to come out for lunch with us.'

Della looks at Robin's concerned face. 'And I've explained to Tash that I don't have time this afternoon, I'm just stopping by for a minute.' Della detects a small flicker of relief. 'I just had a quick question about Leo's estate.'

'Tash, why don't I see you outside in five minutes?' asks Robin smoothly.

'No way,' replies Tash. 'I've hardly seen Della recently, and if she's not coming out for lunch, I'll just make myself comfortable in the corner over here.' She flops down on a large leather sofa to the side of the room.

'It's OK. This kind of involves both of you anyway,' says Della. 'I found out yesterday that Carrie, my next-door neighbour, is acquainted with Robin. It seems Robin helped her to buy the house next door.'

'Did I?' Robin says, looking uncomfortable. 'Well, part of my job is to arrange mortgages, so it's not beyond the realms—'

'She bought that house with Leo's money.'

'Wait, what?' blurts Tash. 'I don't understand.'

'Yesterday, Robin told me Leo's inheritance from his father was used to buy a house. What he didn't tell me was that it was Robin himself who had arranged the mortgage.'

'Robin?' Tash turns to her husband, looking baffled, and in that moment Della realises she knows nothing about this. That this is something between Leo and Robin to the exclusion of their wives.

Robin immediately rearranges his face into cordiality. 'There's really nothing sinister going on.'

'Then why keep quiet about it?' asks Tash quickly.

'Yes, Robin,' echoes Della sweetly. 'Why would you do that?'

'Client confidentiality. I can't just go blurting out everyone's business. I—'

'Bollocks, Robin. You talk about work all the time at home. And this is Leo, our friend.' And then her face falls. 'Oh my God, Della. You don't think Leo and this woman . . .' She doesn't finish the sentence. She doesn't want to say the words. 'This is awful. Terrible. How did you find out?'

Della has already decided not to say anything about Jude. 'Carrie and I had a conversation yesterday,' she says carefully. 'She said she was an old friend of Leo's, and he gave her the money to buy the house. But yes, I definitely think there is something more to it than a friendly gesture. So I thought I'd come back here today to find out if Robin knows anything else.' She looks at Robin quizzically, wondering how he's going to deal with this in front of his wife. Before he can say anything, Tash's phone rings.

'Shit,' she says, looking at the name on the phone screen. 'I have to take this. Important client. Back in a minute.' She ducks out of the room as she answers the phone, her enthusiastic greeting at odds with the look she shoots Robin as she leaves his office.

'I'd say you have about five minutes,' says Della in a dangerous voice. 'I don't think you told me everything you knew yesterday. So I'm giving you one more chance.'

'I *did* tell you everything I knew,' Robin insists, looking angry. 'You can't just show up here and expose me like this in front of Tash. That's not what we agreed.'

'We agreed you'd tell me the truth, and I don't think you've done that, have you?'

'I have. The only thing I didn't say . . . the only thing I didn't tell you was a feeling I had, that's all. And that's got nothing to do with the facts, it's just my own feeling.'

'What?' asks Della, curious.

'I never met Carrie, I just dealt with Leo. I stick by what I said that Leo wasn't having an affair with her, the way he spoke about her. But there was something else.'

'What do you mean, there was something else?' asks Della, wondering if it is Jude.

Robin shrugs and shakes his head. 'A sadness. That's all I can say. Leo seemed sad about the whole thing, and I never understood why.'

When Della returns to her car, Tash is emerging from hers. 'Sorry about that. I needed to take that call.'

'That's OK. I'm done now, anyway.'

'Before you go. I just wanted to say . . .' Tash looks awkward. 'I know Robin cuts corners sometimes. But he's not a bad person.

He's just trying to do his best. For me, for you and for Leo. We're just all trying to make the best of things, that's all.'

Della looks at her oldest friend, sensing that the inexorable slide of Tash's loyalty away from her towards Robin is permanent. Della will never win her friend back, and perhaps it's not a good idea to try. It was only when they were children that she truly had Tash's attention, and recently, she has come to understand she needs that attention less and less. Della replays some of the conversations they've had since Leo died, the way Tash has dismissed her fears without really listening. It has only been since Carrie moved next door that Della has understood what it is really like to be listened to, to be given room to breathe. She smiles at Tash, who she knows means well. 'No hard feelings,' she says, squeezing Tash's arm. As she loosens her grip, and feels the friendship slip away, she mourns the loss. But in future, she wants something more equitable.

The sky is clouding over, and a gusty wind blows rubbish this way and that around the car park. She sits in her car, watching Tash go back to Robin. She thinks about what Robin has said, and how he looked when he said it. She would have dismissed it if it wasn't for the fact that Della has felt this too, from Carrie. That sad smile she has seen several times. The feeling there was something underneath the smile. It could be the death of Leo. But why, then, would Robin pick up on the same feeling from Leo himself?

Chapter Forty-Four

On the road home, as the trees begin to thicken into forest, something happens to the sky. Clouds begin to gather and close in. The sky darkens and rain begins to fall. The wind picks up into something more frightening than a few strong gusts and she can feel the car rock as it is pushed off course. Storms pass over the woods occasionally, but usually Della is ready for them. Normally, she listens to the radio every day, looks at her phone for the forecast, but things have been so stretched recently, so out of the ordinary, she hasn't done either, and now she feels a sharp stab of anxiety at being caught out. It is no joke living in a wood during a storm. You cannot leave the house for fear of being hit by flying branches.

She turns the car around and swings by the school to pick up Alex and Jude, but school has already shut. She sees the headmaster locking the gates.

'We sent them home at lunchtime,' he says as she rolls the car window down to greet him. 'We thought it would miss us, but updated weather reports show the storm changed direction and it's coming directly over.'

Della drives home as fast as she dares, cursing herself for not being prepared. She would have prevented Alex from going in today if she had known.

By the time she reaches the dirt track, small branches and debris are being shaken loose from the trees. She draws up to the house and sees Carrie's car is already there. When she opens the front door, she is relieved to see that Alex is home, for once, without Jude.

'They sent us home from school,' Alex says, looking worried. 'I wondered where you were.'

Della is glad the episode with the moon jar has been temporarily forgotten. 'I haven't been checking the forecast. I guess I've been too wrapped up with everything.'

'We should have Jude and Carrie here with us, shouldn't we?'

Della doesn't want them here. It's too soon. 'Let's see how bad it gets before we panic. Have you looked at what the Met Office are saying?'

'It's a red-weather warning. Danger to life.'

'Well, only if we venture out,' says Della in what she hopes is a reassuring voice. 'Is there anything loose outside? Have you put the kayak away properly? I noticed you and Jude have been out on the pond again.'

'Yes, it's put away.'

Della goes through a mental checklist. The studio, the woodshed. Thank God she finished firing everything. The kiln is probably more sturdy than the studio, and it is locked and bolted shut. And Marmite . . . for a moment, she looks around the floor, wondering where he is, if he is safe inside. Then she remembers, and it is the only good thing about his death, that he is not here to be afraid of another storm, that she is not afraid he will escape in terror and be lost in the woods. The absence of Leo she feels as a slowly deepening dread. This will be the first storm without him. He was always so reassuring to be around. Then, Della has a word with herself. She can do this. She has done this a million times.

'I'll go out and close the shutters. I'll check everything is alright next door, that they know what they're doing.'

'OK. Tell Jude to make sure his phone's charged, and his power bank.'

Della suppresses a smile. She opens the front door, and a gust of wind wrenches it from her grasp. She wrestles it back and knocks on Carrie's door. Jude answers and, for a moment, all she sees is Leo. She cannot believe she didn't see it before.

'Everything OK?' he asks, turning into a boy again.

'Sorry, yes. I just wanted to make sure you know what to do during the storm. Before it really hits, you should charge your phones up, and power banks. Stay away from the windows, keep to the ground floor. Before it gets really bad, *if* it gets bad, you should switch the electricity off. Do you have torches?'

'Yes. And candles.'

'Don't use candles. Battery-powered lights are safer.'

'Oh, OK.'

'And close the storm shutters.'

He looks uncertain, young, and a bit frightened.

Della softens. 'Where's your mum?'

'She's having a lie down.'

Della wonders if that is true. 'I'll help you. See, let me show you how they work.'

Together, they wrestle them closed.

'Is it going to be that bad?' Jude asks, as they complete the ground-floor windows.

'Probably not, but it's a pain to get a glazier out the day after a storm. Better to be safe than sorry. You have enough food and water for twenty-four hours? The storm will hit properly in a few hours. It will pass in the morning. But you should eat something hot now while you can in case the electricity goes off. And fill spare containers with water. Make up some hot-water bottles if you have any. Sometimes they have to shut the electricity and the water off.'

'OK.'

'Call Alex's phone if you need anything. Don't leave the house. There'll be branches flying around. It's easy to get hit.'

She leaves him, wondering if Carrie didn't answer the door because she didn't want to speak to her. When she returns to the kitchen, she sees Alex pulling out vegetables from the fridge.

'What are you doing?' asks Della.

'I'm making a veggie chilli.'

Della swallows down a lump in her throat. Leo always did this before a storm. It was his way of telling them not to worry.

'I'll give you a hand,' says Della.

Della and Alex eat together, listening to the wind gather force. The light in the house is muted because of the shutters, but there is a small window in the kitchen that is not covered. Periodically, they both peer out of it, reporting what they can see. It is when it gets dark that things begin to scare Della.

The sound of the rain begins to recede into the noise of the wind as it changes from a moan to a terrible roar. Della imagines an animal prowling around the house, testing the doors, trying to get in. They both move into the lounge. They sit close together on the sofa, which is pulled well away from the window, a large duvet wrapped around them both. Things begin to hit the house. The walls shake as the roof is assaulted. The shutters on the windows bang loudly, there is a volley of gunshots as something peppers the wood. Then they hear a huge, engulfing sound that seems to shake the earth, like a crashing wave or a collapsing building. Unable to bear it any longer, Della gets up and looks out of the small window near the back door. She can see nothing until a flash of lightning illuminates the wood, showing her a brief view of the trees, their branches torn at impossible angles. And then she sees it: a large, ancient hornbeam has fallen over the path into the woods, narrowly missing the studio. Then it goes dark again, and she can see nothing more.

Neither Della nor Alex can sleep. It is too loud, too scary. They spend the night on the sofa reminiscing about past storms, how they compare to this one. They talk about Leo, what he would be doing now. And then, very slowly, after they have both dozed off together and woken up again, as the darkness of the house begins to be touched by light, they realise the noise has diminished. The rain is falling more steadily as the wind recedes. It is still wild out there, but the worst is over.

'I've been thinking about what you said,' says Della, kissing the top of Alex's head. 'About the raku firing. If I can get good prices for art pieces, I won't have to work so hard on the dinnerware. I called that gallery in New York. They want to commission more work.'

Alex raises her head, which has been resting on Della's shoulder. 'That's great news, Mum.' She looks thoughtful. 'You could make more money with less time.'

'Exactly. And then I . . .' Della's mind drifts to the idea that was dismissed by Tash. 'Well, never mind.'

Alex nudges her playfully. 'Go on. Tell me.'

'I wondered about setting up a little school. Kids, maybe. An after-school club. I don't know.'

'That's a brilliant idea,' says Alex, nudging her again.

Della feels the warmth of the comment fall on her like sunshine.

'But you should teach adults too,' Alex continues. 'Night classes, weekend workshops.'

'Exactly,' replies Della. 'You know, I had the most incredible pottery teacher when I was young. I still remember how it felt to be taught by her. It would be nice to think I could do that, too, for somebody.'

'What was she like?'

As the wind finally dies down, and a weak shaft of sunshine penetrates through the shutters, Della tells her the stories that are never far from her mind. The softness behind the hard exterior, the kindness beneath the gruff comments. How Miss Abramovich allowed Della to explore her creativity, allowed her to make mistakes.

'I suppose that's where I get it from,' says Alex thoughtfully. 'My creative side. Dad wasn't creative at all, but you are. You must have passed it on to me.'

Like a magic-eye pattern she has stared at for the past seventeen years, it is only now that Della recognises the connection between herself and her daughter. Something shared that she can nurture and support.

Eventually, her mind turns to the clean-up. The hornbeam might have to be chainsawed to allow access to the path. She wonders how the studio is, the kiln. Just as she is thinking about venturing upstairs to see if the roof is intact, there is a frantic banging at the door.

Alex looks wide-eyed. 'It must be Jude.' She runs to the front door to let him in. 'Are you OK?' she asks, looking him up and down as he comes into the hallway.

'I'm fine, but Mum isn't,' he says. He looks as if he might cry.

'What's the matter?' asks Della.

'She fell and hit her head. I need to take her to hospital, but a tree has fallen across our car, and I can't use it.'

'Jude, you can't drive in this. There'll be trees down all over the place. Is she unconscious?'

'No.'

'Is she bleeding?'

'No.'

'Then what?'

'I want her to get checked out,' he says, stubbornly. 'She's not well.'

Somehow, Della knows he is not referring to her head.

Jude hesitates, looks at them both, from one to the other, and something about his expression makes Della's heart quicken.

'She's ill,' Jude relents. 'She didn't want me to come here and tell you. It affects her mobility, sometimes. Look, I just need to use your car.'

Della remembers the bruised arm, the throwaway comments about being clumsy. The comment she made yesterday: *Life is short. Shorter than we like to think.*

A quiet, dark feeling settles over Della. 'What's the name of her illness, Jude?'

Jude swallows. 'She has MND.'

Chapter Forty-Five

Della tells Jude to go and reassure Carrie while she sees if the car is fit to drive.

'Mum,' says Alex urgently as she goes outside. 'What's the matter with her? What's MND?'

Della turns to her. 'Motor neurone disease. It's an illness that affects the nervous system.'

'I don't understand.' She reads Della's face. 'Wait . . . Is it serious?'

Della feels the knot in her throat tighten as she prepares to tell the truth. 'Yes. It's serious.'

'Like, how serious?'

'Alex, there's no easy way of telling you this. There isn't a way to fix it. It's an illness that gets worse as time goes on. It affects muscle movement, makes it hard to . . . do stuff.'

'And then what? You end up in a wheelchair?'

'Well, yes, but . . .' Della doesn't really know how to explain it kindly.

Something in Alex changes. A spark of understanding. 'Is she going to die?'

Della feels her shoulders slump. She nods. 'Yes. Yes, she is.'

'But not for a long time, right?' asks Alex.

'It can be quite quick for some people.'

'How quick?'

'Some people live for many years. But some people don't. It depends. It's hard to predict.'

Alex's hand flies in front of her mouth. 'Oh my God. Poor Carrie. Poor Jude. He doesn't have anyone else.' Her eyes fill with tears.

'Listen, Alex, I need you to be strong for Carrie. Jude said she didn't want us to know so I'm guessing that means she doesn't want people weeping over her. Right now, she needs help. Practical help. We need to get her to a hospital.'

Alex grimaces, pulls herself together. 'OK. What should I do?'

'I need you to walk up the track and move any branches out of the way so I can get the car down. If there's anything too big to move, then call me, and if we can't do it together, I'll have to get an ambulance out. Wait for me at the top of the track and I'll pick you up in the car with Jude and Carrie if it's clear enough to drive.'

Glad of something to do, Alex pulls on a coat and puts a pair of gloves in her pocket to protect her hands. She laces her boots up and makes sure she has her phone before she runs up the track. Della goes to the car, which has just avoided being hit by the tree that has covered Carrie's. She opens both of the back doors as wide as she can, and she goes next door.

She smiles briefly at Carrie, who is now sitting up with Jude supporting her. There are dark circles under his eyes. 'We are going to get either side of your mum and lift her together, OK?'

Jude nods.

'Can you hold on to Jude and me?' she asks Carrie, and Carrie nods her head, looking defeated. With difficulty, they get Carrie off the floor and shuffle together out of the house. As they do this Della is dimly aware there is damage to the house, but she doesn't want to look at it or think about it right now.

'Can you take her while I go to the other side?' asks Della. She lets Jude support Carrie, and she goes on to the back seat to help settle her when Jude leans in with her. 'OK?' she asks Carrie. Carrie nods, but doesn't say anything.

The track is free of big branches; Alex is just clearing the last as they reach the top. Della prays they don't get a puncture on the way out. The roads are empty apart from a slew of branches and debris on the tarmac. Some traffic lights are not working. Old and beautiful trees are leaning precariously or are already horizontal. They have to edge past a couple of trees that have fallen into the road, but the main road is wide enough to get down at a decent pace. As they approach the hospital Della has a sinking feeling she recognises from when she came to see Leo, and she wonders if it will always be this way, if she will always associate this hospital with terrible things.

They manhandle Carrie into the building and Della promises to wait while Carrie is seen to and they know what is going on. An hour passes, almost two, enough time for Della to understand a few things about Carrie's situation. Then Alex's phone rings and Jude tells her to come up to the ward to see them. Carrie is in bed, asleep. Jude looks worn out. Della checks her watch. It is almost 8 a.m.

'Why don't you two go and get breakfast in the canteen?' she says softly. 'You can bring me up a hot drink and a sandwich when you're done. I can wait here with Carrie.'

Jude looks unsure, and Della sees his love for his mother, the pull he feels. And she wonders how long they have left together, how much of a man he will be when he has to deal with her death.

Della lowers herself on to the seat next to Carrie, wanting to crawl on to the floor and lie there instead. She is so tired. But Carrie's eyes are open as she gazes at Della with a regretful expression.

'I'm sorry you got dragged into this,' she says, weakly.

'How are you feeling?' asks Della.

'Disappointed that my body let me down. But I'll have to get used to that.'

'How long have you known?'

'About twelve months. It's why I decided to get in touch with Leo. If you hadn't already guessed.'

Della nods.

'It wasn't supposed to be like this. I was the one who was going to die before Leo. Can't even get that right.' She coughs, or laughs, Della can't tell. 'Where's Jude?'

'I told him to get some breakfast with Alex. They'll be back soon.'

'Then we don't have long. Is this beginning to make sense to you? The house? Leo's plan?'

'I think so.' Della feels the burden of understanding that settled on her in the waiting room.

'I need you to love him, Della.' Carrie's voice wavers when she says this. 'I know it's a big ask. That you don't know us. But he's an amazing kid. The best.' A tear tracks its way down Carrie's face. 'Leo said you'd come round eventually. But he didn't bank on . . . he didn't bank on this. So I have to ask. Beg, actually.' Carrie looks at Della, her gaze unwavering. 'Leo was the only person we had in this world. I'm begging you, please love our son.'

Chapter Forty-Six

Carrie and Jude remain at the hospital and Della takes Alex home. The car is silent on the drive back, the road eerily quiet. Next to Della, in the passenger seat, Alex is mute with fatigue or shock, Della cannot tell, but she is grateful there is no pressure to fill the silence with conversation. Her thoughts slide over one another like snakes. She is unable to catch the tail of one before another slithers into her consciousness, demanding her attention.

She acknowledges the enormity of what Carrie is asking. A child doesn't stop being a child when they turn eighteen. You are responsible for them for life. At least, that's how Della sees it. Another thought slithers in. Maybe that's why Leo did what he did. He knew, if she agreed to look after Jude, that she would take it seriously, do a good job. Be a mother to him. But how can she do that, without Leo, in the knowledge that Jude is Leo's biological child, and her own daughter is not? It feels as if the universe is playing a monstrous trick on her.

The thought of running away slides into focus. She is certain, now, that Leo would have done anything to cement the connection between her and Carrie, Alex and Jude. He would have guessed how much his two children would get on. And now he has buried her brother somewhere on their land, she is tied to this place, to this family, whether she likes it or not.

As she weaves in and out of the debris and broken branches on the road, as she drives carefully down the dirt track, she wrestles with these thoughts, and so, lost in herself, she forgets to prepare for the damage to her home. The house has weathered the storm, but a price has been paid. A couple of the shutters have been ripped off the front. The roof is missing tiles. But it is the trees she cries out for. To the front of the house, an oak, centuries old, has fallen. Its crown has engulfed Carrie's car. Della thinks about the nests that have been built in there, the thousands of creatures who have made it their home. Della looks up, to the area surrounding the house. There were hornbeams that circled it, like a close-knit family holding hands. Now, as she looks above the roofline to the spread of green behind, there are gaps.

She takes her seat belt off and turns to Alex. 'I need to go and check the damage in the wood. Are you OK to go in by yourself?'

Alex looks at her, and her eyes are dead. She looks like a zombie. 'Yeah. I just want to sleep.'

Della reaches over and tucks a lock of hair behind her ear. 'Check all of the ceilings for plaster cracks upstairs before you do. Or sleep downstairs. I don't want anything falling on you.'

'Don't worry. I'll be fine.'

Della does worry. Because now, she knows that life can be taken away at any minute. She feels the fragility of it, like a leaf skeleton that has survived for years in the woods only to be crushed under the weight of unthinking feet. She leaves the car, locks it, and walks around the side of the house. Some of the trees are leaning drunkenly against one another. Others are already horizontal on the ground. The earth has been pulled up by their roots, great plugs of soil upended, bristling with root systems that have nowhere to go. There is an intimacy to that space, a place that should be hidden underground, out of human sight. Della wonders if she might find Ethan tangled among the branches, and the urgent need to check before Alex comes out feels overwhelming. She goes from fallen tree to fallen tree, checking the holes they have made, the earth they have thrown up. But earth is all she does see. There is no sign of Ethan. Eventually, she returns to the studio, and Della makes a note to herself to call the tree surgeon to assess the damage and make the uprooted trees safe.

The studio and the kiln have both escaped, intact. Their position has sheltered both buildings from the brunt of the storm. There are torn branches and leaves covering the roofs, but that is all. Della walks past both buildings and follows the path through the wood, wondering how safe she is, if there are any trees that are being held up by their neighbours, their weight caught by a singular branch that is slowly giving way. The desire to know if the path is useable overrides her fear, and she follows it, taking pictures of all the trees that might need the attention of the surgeon. The path is clear. She navigates it all the way to the pond, and stands there, looking over the water, which is now flat and compliant, the surface covered in debris. Small leaves and twigs lie motionless, waiting to become saturated and heavy enough to sink down to the bottom. On the fringes, a branch has come off a large birch tree and dips under the water, still tethered to its trunk by a narrow strip of bark. Della moves around the perimeter of the pond, wondering if any duck nests have survived, and she is astonished to see a mallard sitting on eggs, as if it is an ordinary day.

When she reaches the jetty, she can see it is leaning. She walks along it cautiously, needing to know it is safe before she lets Jude and Alex back here in the kayak. The planks on the deck are sound enough, but she can see one of the piles stands at an angle. She approaches it, kneels down, looks over the side. There is something caught in the structure underneath, a large tree branch, perhaps. She gets on to her belly, not wanting to slide and fall in. She lowers her face to the water, looks in through its glassy surface down to the murk below. There are shadows here, patches of dark and light, and it takes a moment for her eyes to make sense of what they see. She notices delicate fronds that move and wave under the water. It looks like a plant, some kind of pondweed. But it's not like any plant she has seen before. The filaments are too fine. They are beautiful in their way. They catch the light and swirl around her fingers as she reaches into the surface of the pond. The strands slide over her fingertips, caught in the movement of the water. It is only when she feels their softness, sees the colour more closely as she draws them through her fingers that she understands what the filaments are. That this is Ethan's hair.

Chapter Forty-Seven

Della withdraws her hand and stands up on the deck in one swift movement, wiping her fingers on her trousers, as if to rid them of contamination. She becomes horribly aware that only the thin planks on the jetty are separating her from her brother's body, that he is lying, face down in the water, only inches from her feet. Something during the storm must have dislodged him. She can still see his long dark hair creeping out from below the decking, the kingfisher blue of his jacket. She stands there, transfixed by the waving strands for a very long time, wondering what to do. She understands, now, that Leo was telling the truth, that she never saw any sign of disturbed ground in the woods because Leo didn't bury Ethan, he dumped him in the pond.

She thinks back to a few weeks ago, when the ice had melted and Alex had wanted to take the kayak out on the pond. Leo had asked her not to, citing blue-green algae.

'I'm not going to swim in there, Dad. I'm just going to paddle about. Come with me. It's such a lovely day.'

But Leo had been adamant, and he had proposed something else instead, something extravagant, Della remembers. She had thought nothing of it at the time, but now she understands the horror he must have felt, at the idea of Alex being anywhere near the pond. Then she thinks of Alex and Jude being in here together when the pond warms up, jumping off this jetty and into the water. She brings her fingers up to her lips to stop the feeling of nausea that rises up in her throat. Did Leo try and sink Ethan's body and it has somehow freed itself in the storm, or was he hiding it here, hoping to bury him in the woods?

Della thinks, hard. She races to the studio, finds some yellow-and-black tape with CAUTION stamped all over it. With the jetty leaning like that, and the tape, it will look too unsafe to walk on. It will buy her time to think. She runs back to the jetty, wraps the tape around the entrance to make it hard to cross. It is impossible to take her eyes away from the water. The horrible thought that Ethan's body might float into the middle of the pond. She cannot leave it there. But the idea of touching it . . . the very idea makes her double over, breathless, gasping.

She looks at her watch. It is past lunchtime. Then she sees the date. March the twenty-first. Her wedding anniversary. Three weeks to the day of Leo's death. Three weeks in which her life has been demolished.

Alex is still asleep when she lets herself into the house. Della sits, for a very long time, in the kitchen, the colour draining out of the sky. Then, when it is dark, headlights fill the room, sweeping the walls as a car comes down the dirt track. Della gets up, walks to the window, and sees Jude and Carrie get out of a taxi. Carrie is moving well; she does not seem to need assistance. Jude opens the door for them, and they disappear into the house.

When Leo died, Della felt alone. But it wasn't like this. The urge to talk to someone, tell them what she has seen, is overwhelming. It gnaws at her like an ugly, hungry animal. But who can she talk to? She can never unsay what Leo has done. Whoever she tells will carry it, always, just like she has to.

She knows she cannot leave this place with Ethan there. She must stay here, forever, or she must deal with his body before she sells up and leaves, and she cannot do that alone. Della considers calling Tash but rejects the idea immediately. The days of leaning on Tash are over. She must bear the weight of this alone, to protect her daughter, to protect herself. Who's to say the police would believe her story? She is turning the problem over, over, in her mind, when she becomes aware of the sound of Carrie's door opening. Della enters the hallway just as Alex is coming down the stairs, bleary-eyed. They meet at the bottom of the stairs.

'I think I slept too much,' Alex says. 'Who's at the door?'

'It's Carrie,' replies Della, going to answer it.

'They're back?' asks Alex, perking up. 'She must be OK if she's ringing our bell.'

Della opens the door, and Carrie does indeed look better. 'I'm back to some kind of normal, for the time being,' she says, shutting down any more questions. She looks beyond Della, over her shoulder to Alex. 'Jude could do with some cheering up. I told him to take you to the new Thai place on the high street. My treat. I thought you could both do with a night out while Della and I discuss repairs to the house.' She turns to Della and says brightly, 'I figured it would be cheaper to do it together. I don't know who to call.' Then there is a pause, a meaningful look crosses Carrie's face and Della knows full well she has not come here to discuss the house. But Della doesn't make an excuse and close the door, because a possibility is opening up in front of her, like a ray of moonlight on a dark night.

Alex grabs her jacket and flies out of the door, leaving the two women standing opposite one another, either side of the threshold, looking straight into each other's eyes.

'That was kind of you,' says Della. 'To pay for Alex like that.'

'I wanted to finish the conversation we started in the hospital. Or at least, find out what you're thinking.'

As she says these words, Della sees a way out. She knows what must be done, that she must make a deal with this woman. Exchange one life-long commitment for another. She sees how much Carrie loves her son. She understands how desperate she must be.

Well, Della thinks. *I'm desperate, too.*

'Come in,' Della says, stepping to one side.

Chapter Forty-Eight

Della shows Carrie into the lounge and they sit opposite one another, the time for pleasantries over. The days of sitting together like this, drinking fragrant tea, seem a lifetime ago. So much has happened, she is a different person, now. Della feels hardened, whittled down to the meat. A leaner, purer version of herself.

'What happened at the hospital?' Della asks.

'They checked me over,' Carrie replies. 'But I know that one day, the accidents, the stumbles and falls. It will become too much.'

'And then what?'

'Jude and I have a plan. I'm going to enjoy life until I don't. Then I'm going to go to Switzerland. Unless the law changes here, and then I'll be able to die at home.'

Della is shocked by her honesty. 'You're going to . . .'

Carrie meets her eyes with a level gaze. 'I'm going to finish my life on my own terms. I'm very certain of this. I'm at peace with it.'

'But Jude . . .'

'He wouldn't have it any other way. He wants to help.'

Della thinks of the men and women who have been arrested when they return from Switzerland, grieving, widowed. That assisting a death in a clinic in Switzerland is against the law. 'He's only seventeen,' Della says quietly.

'It might not come to that,' Carrie reassures her. 'I may have a fatal fall or get an infection. It might be taken out of his hands. It's going to be hard when I get very ill. I don't want that for me, or for him.'

Della doesn't know how to put the next question. 'How long?' she asks. 'How long do you think you have left?'

Carrie shrugs. 'I think about two years.'

'What about if I helped? If Alex and I got involved?'

Carrie looks confused. 'What do you mean?'

'Between the three of us, it would be easier. Less pressure on Jude, less pressure on you.'

Carrie shakes her head. 'You don't know what you're saying. It's not a week or two. It takes months. Years, maybe.'

'I'm aware of that.'

Carrie narrows her eyes. 'And Jude? Will you take him in? He will need a family after I'm gone. I'm all he's got.'

Della sees the grit in her, the steely determination to do right by her son. 'Yes,' she replies. 'I will.'

But Carrie isn't persuaded. 'I don't understand. You looked like you wanted to run a mile in the hospital this morning. What's changed?'

'I want something from you in return,' Della blurts out, her heart racing.

'What?'

'You once told me you were very good at keeping secrets. Is that true?'

'Yes. I haven't told Jude that Alex isn't his sister, and I don't plan to, if that's what you mean.'

'It's not that. There's something I need to do. If you help me, I'll help you and Jude. If you don't want to do it after I've told you what it is, you have to promise me you won't tell anyone. This is for Alex's sake. And for Jude, because he lives here too. Nobody must know.'

Carrie doesn't hesitate. 'Tell me.'

'Just before he died, Leo killed my brother and put his body in the pond.'

Carrie bursts out laughing. Della sits, frozen, not sure what to say. She waits for the laughter to subside, and then she watches Carrie's face change as her ignorance is replaced by the shock of understanding.

'*What?*'

'Just before he died,' Della repeats in an even voice, 'Leo killed my brother, Ethan.'

'How? *Why?*' asks Carrie, incredulous.

'Ethan has been a continual threat to my safety. Leo knew this when I met him. After we had Alex, he became a threat to her safety, too.'

'Like how?'

'One day, I will tell you. But let's say he's a fan of setting fires.'

'So you moved to a *woodland*?' Carrie lets out another manic laugh.

Della cannot help but smile. She said the same thing to Leo at the time.

Have you ever tried to start a fire in an English wood? he had replied. *It's perpetually damp. You'd have a job on your hands.*

Della continues. 'I think he did it when Alex and I were away. We came home on a Sunday evening, and his face was bruised. He was in a state, said he'd had a car accident. Hit a tree on the top road. But I think Ethan came here. He did that, from time to time.'

'What? And ran him over?'

Della shrugs. 'Or they had a fight. I don't know. All I know is this. The top road borders our land. It's elevated, several metres high. There is a slope that runs from the road to our land below. It goes straight down to the pond. If Leo hit him with the car, or they had some kind of fight up there, if a man fell down that slope, he would find himself in the water.'

Carrie shakes her head. 'I can't believe he would do that. Leo isn't capable.'

Now it is Della's turn to laugh. 'Isn't capable? Look at what he's done. The lies he's told. He's orchestrated this situation between the two of us. Family is everything to Leo. *Everything.* Ethan regularly threatened that.' Della sees him, coming out from behind the trees, Alex, a toddler, high on his shoulders. She screws her eyes shut. 'If Leo was backed into a corner, he would fight for us. I know it.'

'Didn't anyone come here looking for your brother?'

'He's not the kind of man who would be missed. People are generally glad to see the back of Ethan.'

Carrie shakes her head in disbelief. 'I just can't get over it. The idea of it.'

But Della has gone beyond her own disbelief. She has had time to think about the man she married, and the way she can choose to remember him. 'I've decided to believe that he didn't do it deliberately,' she says. 'That it wasn't premeditated.' The idea Leo planned to kill Ethan is too painful to contemplate.

Carrie leans back and rests her head on the sofa. 'I remember a few days before he died, he didn't want to talk. He seemed . . .'

'What?' Della asks.

Carrie shakes her head. 'I thought it was the move. That he was getting cold feet. I never imagined . . .'

'I did wonder if he'd told you.'

'I don't know what I would have done with that.' Carrie looks at her, sharply. 'I'm not sure why *you've* just told me. Wait . . .' A grim look changes Carrie's expression. 'What is it that you want? This favour you need?'

'Ethan's body has come to the surface of the pond. It can't stay like that.'

Carrie sits up, a horrified look on her face. 'What do you want me to do about it?'

'I need help. To get rid of it. Sink it back down. I don't know.'

Carrie's mouth drops open. 'Oh my God.'

'I know. But I can't do it by myself, Carrie. I'm afraid of him. Even if he is dead. And I can't ask anyone else. Nobody must know, and . . .'

Carrie chips in, '. . . and I'm going to die soon, so I'm a safe bet.'

Della lets out a breath. 'Yes,' she admits. 'That's part of it.'

'And what's the other part?'

'You've asked me to do something for you that will have repercussions for the rest of my life. And Alex's life. If I take on Jude I will do it properly. I will love him as much as he allows me to. I will be there for him until I die, and then Alex will be there for him.'

Carrie looks away, her eyes filling with tears.

'But I cannot have this hanging over them, too. Leo did something terrible. It needs sorting out. If Ethan is ever found, it will come out that he's my brother. It will be easy to assume I did it. In the past, I've complained to the police about him turning up here. The complaints will be logged somewhere. If that happens, our children will have nobody.'

'Christ. This just gets better and better,' says Carrie bitterly.

'I'm sorry to drag you into this, but I don't have a choice. You need me to step up and I need you, just as badly.'

Carrie's expression changes. She becomes businesslike. 'You can't sink him down again,' she says darkly. 'He needs to come out of there.'

'If we bury him, there'll always be the possibility he'll get found. Developers sometimes come here, asking if we're interested in selling. Alex and Jude might need the money one day.'

'Then we need to do it properly. We need to do it tonight. When the kids are asleep.'

A wave of gratitude washes over Della. 'What do you think we should do?' she asks.

'Isn't it obvious?' Carrie asks with a sigh. 'Your kiln is big. And it gets very hot. Hotter than a furnace, I imagine.'

Chapter Forty-Nine

Della took a sleeping pill last night. Something she has not had to do for a long, long time. She sleeps through Alex getting up and leaving for school. She sleeps past the morning until the afternoon. She wakes to a quiet house, feeling as if she is underwater. Then she remembers. Swiftly, she puts the memory away. Locks it up, in the dark. Still in bed, she reaches for her phone and texts Carrie.

Are you awake? Are you OK? she types.

Yes, comes the reply. Just.

The kids will be home soon, Della types.

Don't worry, Carrie replies. I'll come over before they do.

Della showers, again. She emptied the hot-water tank in the early hours of the morning and now it is full once more; she stands in the glass cubicle, robotically soaping her skin, shampooing her hair, scrubbing her fingernails with a stiff brush. Eventually, the tank empties and the water runs cold. Reluctantly, she gets out, wraps her hair in a towel and dries herself off. She glances at the black bin bag in the corner of the bathroom. In it, a wet pile of clothes she will never wear again.

She cannot eat. She cannot.

She fights the urge to go back to sleep, to become unconscious once more. She prowls around the house in a pair of joggers and an old sweatshirt, her hair still damp around her neck. She avoids looking out of the back window and into the woods. It is only when she hears the sound of the doorbell that she jumps into action, rigid with purpose. She walks down the stairs, quickly, gripping on to the banister so her knuckles turn white. She opens the door, and before Carrie is over the threshold they fall into each other, wrapping their arms around one another, rocking.

'The worst is over,' Carrie whispers into her hair. 'The worst is over.'

Carrie comes into the house. Della is about to close the door when she sees Alex and Jude appear from the shadows of the dirt track, deep in conversation. 'Shit, they're here,' says Della, a wave of panic engulfing her. She didn't think her heart would find it possible to beat this way again, so soon after last night, for her body to come alive once more with the pulse of adrenaline.

'We've got this, Della,' says Carrie, giving her a steady look. Then she turns to Alex and Jude, who are almost at the house. 'Guess what?' she says in a bright voice. 'We're going away for the weekend.'

'What?' says Jude, dropping his bag. He and Alex stand at the door looking puzzled.

'Della has kindly offered to get the roof fixed this weekend and I need some peace and quiet. I've booked a hotel in London. For the three of us.'

'Me too?' says Alex, surprised.

'I thought it might be nice if you and Jude explored the city while I make use of room service and Netflix.'

'Seriously?' says Jude, looking delighted. 'When do we leave?'

'Now. Della put you on her car insurance. Pack a bag and let's go.'

Alex has a moment of doubt. 'Are you sure, Mum? Don't you mind being left behind?'

Della smiles as widely as she can. 'I want to get the roof sorted out before it rains. And the tree surgeon said he would come tomorrow. I don't like to leave things as they are.'

Carrie shoots her a look and smiles. 'Go on then,' she says to the kids. 'Get yourselves ready.'

It feels like an age, to hold herself together while Alex packs a bag. Carrie, a tote already packed and waiting between her feet, sits with her at the kitchen table. She reaches out and takes Della's hand in hers.

'You going to be OK?' she asks.

Della nods. 'You?'

'I need to sleep for the whole weekend. But when we get back, we need to talk to Alex. About Jude.'

'So soon?'

Carrie nods. 'You and I are going to be freaked out for the next . . . I don't know when. We need a good reason. Telling Alex about Jude and Leo will work in our favour. The kids will look inward. They'll focus on themselves, and they'll ignore us for the most part. If they do notice that we're behaving oddly, it's easily explained.'

Della feels the pull of kinship. She squeezes Carrie's hand in gratitude, and they sit like that, quietly holding on to one another until Alex comes down the stairs, bag packed, and Jude knocks on the front door.

It is barely four o'clock when Della waves them off. She trusts Jude to drive carefully. He will look after both of them, she knows this. She doesn't need to think about Alex or Carrie for the whole weekend. But still, as Della goes back into the house, there is a knotted ball of worry in her stomach.

She opens the back door, and it shuts behind her as she walks towards the log store. She unlocks the door and pulls the wheelbarrow out, then she loads as many logs as she can into the barrow. Just inside the door is a large metal box with a padlock. She uses a key on her keyring to unlock it. She swings the lid open and grabs a handful of kindling, a few firelighters and some newspaper. Muscle memory urges her to lock the box shut, lock the door behind her, but she fights it, leaving everything open as she wheels the barrow to the kiln.

She checks the kiln door is locked and bolted shut, even though she remembers checking it all last night.

She lays the newspaper, the firelighters and the kindling in the same way she has always done in the fire hatch at the back of the kiln. She uses a long chef's lighter to fire up a flame and she reaches into the heart space. She watches a small flame jump, take hold, and begin to explore the paper. She sees the smoke curl. She stays there for some time, observing the newspaper disintegrate under the heat of the fire, the words on them buckling and blackening under the flames. She hears the sticks pop and split, she sees the flames discover the bone-dry logs. It doesn't take long. The smell of the wood is sweet and clean, the smell from the kiln is something else.

She returns to the log store with the wheelbarrow and fills it with another load, opening the fire door and feeding the kiln with more wood. She will sit here all night, splitting logs, building her fire, making it burn bright and hot. The temperature in the kiln will reach well over one thousand degrees.

In the early hours of Saturday morning, when she is certain the fire has done its work, she will stop adding fuel. She will sleep while the flames lose their anger, she will come back here to watch them die. When she decides the time is right, when the lock is cool enough to touch, she will open the door and look inside.

It will be the most astonishing magic trick.

Everything she's been afraid of will have been consumed by fire. There will be nothing left but a pile of ash.

Chapter Fifty

One Year Later

Della breathes in the woods, in awe once again that a place so bare and brown and dead-looking will soon split and twist into the bright urgent green of hornbeam, beech and oak. The silver birch has grown over the past twelve months. Della can see its silvery bark from her bedroom window. Sometimes, when she cannot sleep, she stands in the darkness and seeks out its pale trunk, picked out in moonlight, a sentry next to Marmite's grave, watching over the house.

She pushes Carrie along the path that winds down to the pond. It has been hard to get the wheelchair through here in the mud, but now that the weather has dried up, the path has become firm once more, and Della is grateful for it. This is a daily ritual for both of them, and neither would ever want it to stop. Behind their conversation about the changing season, there is the knowledge that all of this is fleeting. That one day, Carrie might not be well enough to leave the house. They are pollen spores, Carrie says, blown about on the wind, they are feathers on a bird in flight. They do not know when they will fall down to the earth. So they take each day as it comes, one hour at a time. Life has become a collection of victories, sweet moments to be caught, acknowledged and embraced.

Back at the house, Jude and Alex are finishing their first project. They have knocked the walls down that Mrs Winters put up, restoring the house to its original self. They are taking photographs as they go along, making a blog so they can document their progress and attract customers. They are as close as two siblings can get. That is what they believe themselves to be, and Della has no intention of ruining that with the truth.

Their work has made the hallway a large space now, with two staircases that veer in opposite directions, making the house seem grander than it is. There is now a gap in between the stairways, where something needed to go. For a while, they put a little table there, and one of Della's jugs for flowers. But Della has always disliked the idea of flowers dying for her enjoyment, so she found the pieces of Leo's moon jar, welded them together with lacquer, and picked out the fractures with gold. Kintsugi is a well-known Japanese mending technique. Della never had cause to put it to use, always preferring to mend her pottery invisibly or throw her mistakes away. But to glorify imperfection like this, to pick it out in gold, means something now. It has its own powerful beauty. The moon jar is the last vessel she made in her old, subdued style. Now, everything she creates sings in colours forged by flames.

Della stops at the edge of the water, puts the brake on Carrie's wheelchair, and for a moment, they say nothing to one another, breathing in the spring air. It was Carrie's idea to do this every day. Della would have been happy never to see this pond again, but Carrie was insistent. That terrible night cannot be their lasting memory of this place. It must be blotted out by something good. Della leans over, makes sure Carrie's hands are not cold. Last year, at the end of the summer, she brought a chair up here, for herself, so they could sit side by side, holding hands. It is hard to explain, but Carrie is a mother, a sister, and a daughter to Della, all at the same time. She is half of her, more than Leo ever was. More than Tash could ever be. She knows that this bond, formed overnight in a matter of hours, will last until the end.

They do not talk about that night, ever, but Della knows they both think about it. They both dream about it, she is sure. For Della, it happens in abstract: wet hair against pale skin. The shock of cold water as she lowered herself in. The need to feel with her hands, the urgent desire not to look, because to see his face would break the suspended reality she had constructed for herself. It was the only way she could do it. And then Carrie, talking, talking to her all the time, in a low, sure voice from the edge of the pond. Della can't remember the words, but they felt like hypnosis, like a river that carried her through that night, guiding her, bearing her up as they gathered the corners of the picnic blanket between them once more and pulled it through the woods.

She was glad it was dark. So glad she couldn't see.

Carrie had been helping her close the kiln door when she touched Della's arm in the darkness. 'I've just had a thought,' she said, a note of trepidation in her voice.

'What?' Della said in a desperate whisper. She was wet. Freezing cold. Her teeth chattered.

'I know you don't want to look at him. But you need to be sure.'

Della had let out a noise of despair. 'It has to be. Who else would it be?'

'All I'm saying is, it could be a huge coincidence. That some other man fell in and drowned there.'

'It can't be. I saw his hair.'

'Plenty of men have long brown hair. Look, Della. You have to be absolutely certain, so you never have to worry about Ethan again. So you can sell this place if you choose to do it. So you never wake up in the night in a cold sweat, wishing you'd checked.'

Della had sobbed. She'd thought it was over. 'Please, Carrie. Don't make me look at him.'

Carrie had pulled her into her arms, then. She had held her tight. 'If I could identify him myself, I would do it for you,' she said. 'I would. You have to be brave. One more time.'

'I can't,' Della pleaded. 'I can't look at his face.'

They had stood together, Della snivelling. An owl hooted in the distance and Della wanted to have a life like that. To be free, among the trees, to be afraid of nothing.

'What about a photograph?' Carrie said eventually, her voice filled with doubt. The moonlight had caught the surface of her eyes. She stared, unblinking at Della, waiting for her to understand. 'I can go in there and take a photo with my phone.'

Della felt sick.

'Does he have any marks? Jewellery he always wore?'

'Yes,' Della says, remembering. 'He has a tattoo. On his neck. It says *Love Burns*.'

'OK, I'll see what I can do,' Carrie said. But Della heard the reluctance in her voice, the fear. And then, for no reason that Della could account for, a memory of Miss Abramovich surfaced, the day she picked Della up from hospital and took her to see the ashes of her home. They had stood together, facing the devastation. *Look at it, Della*, her teacher had said. *If you see it, you will be able to accept it.* Della looked at the open door of the kiln, a wash of understanding coursing through her. Each time her brother came back for her, she had searched for the boy she once knew, willing him to step forward. But the boy had gone, crushed under the weight of the man he had become.

She had caught Carrie by the arm, then. 'Don't worry,' she told her. 'I'll do it.'

Carrie covered Della's hand with hers. It, too, was cold and wet. 'Just think,' she said. 'When you know for sure, you can get on with the rest of your life. Imagine that, Della.'

Della imagined it. She imagined living here, as free as that owl. She imagined, years from now, other children running through the woods. Children she taught at the school she knew she would set up when all of this was over. Children that belonged to her daughter, perhaps, or Jude. She imagined an open door, welcoming in the sunshine, wet paw prints on a cool, stone floor. And for a moment, in the darkness, her clothes sodden, her face streaked with mud, Della felt a wave of joy so intense, so pure and true, it felt like a lightning bolt, and she knew that it would leave its mark on her for the rest of her life.

AUTHOR'S NOTE

I am lucky enough to live near woodland and I walk in Highgate Wood and Queen's Wood in North London most days. While they are not as expansive as the woods described here, they are ancient and beautiful and they inspired the setting of this book.

In Highgate Wood, there is a little house. Every night at dusk, visitors are locked out of the wood and I often wonder what it must be like to live in that house, to enjoy the woods when everyone else has gone home. Hopefully, life there is less dramatic than Della's.

For those of you familiar with the world of pottery, you might know that a wood-fired kiln is usually bricked up for firing and rarely has a door of the kind I have described. I did find a couple of examples of small, hinged fire doors so I took the liberty of making the door on Della's kiln much bigger in the interests of plot. I hope kiln aficionados will forgive me.

READING GROUP QUESTIONS

1. Do you think Leo was a good husband?

2. Discuss the friendships between Della and Tash, Robin and Leo. Who was a good friend and who was not?

3. Was Ethan someone to be pitied or feared?

4. Do you think there was a similarity between Leo and Ethan or were they very different people?

5. Was Della a weak or strong person?

6. In what way does colour play a part in the book?

7. Do you think Della had a right to feel angry with Carrie?

8. What role did pottery play in Della's life?

9. Was Della right to keep the truth about Alex's father to herself?

10. How do you feel about Ethan's death? Was it something to mourn or something to celebrate?

If you enjoyed *These Dark Places*, why not read *The Vanishing Tide* by the same author? Turn the page for an exclusive extract.

Prologue

It is always the same. The sun is setting and there is no sign of her yet. She sits on the sea-wall, back to the lagoon, kicking the heels of her sandals, waiting for Clare. She has developed a quiet patience for her sister's timekeeping, but the baby will be awake soon and she must get back. Her gaze tracks the cockle wagon as it trundles down the long stretch of sand, the men sitting on the edge with their rakes and buckets, their legs dangling and swaying as they laugh and joke. Their voices become faint and begin to recede into the wail of the seagulls and the advancing tide. She squints into the sunset as it suddenly stops: a solitary man leaping from the back, tearing into the water.

This is when the shouting begins.

The wagon becomes alive with men, jumping onto the sand and sprinting through the sea, kicking up foam and stone like so many wild horses. They surround the object of their disquiet. One of them, still a boy, turns and vomits into his hands. She sees them gather a dark shape and heave it clear above the water. It is only when that beautiful hair falls back into the waves like an inky waterfall that she knows Clare isn't coming back.

Chapter One

Isla, March

Sliding the key into the lock was harder than she thought. Isla had waited almost ten years to enter this house and now she didn't need Astrid's permission, she still felt like an intruder. A salty wind stung her skin as her wrist angled itself against the doorknob, a complicated sleight of hand only three people, now two, could perform to get the key to turn. A click gave way to a groan as the door swung slowly in.

Isla put her rucksack down, hung her coat on the only hook in the hallway and considered her inheritance. The old leather armchair was still there in the sitting room, but the floor was uncluttered by the mess she remembered as a child. It had never been this tidy when she was growing up. The air didn't smell as if it had been sealed up against the world and there were no strands of tobacco scattered across the coffee table; the bowl containing Astrid's Rizlas and her carefully wrapped chunks of resin had gone. It could have been an ordinary room where a normal family might live an unremarkable life. The deception was unsettling. The only thing that looked familiar was an enormous metal shelving system running the length and height of the wall. Hundreds of art books, hurled together and threatening to topple at the lightest touch. She looked at the titles and recalled that several of them had once been aimed at her head, one after another, whizzing by in a blur of colour.

She opened the door into the dining room, quickly averting her eyes from the painting above the fireplace – a habit from childhood she could not shake off. It had always given her the creeps. Maybe she would have liked it more if somebody else had painted it, somebody nicer. It was worth more than the house, she knew that, and the house was worth a fortune. You weren't allowed to build this close to the shoreline any more and the view to the sea was stupendous. Astrid had regularly fended off estate agents who came knocking. The building, more than a hundred years old, needed renovation and was ripe for profit. She never let them down kindly. Upsetting people who wanted something from her was a sport in which Astrid excelled. Now it was Isla wandering through the rooms like a prospective buyer, noting the jobs that needed to be done, the cracks that had to be filled. It wasn't too bad. The white weatherboard on the beach side was peeling, but the skeleton of the house had endured. She would enjoy doing something with her hands while her mind considered what to do with the absence. Loving Astrid had been a burdensome task. London was too far from here to make social calls, especially when you knew you weren't welcome. Although Astrid seemed to tolerate a phone conversation once every couple of months, it was always Isla who made the call. Astrid had never courted anyone's company but her own.

The house felt unnaturally cold. A damp breath of wind snaked around her neck, stirring the curtain drawn against the window, making her shudder. Spring came late this far north, and she cursed herself for leaving her warmest jumper behind. She had spent almost two decades of her youth here and on the few occasions she'd returned, it was always in the futile hope that the weather would be as warm as the capital. She'd forgotten how the cold crawled into your bones and squatted there till summer. Isla peered back into the hallway to see if she had left the door open. It was shut.

The last time she'd visited, she had brought wine and flowers. It had been a significant birthday for Astrid; Isla had felt there should be some acknowledgement, even though Astrid had not remembered Isla's birthday for years. Astrid had given her a curt nod of appreciation when she'd handed the flowers over. There were only eighteen years between them. They should have been more like friends. But, just as before, she'd found herself cold and alone for the weekend while Astrid painted in the studio. Isla had used the time to brood. She was past forty and still with no family of her own. She didn't want to be here. Astrid didn't want her here. No wonder she couldn't hold down a relationship – she had never been shown how to care for anyone else. Astrid was all she had, all she would ever have. Isla was suddenly floored by the understanding that this would never change. She had lost her opportunity to make her own family; she'd been too busy moping over the mess she'd left behind in this house.

Two days later, when she saw the flowers lying on the kitchen countertop, wilting in their cellophane, something inside her snapped. This would be the last time. If Astrid wanted her company, she would have to ask for it. The request never came, and when the time stretched between them it had been more a relief than a heartbreak. As Isla looked around the place, remembering that weekend, it struck her that Astrid had always been incapable of nurturing the living, and she had passed this affliction on. It was probably the only thing they had in common.

A faint chemical scent she couldn't put her finger on drew her to the foot of the stairs. There was a large circular stain on the oatmeal carpet, pale grey in colour – not what she'd imagined.

She crouched down and touched it, conscious of being close to something very profound. It was dry and crisp and when she drew her hand back, a fine white powder coated her fingertips. She wondered who had taken the trouble to do this. It must have been hard to clean.

She stood. Using the stairs would be difficult without thinking about Astrid's last moments, but even so, as she stepped over the stain, a small seed of excitement began to grow in the pit of her stomach. Maybe the information Astrid refused to provide when she was alive could be prised from this house now she was dead. Astrid had always delivered the truth like an unwanted meal. It didn't matter if it was unpalatable to the recipient; you were to eat it all without complaint. If Astrid had wanted to tell Isla about the circumstances surrounding her Aunt Clare's death, no doubt she would have taken delight in frightening her with the gory details. But to refuse to talk about it at all – well, that was something else. The story of Isla's father had been repeated like a folk song throughout her youth: *He was a waste of space, he didn't care, he's gone, gone, gone.* Astrid could have used his death to curry sympathy, but she didn't. It was the women who mattered in this family. Men added a layer of complication. It was a lesson Isla was still trying to unlearn.

As she reached out to steady herself, she noticed the finial at the end of the balustrade. The tip was missing, broken off by Astrid's fall. Isla touched her own head and winced at the thought. She had felt fine about coming alone, staying here by herself. It hadn't crossed her mind to book into the only hotel in the village, but when she started to walk up the stairs she felt a resistance, the flex of a muscle, willing her to go back down. Halfway up she paused, unsure what to think. Astrid was gone. Isla would never again bear the brunt of her disapproval. But the house was charged with friction. She could feel it gathering round her like mist rising up from the sea.

She said out loud, 'This is my house now.' The words sank through the air like stones through water and before she finished saying them, she knew it wasn't true.

ACKNOWLEDGEMENTS

To my agent, Rebecca Ritchie, my editors, Victoria Pepe and Victoria Oundjian, and the wealth of copy-editors and proofreaders who spend many hours considering my words and correcting them, thank you for the support you continue to give my work, I really do appreciate it. Thanks, also, to Nicole and the APub team for marketing and publicity, and to Emma Rogers, who always does a spectacular job designing the covers of my books.

I am indebted to my beautiful friend Rosie Ruddock of Stable Yard Pottery for teaching me how to throw a pot, for checking my pottery facts and answering questions I had about clay and glazing. Rosie, you need to get another job now so I can nick it for the next book. My North London writing group gave me invaluable advice on a very early draft of this book. Thanks in particular to Tammy Cohen, Marianne Levy and Anna Mazzola for their wise and witty words, to Robert Graves for gently explaining that fingerprint technology doesn't work when you're dead and Sarah Lawton Coombs for her disturbing knowledge of human decomposition. To Anna Wise and Tami Hoffman, my reading group buddies, thanks for your friendship and the high-quality cheese and wine. To the ladies of the pond, still sipping and dipping, it's such a treat to still be swimming with you all.

Big, big love to Sian Hurst, my woodsy walking wife. The hours we spend in Queen's Wood with Maggie and Luna on the boozy bench are the best! To Lizzy, Rex and G Walton, special thanks and love for being Milly's Sheffield family and looking out for her this past year, and for always having a bed ready for me. Jim, thanks to you for adventures on boats, in bars and on The Loop. To Mum, who is always there for me and who is a brilliant source of information for anything medical, love and thanks for the work you put into this one. I owe you.

Sat, Milly and Ruby, who shape my family in the best possible way, my deepest love to all of you, always. You make me so proud it's hard to put into words.

ABOUT THE AUTHOR

Photo © 2024 Tom Willcocks

When she's not writing fiction, Hilary Tailor runs a design consultancy specialising in colour and trend forecasting. She has worked with Adidas and Puma and sits on the Pantone View colour committee. Hilary was raised on the Wirral Peninsula and graduated from the Royal College of Art. Her debut novel, *The Vanishing Tide*, was published in 2022 and has thousands of five-star reviews. *These Dark Places* is her fourth novel. She can be followed on Instagram @hilarytailorwrites and has a website: www.hilarytailor.com.

Follow the Author on Amazon

If you enjoyed this book, follow Hilary Tailor on Amazon to be notified when the author releases a new book!
To do this, please follow these instructions:

Desktop:

1) Search for the author's name on Amazon or in the Amazon App.
2) Click on the author's name to arrive on their Amazon page.
3) Click the 'Follow' button.

Mobile and Tablet:

1) Search for the author's name on Amazon or in the Amazon App.
2) Click on one of the author's books.
3) Click on the author's name to arrive on their Amazon page.
4) Click the 'Follow' button.

Kindle eReader and Kindle App:

If you enjoyed this book on a Kindle eReader or in the Kindle App, you will find the author 'Follow' button after the last page.